THERE YOU WERE

A PRIDE & PREJUDICE REIMAGINING

MICHELLE RAY

Quills & Quartos
PUBLISHING

Edited by Marcelle Wong and Regina McCaughey-Silvia

Cover Design by Cloudcat Designs

ISBN 978-1-951033-79-8 (ebook) and 978-1-951033-80-4 (paperback)

To Lauren & Jen who loved this story first.
-and-
To Miss McElligott and Mrs Littenberg who inspired my love of
Shakespeare, dramatic teaching, and the character Miss Taylor.

CONTENTS

CHAPTER ONE

Longbourn Village, 1794

My earliest memory is of people staring at us. They always stared at us. Not that the sight of a six-year-old girl walking with her four-year-old sister was so unusual. No, it was the scandal of our mother's disappearance, worsened by our family background and heightened by the fact that we were always unescorted, always unchaperoned and, in my case, usually ill-behaved.

We were not the wealthiest in Hertfordshire. That distinction belonged to the Earl of Broxbourne and his family, the Fitzwilliams. But our free spirits, combined with the size of our estate and all of the expectations that came with it, baffled and disappointed people by turns.

Some said I ran wild. Some said I would grow out of it. I always wondered what *it* was, since I behaved just the same as many of the young boys in Meryton, but somehow I saw more upturned noses, and received glares from more withered ladies in beaded black dresses who clucked their tongues and whispered about my poor upbringing just loud enough for me to hear it. When I was little, I would stick out my tongue. Sometimes I would cry.

Once, Jane—ever my protector—walked right up to Mrs Oakley, a merchant's wife, after she began reprimanding me, and told her to look after her own granddaughter who was getting quite a name for herself in the village. Mrs Oakley whipped out her umbrella and hit Jane so hard across the face that you could see lace marks on Jane's cheek for an hour. The indignity must have been severe, for Jane had never earned a punishment of her own accord. But Jane merely put one hand on her face, the other around my shoulder, and led me towards Longbourn with her head held high. If I was not already sure Jane would protect and guide me no matter what, that convinced me.

Two saving graces of our youth were that Father hated social gatherings and that he had renounced religion. As a result, he never took us to church where stillness was required and gossip abounded. I found my religion in the woods. To me, all the evidence I needed of God was in the travel of an ant colony or the spring thaw. During the brown stillness of late winter, one could feel certain that God had given up on our silly planet, and that everything on Earth would be left forever frozen and dull. But if you look carefully, you can see little bulges on the trembling tree branches. That is hope. That is the promise of heaven. That can give anyone in tune with the earth the impetus to get out of bed on a frosty morning. If you have patience and an awareness of what is coming, you will be there to witness the first pale green poking out of those bulges on the twigs. And in a matter of days—moments in the life of the planet—the green grows and explodes until you cannot look through the woods and see anything. It is covered with luscious life that calms the feeling of dread, of forsakenness, and ignites an excitement for running out into the woods and staying until the leaves turn orange and fall to the ground again. But most people cannot see the change begin and do not feel the glory. They coop themselves up in freezing cold buildings and pray for a salvation that is mere steps away.

Jane always preferred to be indoors. The genteel pastimes of young girls were well suited to my dear sister, but I taught her to also marvel at the ever-changing clouds above and to feel the beauty of life in a tree trunk. We would sit so still that deer might come and pause to eat off a nearby shrub; we taught ourselves to swim, and we spent hours weaving myrtle branches into crowns. We called ourselves the Princesses of Longbourn.

Our family circle included Edward Gardiner, my wayward mother's younger brother who came to live with us after she left. Uncle Gardiner, who was just a boy when I was born, seemed more like an elder brother, but he was so quiet and sombre most of the time, it was as if he was scarcely there.

Uncle Gardiner and my father appreciated nature in terms of its yield for their profit. Counting crop yields satisfied their urge for movement; sitting still long enough to watch a bird build its nest would drive them to distraction.

Mysteries and secrets were a part of my childhood. I knew not to ask questions, and those around me did not offer much information on any topic, at least not directly. All I knew was from whispers others assumed I did not hear. Jane told me to ignore what people said, as the information was not always accurate, but I could not help myself. I was left to guess and make inferences about everything from why my mother left, to why Jane and I did not have a tutor at the house like proper young ladies.

My father never asked me if I wanted to learn from Miss Taylor, likely imagining that I would fight him on the matter. Rather, one fine autumn day when I was seven years old, he uncharacteristically took Jane and me on a ride in his gig and stopped in front of a cosy brown house. He told us to knock on the door and, before we walked three paces, had already pulled away. I have often wondered if it was due to trust or carelessness or a desire not to be bothered with me more than necessary.

I was not sure exactly where we were or why, but Father had given us an order. Neither Jane nor I could reach the knocker, so I banged on the door with my fist. The door opened at once, and before us stood a small woman with blue eyes made larger by extremely thick glasses. She smiled kindly and reached out her hand. "The Miss Bennets, I presume?" she said, shaking my hand and then Jane's with even more warmth. Her hands were smooth, so I knew right away she had never been a farmer's wife.

My father chose Miss Taylor, a former schoolteacher, to read with us and teach us whatever she deemed important. He had intended for us to spend a short time together, but our visits continued well after he stopped paying her, and well after Jane decided she would rather spend her time in the drawing room with our neighbour Charlotte Lucas.

Our father had meant for us to acquire a basic education, but Miss Taylor stressed a rich vocabulary and an appreciation of great literature. "Never settle for simple words or simple books, Elizabeth," she would say if I described my day as fine or bad. She skipped mathematics altogether, which I regret every so often, but I have never regretted a moment spent with her. She loved to walk through the woods reading different authors' descriptions of nature. Miss Turner's thick glasses and grey-black hair,

4

which she let flow only when reading aloud, come to mind every time I hear mention of my favourite writers. There was no one quite like her in Meryton.

Father never asked how we spent our time, nor if we were happy to be taught by her. On that first day, he came to her house at mid-morning to return us home, and announced that from the next day on, Jane and I would leave in the afternoon and return home on our own. As we rode together, I could not bear the silence, and shared that she had stacks and stacks of books. He pressed his lips together, keeping his eyes fixed on the empty lane. Jane cleared her throat, a signal that I was to stop speaking, yet I could not keep from sharing that she had piles of books in every part of the house, including next to the stove, which seemed rather dangerous! I told him how Miss Taylor put leaves in her hair when we took a walk, and that she served us biscuits sweetened to perfection with molasses. I had wanted to thank him for sending me to learn with her, and to promise that I would work very hard, but he gave a disinterested wave of his hand and looked away. "That is enough, Lizzy. You know better than to speak before being spoken to."

Not long after my visits with Miss Taylor had commenced, I overheard a conversation between my father and our neighbours, Sir William and Lady Lucas.

Lady Lucas was a plain woman whose constant judgment emphasised her severe countenance. Perhaps my father tolerated her because he enjoyed Sir William—as much as he enjoyed anyone. They were our only callers in those days, and Father was less sullen whenever Sir William, lanky and bald but for tufts of hair just above each ear, darkened our door. This visit was tense, however, as they were when Lady Lucas had a particular criticism to share.

"Having Elizabeth and Jane educated at home by a tutor would be much more appropriate. And my understanding is that they merely read. In English! When will the girls learn French or Latin? When will they learn to paint or play an instrument? My Charlotte is already learning the harp."

"Jane is nine years old." My father sneered. "I highly doubt that she could even reach the strings."

"Sir William, tell him!" Lady Lucas said, her voice scratching at my brain like when Hill sharpened knives.

Sir William rarely offered an opinion, but straightened at his wife's reprimand. "The harp aside, Bennet, my wife has a point. Put down the flask and listen to reason, for once."

I was shocked by this direct comment on my father's drinking, but even more so by what came next.

"You let those girls run about the fields and woods shouting just like boys, and Elizabeth has a most unruly manner," added Lady Lucas. "I have heard talk of it even from my servants."

"Why do you allow gossiping servants, dear lady?" A gorgeous moment of silence during which I could picture Lady Lucas's face squished with disapproval, not her most attractive expression. "Hill will not have Elizabeth in the kitchen, and there is no one to teach her needlework."

"Your wife could."

A less welcome silence. Then the bang of a flask on the side table. "No," was all my father offered and I wondered why, but would never know.

Incredibly, Lady Lucas pressed. "Every woman must know how to sew, knit, cook, and supervise a household. Whether high or low, this sort of knowledge is of great advantage."

Sir William added, "Gaining such information would

not interfere with intellectual advantage or even of elegant accomplishment. A well-regulated mind can find time to attend to all."

At this, my father actually snickered. Though I was young, I knew what he thought of the silliness of our neighbours.

"They need a woman's hand to guide them along." Lady Lucas sniffed. "Before you know it, you will be worrying about their marriages and you will not wish to manage such a thing on your own."

Sir William cleared his throat. "Our girls must marry well."

"And I will have my own daughter to marry off. Perhaps two if this one is yet another girl."

Lady Lucas was heavy enough with child that I had been surprised she ventured out of her home, and realised my educational situation must have been dire if she had risked the three-mile journey to our house for this discussion.

They continued to grumble and argue until, rather unexpectedly, the conversation drew to a close. I daresay my father was the cause, having found some way to offend Lady Lucas, who stormed out, her husband trailing behind her.

When Lady Lucas barged through the door, she nearly ran into me, and startled so strongly her hands flew above her head followed by the clutching of her chest. Once recovered from her shock, she shouted, "Oh my nerves! Proper ladies do not eavesdrop! Go find Jane and try to get her to go outside and take some air." The irony was not lost on me.

My youth was marked with such exchanges. Everyone was always concerned about the poor, motherless Miss Bennets who ran wild while their father drank all day. Jane and I stayed outside as much as we could to enjoy our kingdom of nature together, where no changes mattered but the seasons. We dreamed of what we would do if we ever broke free of Meryton and our family's expectations and disappointment. Never could I have imagined that circumstances would bind me to the very lands and people I most loathed.

CHAPTER TWO

1806

My life changed one autumn day when I was fifteen. I ran into the house and forgot to leave some of the dirt outside. At least, that is what Hill snapped at me as I flew through the kitchen. I attempted to escape up the stairs, but she grabbed my arm and yanked me back. "Why cannot you act like a girl of your age? Why do you not desire to dress nice and act like a lady?"

I shrugged, which just seemed to irritate her all the more, and she boxed my ear. "You must take a bath."

"I shall use the pitcher and sponge."

"Not today," she said.

Hill and I had had countless arguments about how clean I was at any given time. I still maintain that there is little difference between stream water and well water when it comes to bathing, but I now admit that heat, soap, and scouring make a real bath superior.

I waited impatiently while Ruthie, the young kitchen maid who looked miserable most of the time (but never more so than when she had to assist me) prepared my bath. At last she filled the tub, helped me off with my clothes, and left the room with a perfunctory curtsey. I dipped in my toe. Scalding hot. I swore under my breath. "Those women wish to kill me."

As I stood naked and shivering beside the tub, I heard a carriage coming down the road. I reached for my shift and heard Hill call through the door, "If you think you are coming out here before you have washed thoroughly, you have quite sorely mistaken the matter."

She outweighed me by quite a bit, so I scowled at the tub and tested the water again. It was cooler by a degree or two, so I sucked in my breath and slid in. When I rose up again, gasping from the heat, I heard a woman's voice, gentle and young. My heart skipped.

My mother?

Of course it was not. It could not be. But who? I would not have been ordered to bathe for relatives, and my father rarely had callers.

I grabbed for the soap, cleaning myself as quickly as my arms would move, wetting my hair and scouring my neck with a scratchy sponge where Hill was sure to check if she was so inclined (and she was often so inclined). I leapt up, splashing water all over the floor, and wrapped myself in a soft towel scented with lavender, one reward for all of this inconvenience. I tugged a comb through my tangled hair, hearing the snap of strands and getting it utterly stuck. I called for Ruthie, who finished the job better than I had hopes of doing, but refused her offer of a plait. I did allow her to help me on with my corset. I dragged my skirt in a puddle on my way into the hall, and ignored the silent reprimand in Ruthie's furrowed eyebrows.

Tiptoeing down the stairs, I peered into the sitting room. My uncle was back from visiting…somewhere. I had been told, but cared nothing for his doings since he cared so little for mine. He was so stiff and quiet that one could never know him.

Everyone in the room was acting peculiarly. My father flashed a rare grin as he shook Uncle Gardiner's hand. Uncle Gardiner appeared happy. Hill, whose emotional range went from annoyed to angry, stood in the corner with Ruthie, dabbing one eye with her apron. Jane sat in the corner, her lips twitching as she attempted to hide her smile.

And then I spotted the source of the change. There stood a young woman wearing a light yellow dress that looked as if it would float away in the slightest breeze. Her movements were gentle and precise, and her smile took up her whole face. Her wavy chestnut hair was pinned up with flowers. It was clear she was a regular bath taker.

Jane beckoned. "Lizzy, come join us."

Everyone's heads snapped to me. My cheeks burned at the attention, so I turned to Jane, running right into a chair.

Jane cleared her throat. "This is—"

Uncle Gardiner took a half step closer to the stranger. "Lizzy, may I present to you my future wife, Miss Margaret Hawkins."

If my uncle had told me that Lady Godiva was standing before me, I could not have been more stunned. Jane giggled, and the others followed suit. I am not sure what my face looked like, but my cheeks caught fire when the maiden smiled in my direction.

"How do you do, Miss Elizabeth?" Her voice sounded like a melody. She approached, bringing with her the scents of roses and powder. I curtseyed, thinking there was no way she enjoyed a good mud fight and fishing the way I did. But there was something about her. Something that made me glad she would be a part of my life.

It was rare that Jane had strong feelings about anything, but even more rare that she would disagree with our father. I knew it could not be anything good when I heard them arguing in the drawing room one afternoon shortly after Uncle Gardiner's shocking announcement.

"She is coming! No discussion!" I heard my father say, his tone brooking no disagreement.

The door flew open and Jane almost knocked me to the ground. She stopped just long enough to see that I was not bleeding before she fled towards the stream that separated our land from the Fitzwilliams' estate. I ran after her, as I always did, crunching through the dry grass. The brisk walk took a mere five minutes, but by the time I arrived, sweat was sliding down my spine. Once in the woods, cooler air enveloped me, as did the welcome scent of moss and mud. Jane stood facing the slow-moving water, her head bowed. Only once I was near could I see the shaking of her shoulders and hear her soft weeping.

"Jane?" I wanted to pull her to me, but sometimes she preferred to be left alone. She did not turn or acknowledge my presence, so I stared at the water, counting the smooth submerged stones and wondering if I could leap across the stream without muddying my shoes. It had not rained for a few days, so I suspected I could.

Jane's sniffs slowed. "They have no right. No right!" A sob burst forth, and she covered her face. I stared at a leaf struggling to free itself from a rock, knowing she would calm herself and tell me more when she was ready.

Drying the tears on her face, she knelt, eyes fixed on the opposite bank. "I do not understand how he could want that woman at our house."

"Who?" I asked.

"Our mother."

"Our mother?" I sucked in a sharp breath. "I thought she was dead."

"Why would you think she was dead?"

"I…" Because I could not imagine why else a mother would never write or visit. Almost fifteen years and not a word. I had never been told why she had left in the first place, and somehow thought, or maybe hoped, that everyone said 'she left' as a euphemism for dead. Being dead explained it. Being alive and turning her back on us was incomprehensible.

I shook my head, trying to make sense of this revelation. "And Father knows where she is?"

"Yes."

I paused, hoping that what I was wondering could not be true. "Did Uncle Gardiner?"

Jane nodded sharply.

I hesitated before my next question, hoping I was wrong. "You did, as well?"

Jane squinted at the stream as if willing it to dry up and for the earth to crack beneath it. "Vaguely."

"Why did you not tell me?"

"Do not ask about her. I swear, Lizzy. Do not."

I tucked my lips between my teeth, then ran off.

Whether full of joy or rage, among the trees I always found answers…or at least peace. I sat on a bed of moss and listened to the gentle rustle surrounding me, considering what I had been told: our mother was alive and everyone else knew where she was. Even Jane. While our father and uncle constantly disappointed me and hid things, Jane never did. That Jane—my ally, my dearest friend—knew and never told me was the ultimate treachery. How could she?

All my life my mother had been a spectre in the house. I had learned not to ask about her, as my questions and comments were typically met with pained silence. My mother was agony and discomfort, and it was best not to wonder about her. Now she was coming.

What could I do? Nothing. Simply meet her and see. See why she left me. See what she was like.

And yet. And yet!

I closed my eyes and attempted to breathe. The green canopy above my head soothed my mind. A breeze fluttered the leaves as if whispering a gentle 'shhh', the sound a mother would make to her child...if one had had a mother's care. I refocused, listening to the birds chattering in the high branches. I opened my eyes, watching a crossbill swoop to another tree, then a second and a third.

Jane approached and held out a hand. I took hers in mine and she squeezed, then began walking.

We slowed at the little hunting cottage we had found years ago, which was just far enough off from our house to have served our needs on many such nights when it was best not to be inside with the others. No one would come out and look for us tonight. No one ever did.

We sat down on the logs outside the cottage and watched the sky darken and the stars emerge, first one, then another, then so many you could count them until the sun came back and never finish counting. It reminded me of a black pond with floating candles. Lightheaded from fatigue and hunger, I felt as if I were swimming among them.

Though many summer evenings remained hot and close, this night the temperature had dropped. I heard a noise and realised it was my own teeth chattering.

"Let us take refuge inside," Jane said. There was wood in the fireplace and somehow we managed to light a fire, sitting close to warm ourselves. As we watched the firelight dance, she asked, "Better?"

I shrugged, pulling my arms tighter around myself.

"I ought to have told you I knew," she said, her forehead creasing with consternation.

I sighed, trying to let go of my anger. "Yes."

"No more secrets. Ever. I promise." She reached out for my unfashionably suntanned arm.

I nodded and closed my eyes, wanting to believe her.

A CLATTERING AT THE DOOR AWOKE US BOTH WITH A START.

A man's frame filled the doorway, his features obscured by shadows. "What in blazes!"

I scrambled to my feet, taking in Jane's startled eyes, her mouth agape, the very idea of trouble turning her to stone as it always did. I considered rushing at him, waving my arms like the heroine in one of my novels when confronted by a bear, but his long coat and tall shining hat gave him out to be a gentleman rather than a local ruffian come to compromise us. The gun ought to have terrified me, but as my eyes adjusted to the light, I could see that he was dressed for hunting. And we were in a hunting lodge. His, perhaps?

"Who are you?" he barked.

"Who are *you?*" The words spilled out before I could check my tone. He stiffened, but before he could say anything else, I grabbed Jane's hand and yanked her past him towards the open door.

"Stop, I say!"

We ran, peals of laughter escaping me as I looked over my shoulder, only to slam into someone outside and tumble to the ground. The damp from the night immediately seeped into my skirt, and I knew Hill would be furious with me for being a disaster once again.

"Miss Elizabeth?"

I looked up. Registering his identity, I accepted his outstretched hand and allowed him to help me to my feet.

James Fitzwilliam was the second and youngest of the Fitzwilliam sons. Not heir to the earldom, he was set to join the regulars as a lieutenant colonel as soon as he came of age.

"You know this creature?" asked the stranger, who had followed us outside.

"This creature," I said, hands on my hips, "is his friend and neighbour."

Jane cringed at my impudence—a flaw she had reprimanded me for so often that it was nearly comical—but James Fitzwilliam, whom we had known since we were born, smiled. "This is Miss Bennet and her sister, Miss Elizabeth Bennet."

The stranger looked Jane over. She gave a proper curtsey, her cheeks flushing.

"This is my cousin, Mr Darcy." An awkward silence fell. "We were hunting!" he added in a bright voice.

"Hunting what?" I asked, matching his enthusiasm.

Jane took hold of my arm. "We must take our leave." Pulling me away, she paused to offer a perfunctory curtsey so as not to be rude. I waved, which made Jane hiss, "Lizzy! Honestly."

CHAPTER THREE

I was not involved in my uncle's wedding plans, and for that I was thankful. Mr and Mrs Hawkins were paying for the affair, although it would take place in Meryton. I had half a mind to protest the pink gown Margaret had commissioned for me, as I hated pink, but she had such a way of talking that a person could not dream of arguing. I wondered if that was how my uncle had become attached. I had not even known he was contemplating marriage, much less courting anyone. To my shock, my practical uncle had become a romantic—bringing her flowers and copying sonnets onto fine paper.

When she and her parents arrived at our home the week before the wedding—with the plan for Margaret to remain, and for Margaret and Uncle Gardiner to live in our house until he inherited it upon our father's death—I saw her effect on him. His shoulders relaxed. He looked up from his books. He left the worries of Longbourn aside and spoke. In complete sentences.

It was odd. He showed little emotion on the whole, but

somehow always had a tender look or touch for this young lady. He smiled when she was near, a smile that reached his eyes. Even his posture, so stiff one thought he might be wearing a too-tight girdle, softened as he went to take her hand or place a kiss upon her forehead. His very soul seemed to relax, whether they were seated side by side or across the room. I never would have matched them, but he certainly was much more pleasant to have around now that they were.

I loved the changes I saw, yet I wondered if Margaret would try to act like my mother once she became the lady of the house.

A DAY BEFORE THE WEDDING, SHE ARRIVED—MY MOTHER, that is. Everyone had been on edge for days with the anticipation of it. Even the birds that lived in the eaves seemed agitated. Jane had not eaten a bite for days and I feared by the time my mother actually arrived, Jane would be too ill to see her. Any time a carriage passed on the road, *I* felt ill.

At last, I saw through the window of the bedroom I shared with Jane that a curricle approached bearing a single female passenger. She was wearing a light blue jacket and a matching blue bonnet. I could not make out her features and wondered if I looked like her. Or if Jane did. Or Uncle Gardiner. Would she be kind? Cruel? Weak-minded? Brilliant?

The horse turned off the road and neared our house. My father called for everyone to come outside. I took Jane's hand like a child half my age, but could not help myself as I followed her down the stairs. With my free hand I checked to see that my dress was in order.

The others were already outside, lined up. Jane

smoothed the curls by her temple, her eyes lowered. She squeezed my fingers so tight they began to throb but showed no other sign of emotion. I followed her gaze towards the figure that grew larger by the moment. My father cleared his throat and Margaret whispered something in Uncle Gardiner's ear, which elicited a nervous laugh, quickly stifled.

My mother was close enough to study now. Her hair was light like Jane's; her posture, so straight and proud, was like Uncle Gardiner's. Her mouth was like mine—thin lips that curled under into half-moons in the corner.

Having no servant with her, she drove herself in a curricle that looked more fashionable than practical. She pulled on the reins and the black mare slowed to a stop, the carriage rolling back until her gloved hand pulled on the brake. As she stepped down, my father extended a hand to guide her to the ground. How could he be civil to her? I never presumed to understand my father.

She neither smiled nor moved. Her eyes flicked from one person to the next, dancing between Margaret and me for a moment. The backs of my knees began to sweat and my limbs lost their feeling. I knew I should say something but could not force air past the lump in my throat.

Margaret stepped forward. "Mrs Bennet, how do you do? I am Miss Hawkins."

My mother slipped off her beige glove and clasped Margaret's hand. They smiled and then, to my surprise, my mother hugged her.

My uncle stepped forward, and hugged her as well. Jane stood frozen like a deer spotted by a hunter. I attempted to wriggle my fingers free, but she continued holding on. "Jane?" my mother asked. "Oh what a beauty!" To no one and everyone, she said, "I have always maintained that a man would have to go a long way to find a beauty like my Jane. And with such a figure!"

But what did she think of me? My heart began to hammer and I stood unsure of whether to move forward myself. I wanted to. I wanted to hear what she thought of me. Did she think me a beauty? I scoffed at the notion even as I realised how much I wanted her to think well of me, to be proud of me.

Jane's grip on my fingers loosened, and pain shot through my hand as blood began to flow once more. I flexed them, trying to ease the pain, as she approached me.

"And you must be Elizabeth," she said. "My goodness, it has been so long."

I bit my lip to keep from answering too impulsively. Was I supposed to say, "Yes, it has," or "No," or "Indeed, and that is why we despise you"?

She directed a bright smile to the others. "Well, she will never be as pretty as Jane, but I daresay she has grown up very well. Very well, indeed. When I leave, child, I shall give Ruthie directions for some creams to rub on your face. We should have that tan cleared up in no time."

I was caught between calling her rude and laughing, but before I could do either, she levelled her gaze at me. "Not much of a talker, are you, Elizabeth?" She turned to Jane. "She does have all her wits, does she not?" At Jane's nod I did laugh, likely deepening my mother's suspicion that I was feeble-minded. She fluffed her skirt. "Shall we retire inside?"

Hill rushed forth with a surprising amount of speed for her size, hugged my mother, took a bag in one hand and my mother's hand in the other, and the two of them charged up the stairs like girls half their age, which was just about the most shocking thing that had happened thus far.

THAT AFTERNOON, I WAS SITTING IN THE GARDEN WHEN MY mother walked out, unaware of my presence. She looked out at the surrounding hills that rolled in green waves, and a smile crept onto her face.

I cleared my throat.

"Elizabeth. Oh, my. I did not realise you were out here." Her smile slid away, replaced by pursed lips and a cock of the head.

I twisted my skirt between my fingers. "I was hoping we could speak." I wanted some answers about my past. If I could stop being angry for just a few moments, I might learn more about why I had spent my childhood alone.

My mother flushed and her eyes darted about as if looking for an escape. She smiled awkwardly. "I was going for a walk." She paused, as if awaiting a response. "Would you care to join me?"

"With pleasure."

"Good." Her tone suggested that she was anything but happy. "I missed these woods and hills while I was away. A wonderful place to escape."

"Jane and I wander through them all the time."

"You do?" She smiled. "I brought you both out when you were babies. My brother and Matthew never liked it half so much, but you girls always did."

"Matthew? Who is Matthew?"

There was a long silence. I looked at the woman who had borne me, seeing her face contorted with emotion I could not understand.

"Has no one ever spoken of him?" she asked softly.

My anger at her and my father flared. No. I had known nothing of my mother, and evidently, of some person called Matthew. Where was he? Why had my mother chosen to take care of only him?

I clenched my fists and felt my cheeks catch fire. "No," I said, my voice cutting. "No one speaks much about anything of consequence to me, it seems."

My mother studied my face. "Matthew was my—our son. He passed—" She sucked in a sharp breath. "Truly, no one mentioned Matthew to you?"

Perhaps I should have felt concern or sadness that a child—one I was related to, no less—had died. Instead, my fury grew. "Who would tell me? Father? My uncle? Hill? They hardly care about anything except that I stay out of the way!"

I strode ahead, emotion lengthening my stride. I sensed her following me, making me feel powerful, so I did not slow down. After a few paces, I no longer heard her footsteps, but I kept walking nevertheless.

"Do you wish to hear about him or not?" she called out. "I cannot tell you if you are bent on running away."

I stopped. To return to her would admit defeat. I kept my feet firmly where they were.

I heard her exhale, her breath catching at the end. A sob? I swivelled to see. She was leaning against the mossy trunk of a tree dabbing her eyes. "He was yet small when it happened—a fever took him. Days and nights of nursing him, the one who should have been the heir to this estate, and in the end we could not do enough for him. To see our child die...I was undone by it, and your father changed, too. He grew cruel and began drinking to excess. Does he still drink?"

I nodded, not willing to go into the details of his behaviour.

"The years were difficult following Matthew's death." Her lips pressed together. "Despite my own grief, I attempted everything to fix it. Ignoring your father, humouring him, fighting with him. It did not matter what I did. He yelled at me rather than speaking. The more we fought, the more he drank. I endeavoured to give him another heir but instead…"

She trailed off, but I knew. Two girls born. No heir.

"So after the disappointing birth of another daughter, then what? You left?" I asked harshly, not sparing the least thought for her feelings.

"No, it was not entirely— When Jane was very young, I ran off with her and stayed with my sister, Mrs Philips, in London for a few months. "

"You took Jane with you?" I asked, jealous to the centre of my being.

She seemed to know my thoughts. "One child is different than two. Jane was such an engaging child, she could be no trouble to anyone."

Unlike me, who was a trouble to everyone.

"If you hated my father so much and had Jane with you," I said, my voice catching, "why did you return? Did Father drag you back?"

"No." She studied the ribbon of her bonnet. "I believe he might have been glad to be rid of me, but my sister's husband grew weary of us. I had no money to live on. Your father took us back. We decided to try for more children."

She blinked rapidly and turned her face away from me. "I thought, I truly thought, that more babies might settle him. I thought if I could bring him an heir, it could allow him to rest easy. I had you—"

"Not an heir."

She nodded. "And then a miscarriage. He was cold and sarcastic. I…I could endure no more."

I plucked a leaf that landed on my shoulder. "Did you wish to take us?"

"You know as well as I—as well as he—that I had no money and no legal claim to either of you. A man keeps his children."

"Would you have taken us if the law was on your side?"

Her gaze shifted away quickly as she said, "Of course."

Liar.

My hands balled into fists, but I forced my voice to be calm. I had to know all the details I could learn. "How did you manage on your own if the money was his?" I asked, my tone full of disbelief.

She let out a long breath. "He saw fit to give me an allowance of fifty pounds a year. It is enough to live modestly."

"Where?"

"London."

I waited for more, but she added no specifics. London. People we knew went to London for business and pleasure, for quick adventures or for the Season. My father never went. He claimed that spending so much time with others would give him apoplexy. Lady Lucas often advised that my father ought to send Jane, but he said that, at seventeen, she was still too young. Hill, in a rare moment of gossip, surmised to Ruthie that the expense would be too great. She had friends in service at the Darcy and Fitzwilliam houses, and was often told of the vast sums spent on gowns and parties and balls, to say nothing of the expenses the young men incurred while gambling. I had believed this, and although it might be true, for money was of ongoing concern to my uncle and my father, I pondered if he was also hoping Jane would not cross paths with our mother.

I inched closer. "Did you miss us?" My voice sounded young and needy. I crossed my arms as if that could protect me from a negative answer.

She looked at me, her face impassive, and brushed stray hairs away from her forehead. "You were part of an unhappy time. I shut the door on it long ago."

Wave after wave of hurt crashed over me. It had been easier when I thought she was dead. Better to mourn someone I had never met than know she was alive and did not want me, that she did not care for me. The very thought of me—her own child—made her miserable. I wished she was, in fact, dead.

Without warning, she turned back towards the house, leaving me alone. Again.

CHAPTER FOUR

T he next morning, I awoke to a scream from below and the pounding of feet on the stairs, followed by yelling. I rubbed my eyes, threw on my robe, and ran downstairs.

Margaret, usually the picture of calm and beauty, was in a corner of the kitchen sobbing. "A wedding is still a wedding without a cake," Uncle Gardiner said, pressing his head to hers more tenderly than I thought possible.

Hill was staring at the remains of what promised to be brandied heaven. "How could you be so stupid?" she hissed at Ruthie.

Ruthie stood quaking, her face pale. "I'm sorry. I'm sorry. I'm so sorry."

As they were otherwise occupied, they did not notice as I reached for my favourite Bath buns and a red apple. I paused to consider my chances of securing some jam.

Hill's head snapped in my direction. "Goodness, help me!" I knelt on the floor next to a quaking Ruthie and began picking up the biggest chunks of heavy fruitcake, still steaming on the floor.

"Perhaps you can make another one," I said.

"I haven't the ingredients, and it takes three hours to bake, not to mention the time for mixing. That poor, sweet girl."

I felt sorry for her and decided not to cause her any trouble that day, instead spending the hour before I was sent to dress doing what I could to help them, carrying heavy platters and setting flowers on the long table in the garden. Hill must have told me to be careful a million times, but rather than roll my eyes, I smiled broadly, tightened my grip, and marched on. At last Hill nudged me, saying, "Time to go get dressed."

I swivelled on the heels of my comfortable boots and wiggled my toes for what I feared might be the last time that day, knowing that fancy slippers and a gown that required stays awaited me.

A few minutes later, there was a knock at the door and my mother's voice called, "Elizabeth, have you any need for assistance?"

I paused, desiring to decline, but completely unable to fasten my top button. She entered the room and smiled, so I dropped my gaze to the floor.

I felt her fingers fiddling with the buttons at the back of my neck. "There," she said. Then she began to fix the crooked ribbon I had in my hair.

I jerked my head away from her touch. "I can manage."

She dropped her hands and I chewed my lip, not sure whether to apologise. Without another word, she turned and left the room, stopping at the top of the stairs before beginning a slow descent.

The door to my bedroom opened a crack, and Mrs Hawkins peered in. "Miss Elizabeth, you look lovely."

"M-hmm," I said, but my face must have betrayed me.

Mrs Hawkins kindly forbore to say anything of my mother and instead leaned in to help me.

"Look here, your bow is crooked," she murmured. With one quick tug she put it in its place. My stomach tightened along with the bow. She looked at our images reflected in the mirror and smiled. "You look beautiful." She squeezed my shoulders and left the room.

I hurried down the stairs and saw my mother standing in the alcove. I knew I ought to say something kind or simply go outside, but instead I walked over to my mother. "Helping with one button does not change anything."

"I know," my mother answered, pulling at her sleeves.

"I do not need your help."

"I know." My mother looked down and her pained face urged me on.

"You come here after fourteen years—you do not know me. You know nothing about me."

From nowhere, my father appeared. In a low, eerily calm voice, he said, "Apologise to your mother, Lizzy. That is not how *I* raised you to speak to anyone, let alone to your family." I suspected that his emphasis on 'I' pained my mother as much as it hurt me when he called her family.

"Sorry," I said quietly. Likely we both knew I was not, and I had much more to say that would go unsaid.

My mother nodded in response, and he walked away.

When I thought I was calm enough, I stepped into the sunlight. I had offered to walk the short mile to the church, and took my time doing it.

I could see Jane by the church door, standing with James Fitzwilliam's sisters, Lady Mary, Lady Kitty, and Lady

Lydia, the daughters of the Earl of Broxbourne, the most exalted personages in our humble county. Exalted they were, indeed; I was surprised they should have thought my uncle's wedding important enough for them to attend. Then again, my father had more friends than I realised.

Jane, her blonde hair sparkling in the morning light, was still and serene, as a young lady is meant to be. "Jane!" I called out, realising when the three earl's daughters stared at me that I was too loud, too unladylike.

With a small smile, Jane glided in my direction, another quality that I admired. My walk was more of a lope, and I wondered if Jane might tutor me in the art of grace, though I recalled the time she tried, without success, to teach me to set my teacup down without a clatter.

Jane kissed my cheek, telling me how lovely I looked. Margaret had wanted our dresses to mirror hers, but the ruffles and lace which made Jane look angelic only made me feel hot and uncomfortable. It was unfortunate, as this gown would now be part of my repertoire for assemblies and holiday gatherings.

Movement over her shoulder caught my eye, and I spotted James's lanky figure coming towards us, a tall, dark, and decidedly forbidding man at his side. The very man from the hunting lodge!

"Miss Bennet," said James, addressing Jane.

Jane nodded primly in reply.

He turned to me and winked. "Miss Elizabeth. You look…well-adorned." He had rarely seen me in such fripperies, as my taste went towards plain and practical.

"You be quiet," I said, slapping at his arm, a gesture Jane did not approve of. At seventeen, she was even more concerned with propriety than when we were younger, needing to make an impression on any eligible young man or female family member who might be looking for a match. I ought to have been similarly behaved, but I found myself unable to make my mind, mouth, and body work in concert.

"Mr Darcy," I said, acknowledging his companion. "How was the hunting?"

Looking down his nose at me, since I was considerably shorter, he said through a too-tight jaw, "Tolerable, though these lands are not nearly as full of quarry as mine."

"Darcy," James said with an amiable laugh, "no lands are as fine as yours, and yet the rest of us do seem to manage. And that buck you shot was rather sizeable."

I knew gentlemen were in the habit of shooting deer for sport, though the practice never did sit well with me. I loathed seeing those gentle creatures' heads mounted on walls, their glass eyes no replacement for the kindness in the living.

Lady Broxbourne said, "Miss Bennet. Miss Elizabeth." Disapproval iced my name in particular. "Gentlemen, let us move on and permit Miss Elizabeth to finish dressing."

"But I am, Lady Broxbourne," I said, my voice trailing off as her piercing gaze drifted down my body and rested on my still-booted feet. I could hardly breathe. I had left my boots on, meaning to change before we left, but was distracted by the argument with my mother. Utterly humiliated, I froze, uncertain what to do. Lady Broxbourne sailed away on Mr Darcy's arm, her nose high.

Jane had turned pale. "Has anyone else seen?" she asked, her eyes darting about.

"I hardly know. Oh Jane! What shall I do?"

James leaned close. "I shall go to your home and secure your proper shoes."

"You cannot. You will be sweaty and filthy, and your mother will kill you."

He bit his lip and spotted the carriage driver. "Someone will loan me a horse. I am sure of it." And with no further discussion, he was off.

He returned just before we were required to take our seats in the front, tossing them at me before scampering past us all. My heart had been in my throat while I waited, sure my father would notice and scold me in front of everyone, but Jane had told me to stand behind a statue and be still for once, and it had worked.

The ceremony was brief, but people had enough time to work up a surprising amount of emotion. At one point, Uncle Gardiner reached over to Margaret's cheek and brushed away a tear, which made my heart flutter. Would I ever have someone like that? Someone who cared for me, and not just because they were obligated to do so by blood? Then again, blood guaranteed nothing.

MARGARET AND UNCLE GARDINER SPENT THE REST OF THE morning and afternoon at our home talking to guests while holding hands. A few times, I noticed the pair walking alone just far enough from the crowd that no one desired to bother them. I thought it rude, seeing that they had the rest of their lives together, but the others did not seem to mind. I would never understand the rules of society.

I wished to pass the time with Jane, but our mother insisted on keeping her close. She seemed to lose no opportunity to forward Jane to the odious Mr Darcy, who was heir to a large estate and even larger fortune. Despite her beauty, Mr Darcy seemed to have no interest in her. I sometimes wondered if being too handsome might be a disadvantage. Was Jane's reserve interpreted as arrogance, her looks somehow intimidating to him?

James Fitzwilliam and I spent most of the party together, as both of us were avoiding our families. My mother's presence added to the curiosity of the small crowd, and their stares and judgments pained me more acutely than usual. I had known James forever, but he seemed different that day. Perhaps he looked older; I had not seen him for nearly two months, as his family had gone to the Lakes. Perhaps it was that he kept staring at me. Whatever it was, it made my skin prickle and want to stare back at him. And when his eyes met mine and his smile deepened his dimples, my heart hammered so hard I felt sure he could hear it.

At first, we remained with the crowd, laughing and eavesdropping after eating cold ham and the delicious rolls that Hill had spent days baking, but that grew tiresome so we went to the barn. Somehow his hand found mine as we watched a foal snuggling up to her mother. I did not move my hand away, and I did not breathe much either. His thumb stroked my hand as we stared straight ahead. Then he reached under my hair, his warm fingers bringing chills to the back of my neck. His lips pressed to mine and the world exploded in a thousand colours.

I pulled back and looked at him, breathless.

"Have you ever been kissed, Lizzy?" he asked, and when I shook my head, something shifted in his face. He studied the colt in silence.

The barn door opened, and Mr Darcy appeared. "Here you are, James." Then he saw me, and his face darkened. "James, I must insist that you come with me at once."

"Pardon," James said, and as they departed, a few words floated back to me, 'impropriety', 'indecency', and 'future', among them.

THE MORNING AFTER THE NUPTIALS, I KNOCKED ON MY mother's door, knowing she would be packing but struck nevertheless by a pang at the sight of her trunk.

"Will you stay?" I asked by way of a greeting, shutting the door behind me. "Since Father has changed?"

"Changed?" Her eyes grew impenetrable and she dropped her hands to her sides. "I do not know how much people change, Elizabeth. Besides, I never loved him. Heavens, most of the time I did not even like him."

I winced. "Why did you marry him?"

"He had an estate and I wished to raise my station."

There was so much to ask about that, but I had a more pressing question. "Do you hate us because we are his?"

She swallowed hard and my breath stopped as I stood fixed in her gaze. "You look like him."

It was like being slapped by a wet hand. I wanted to walk away but felt rooted by confusion and the desire for her to keep talking, no matter how much it pained me.

Too late she added, "I do not hate you."

Like a pitiful kicked puppy that comes back to its master's feet, I asked, "May I write to you?"

"I do not know that that is a prudent idea."

My face went slack and I reached to steady myself on the dressing table. "Why?"

"My life is set a certain way now."

I felt an ache creep all over my already stinging self. "But cannot it be set differently?"

"Why do you wish to write to me?"

"So you can know what is happening here." I wanted her to hug me, of all things.

"Elizabeth, it is too hard for me to know," she said, her voice distant. "I cannot return, and I cannot be thinking about life here."

"But you returned for my uncle."

"Edward is my brother."

"Oh," I replied, spinning away.

"You do not need me. You are grown now."

I shut my eyes tight. "I am not quite grown."

"Nearly. What can I do for you? My only job would be to find you a husband, and yet, circumstances being what they are, my very presence could only damage your prospects. Or so I have been told."

I wanted a mother more than a husband, and felt young and hurt and sorry and ashamed that she did not even wish me to write.

I ran.

JANE FOUND ME ON OUR HILL. I HAD BEEN THERE FOR hours. At first, I kept my eyes fixed on our house and spotted a groom bringing my mother's curricle around to the front. Then servants emerged, likely with her trunk and bag, though I was too far away to see. Multiple figures exited next—servants in black, my family in colour. The woman in light blue was my mother, wearing the same gown she had worn upon her arrival. She rode away and the rest returned into the house. I could not bring myself to do the same, and stared out at our valley and at Meryton.

Jane sat without a word and handed me a roll left from the wedding party. I choked the food past the lump in my throat. "Our mother said I could not write to her," I whispered, watching the summer sun refusing to set.

She let out a plaintive sigh and then put an arm around me. "I have something to say that might upset you even more," she said, and I braced myself. "Our aunt and uncle have suggested a change of scene by living in London for a time."

"Aunt and Uncle Philips?" I asked warily. Our mother was so very different from both her sister and her sister-in-law; likewise my two uncles were men of wildly contrasting personalities. I often wondered: was it the inherent natures of my relations that had dictated their choices of partners? Or was it the choices they made that twisted them into becoming such different sorts of people? The latter gave me pause as I considered my own prospects, worried that the wrong husband would change the very essence of who I was.

"Yes, but Aunt Philips was so kind in her letter. I have great hopes for the scheme."

"What a lark! When do we leave?"

Jane lowered her eyes. "Not 'we'. They only invited me."

The blood rushed from my head. Jane and I had never been apart. "Why?"

"It is a chance to meet potential suitors. Our aunt and uncle do not believe I will have the right opportunities due to Father's refusal to socialise and travel."

"I am nearly of age. I could meet people, as well." She paused as if formulating an excuse that would hurt me least, and then I realised. "They do not wish for me to taint your prospects with my behaviour."

Jane's eyes flicked to mine and then to the horizon. "This is best, Lizzy."

I leapt to my feet. "You are as cruel as they!"

"None of us are cruel, dearest," she said, rising. Her tone was even, accustomed as she was to my outbursts. I was, unfortunately, proving everyone's point.

"But the Season is not for months. Why not leave later?"

"I desire to live in London for a time beforehand to buy

new clothes and to be schooled in etiquette and to learn dances I am ignorant of. I do not wish to embarrass myself."

I lifted my chin, anger coursing through me. "They are vulgar and rude. What sort of promising young man would call on you if you are with them?"

Jane tucked her lips between her teeth and blinked a few times. "More than will call on me here."

With that she walked down the hill.

CHAPTER FIVE

By the end of autumn, Miss Taylor and I had finished the last of Shakespeare's works. She loved plays, and we enjoyed acting them out. She said it was the only way to capture their greatness. After reading one of the Histories, which I rarely enjoyed, she asked me what I thought. I wrinkled my nose, and she flew into one of her playful rages. "A play or a piece of literature can be horrific, scintillating, uplifting, or outrageous. If you prefer to be colourful, you might say it was duller than the razor of an inept barber! But never, my pupil, never shrug or wrinkle your nose. And, heaven forfend, never say it was boring or nice. Words are power. Make your words strong and long!" She ended with her fists in the air. I let out a guffaw, which made her laugh as well.

Time crept by in the weeks after Jane left, even with an occasional visit to my tutor; I was certain I would die from the silence and waiting. Though Jane and I had made up from our row almost immediately, and the scant days before her departure had been filled with tears and hugs and promises of regular letters, the rending from my dear sister was painful almost beyond endurance.

Winter was dreary and even when spring began in earnest, I found little joy in the waking of the earth, too impatient to watch leaves or ants, too anxious to study the birds as they flew overhead towards their northern homes. I found comfort in the routine of my chores, and even allowed Margaret to teach me to knit. Her work was fluid and perfect. The needles click-clacked together and a little jumper miraculously formed between the wooden sticks and her milky hands. My needles, on the other hand, did little more than touch before I had a knot in my yarn. I would throw the yarn and needles to the floor and storm to the window. Each time, Margaret would gently set down her work and reach for my discarded jumble to undo the latest tangle. "It took me quite a long time to learn to do this, but now I love it. Imagine how wonderful it will be to see the baby wearing something you have made."

"We will be lucky if I have made so much as a cuff by the time it is born," I replied as I sank back into my chair.

We exchanged the same words daily, although I varied the clothing part I would finish. She mustered up a laugh each time. She amazed me.

Letters arrived from Jane—though not as often as she had promised—and I both loved and dreaded each one. The stories were diverting, but envy coursed through me like poison. It was not for wanting to be in rigid social settings, but the opportunities to have new experiences and to walk new lands. She and the Philipses had been to the Lakes, and Jane had spent the Season attending all manner of gather-ings. A number of young men had expressed interest in Jane, whose beauty was much discussed, yet she had not received any proposals. She claimed to be content, as she had not found any man amusing enough or kind enough to make her wish for an engagement, but I worried she was hiding concerns. Our family situation was unlikely to make her prospects easy, for our mother's departure had sullied our reputation, and our father's lack of money made us even more undesirable. Still, her looks and disposition might help her overcome these obstacles. The Philipses and Father had decided that this new arrangement was agreeable enough to consider allowing Jane to stay on indefinitely, a fact which sent me deeper into sorrow.

As the weather grew warmer, Margaret and I began to venture out together into the woods. I showed her my favourite spots around our land, and she told me the Latin names for all the plants. By early summer, Margaret became too fatigued to walk very far, so I sought companionship from James Fitzwilliam. It was only a twenty-minute walk to his house; I thought I could simply speak to him, not having been instructed in such matters by my father, who told me nothing, or by Margaret and Uncle Gardiner, who most likely assumed I knew. The servant raised his eyebrows when I knocked on the door and James's mother scowled as I stood in the foyer, but loneliness pushed me to bear her irritation for the moments it took James to come down the stairs.

"Miss Elizabeth," he said, his pond water eyes pinned to his mother, having lost their usual warmth. "To what do we owe the pleasure?"

I stood dumbly, having no answer I felt comfortable sharing in mixed company.

"Do you need an escort back to your house? An ankle injury on your walk back from Meryton, perhaps?"

I nodded, and he proffered an elbow.

As his coat pressed against my skin, I thought I might

faint. James had overtaken my mind too often these past months. At meals, I envisioned him sitting across from me talking and laughing. As I wandered through the woods, I thought of his hand covering mine. As I fell asleep at night, I pictured him leaning in for a kiss. I would blush in front of others, for no reason as far as they were concerned, and would make excuses about the heat or a fright. When I was alone, however, I relished the catch of my breath, imagining his reaching for me again. With his actual body touching mine, and my head spinning, I wondered at the prudence of this visit.

"What truly brings you to my house?" he asked after we were far enough not to be heard.

"Jane has been living with my aunt and uncle, and I have no one to talk to. It is exceedingly lonely, and I recall your joy at accompanying us on walks through the woods and fishing and the like."

He dropped my arm. I thought he meant to turn me away, but he glanced at the house then said, "You cannot come to my house alone again. We can agree upon times and places to meet."

"By letter?" A letter brought from house to house by servants when we could make the journey in person more quickly seemed absurd, but I knew he was right and hoped our epistles would not be intercepted.

He rolled his eyes. "Have you been taught nothing of propriety, Lizzy? Only engaged couples may exchange letters." Perhaps seeing my wounded feelings reflected in my expression, he softened. "We will agree in advance and hope no impediments present themselves."

Away from the confines of expectation, he was his loose, energetic self. We met as often as we could to walk and talk, me of Jane and my reading, him of his family and his impending departure, his father having purchased a position for him in the Dragoons. James would soon be Lieutenant Colonel Fitzwilliam—a dashing title, in my opinion. His father had insisted that he would not buy his way further up the military ranks, which did not trouble James at all. He claimed to like a good fight, and declared that beating the French was much better than stirring up trouble in the local public houses.

My pleasure at seeing James began to overpower my feeling of loss over Jane. While I continued to re-read Jane's occasional letters until my fingers had smudged half the writing, James's friendship became very important, not to mention that my breath quickened at the thought of him. I marvelled at wanting to be near a man so much that my limbs buzzed with anticipation or having my body burn at the thought of him. I had read of Tristan and Isolde's willingness to die for one another, and of poets professing that their loves were more beautiful than spring or fields of flowers, but I did not feel more stirred up at those words than if I were studying the migration of birds. Never had I imagined that the desire to touch or be touched would fill so much of my mind. James and I had kissed nearly a year earlier, but not since then. Had I offended him? Did I want to kiss James in particular or simply any man of better than average looks? It was difficult to say, as I encountered few men, and even fewer were attractive.

James answered those questions one afternoon as he skinned a rabbit he had caught and killed. He leaned over and gently pecked my cheek. To think of it now, the scene was both laughable and disgusting, but at that moment it seemed the height of romance. The scent of his skin—grass and musk—when I kissed his neck made me flush from head to toe. He threw the rabbit aside, washed his hands in the stream and ran back towards me, wiping his hands on his trousers. He took my face in his hands, and I almost gasped as he pushed his tongue into my mouth. I began to pull away, but then supposed I was meant to like it. I allowed him to continue, forcing myself not to wince or grimace. How had he learned to kiss like that? Had he been with many other girls? Who? Was I worse at kissing than they had been? But this was my first real kiss, and I lacked practice!

He pulled back, his face smooth with contentment. So I was not inept. I let out a calming breath, and a smile tugged at the corner of his lips before he threaded his fingers through my hair, pulling me close again. As his lips touched mine, all thoughts melted away.

From that day on, the destination of our outings was less important. No one seemed to mark that I was gone, and they were accustomed to my running off for hours at a time as it was. Eventually, however, Margaret noticed a change. "Young ladies do not spend time unchaperoned with young men," she said when I confirmed that I had, indeed, been alone with James. "Your reputation would be ruined if anyone knew. All you have is your reputation. You could ruin your sister's prospects of marrying well, too."

I knew this was true, but could not help myself.

"Have you touched?"

My immediate embarrassment confirmed it, and she sat down to ask what I had been taught about the relations between a man and a woman. As it was very little, I was shocked by her explanation. She blushed throughout the conversation, but repeated, "It is important that you know. You do not want to get yourself in a family way."

I was reluctant to spend time with James after that. I did not meet him at the pond as we had planned. I stayed indoors for a number of days, using the rain as an excuse, and I could hardly look at James when he finally arrived at my house and asked if we could sit a moment and talk. Margaret escorted us outside but made herself comfortable on a chair a fair distance away. Nevertheless, we kept our voices low and our gestures non-existent.

"Have you been ill?"

"No."

"Did we have a fight?"

Though I was nervous, the question made me smile for a moment. "No. I... We cannot be doing those things anymore," I whispered.

"Why not? I thought you liked them," he whispered back, his warm eyes twinkling at what I guessed was the memory of our shared pleasure.

"I do, but I do not want to have a baby."

He reared back, running his fingers through his unruly chestnut hair. "Nor do I, but we are not doing anything that will get you...that way."

"Yet."

He stared at me and then at his feet. Stupidly, all I wanted was to kiss every inch of his thin, long neck. He asked, "Cannot we spend time together nevertheless? Just walking. I have grown accustomed to it, and I-I would be lonely if we ceased our excursions."

"Just walking, though."

"I promise."

Sometimes we kept our promise. But no matter how heated things became, Margaret's sobering description of where all the kissing led allowed me to put a stop to it.

Then, on my sixteenth birthday, James and I were caught in an indelicate position.

Between dinner courses, we had decided on a stroll

through the gardens, soon losing the sounds of the gathering within. We continued out the garden gate and, obscured by the high stone wall, we were foolishly overcome with desire. My uncle, who had volunteered to fetch us for jam tartlets, came through the gate and gasped. I dare not describe what we were doing, but it was enough to send him bellowing into the house and my father back out with a rifle before we were entirely buttoned and laced.

"You will marry my daughter, sir, immediately!"

James, so flustered that he had left his waistcoat on the ground, merely stared. His mouth, which usually had an impish smile pulling at its corners, was working around as if searching for an explanation, though there was none but the obvious. "Sir—" James sputtered.

"There is no other way. You will take responsibility for your actions!" My head was still swirling when Father grabbed me by my arm and thrust me towards Uncle Gardiner and Margaret, standing red-faced behind him. "Go home and tell your family I shall call on them to work out the details on the morrow."

My birthday celebration had ended in disaster. The following hours were even less pleasant: words were shouted at and about me, and I was ordered to answer for myself, but any time I attempted to speak, I was instructed to be silent. It was so unpleasant that one of the servants broke her usual remove to look at me with sorrow as we passed in the hall.

Late the next morning, I was sent to the carriage where my father was waiting. Though walking to the Fitzwilliams' home would have been easy, at least the brief journey minimised the opportunity for more yelling. I was relieved by my father's silence. My head already throbbed. My stomach ached. My eyes were swollen from crying most of the night. When the sun rose, I was still fretting. Taking responsibility meant marriage, but was I ready? It no longer mattered. What if James refused? I would be ruined. If he agreed, I would be married to James! He was just a friend. A future soldier. A young man not yet established in the world. An older boy who made my heart slam within my chest whenever he came near, but was he the man I would have chosen to marry? I was not sure, yet it seemed I no longer had any choice in the matter.

We were escorted into a grand reception room and exchanged greetings, though not pleasantries. The earl looked as grave as my father, and his wife looked positively murderous.

After some heated words, the countess interjected, "Your daughter entrapped our son into a marriage that is only advantageous to her. Perhaps you planned this to elevate your own status!"

"Mother!" shouted James, his eyes sunken and shadowed as if he had not slept all night either.

"This is what you think of me?" I bolted upright. "That I whored myself to gain land or title?"

The room fell silent but for the gasp emanating from the countess.

I was too angry to let propriety silence me. "It is a strong word for a strong accusation. Reprehensible, in fact. James and I—" I realised there was no explanation that would not expose us both to further humiliation. "Our actions were—" I looked to him.

James met my gaze. He was biting his lip, his face paler than usual but for the pink tinging his soft cheeks—cheeks I loved to stroke with the back of my hands and press my cheek to. After what felt like an eternity, he drew himself up to his full height. "There was no taking advantage on either side."

My father's lips thinned, his nostrils flared. "I would think a future lieutenant colonel in the regulars would be more honourable than this."

"My son should have had more sense," said the earl, "but I cannot say I am entirely surprised. James has always been impulsive. I had hoped that the Dragoons would teach him a modicum of control, but his departure is now too late to be of real significance."

Hurt played across James's face, but he remained silent, biting his lip again.

For once, I stayed silent as well. We were told to step out while the parents made arrangements. We could have argued, but our fate was decided the moment we walked out past the garden. No, the moment I asked him to walk with me all those weeks prior.

"James," I said once we were alone, "I did not trap you."

"I never suggested you did." His brow was furrowed and every muscle was tight from his jaw to his shoulders to his very feet, which he set into motion with pacing.

I could not breathe, trying to think of being with this person for the rest of my life. With any person. "Do you not think we are too young for marriage?"

He stopped pacing. "My mother was fifteen when she was engaged."

"Romeo and Juliet, too, only that did not work out so well."

His eyes narrowed. "This is why women should not read novels and plays. Your imagination runs too wild."

This gave me pause. James knew I was an avid reader. Would he expect me to set all of that aside once we wed? I had to hope that his lack of kindness—the kindness I loved so dearly about him—and his thoughtless words were due to a general panic, and no indication of future behaviour or a truer self he had kept hidden.

"You are sixteen," he said, "which is not scandalously young. I am eighteen and about to embark on my career, so there is security in that. Do not fret."

I laced my fingers together and tugged, the mild pain focusing me. "I do not wish to marry." His eyes met mine, more sunken and wounded than ever I had seen them. "Not yet, James. It is not you that I object to, but…there are so many things I-I planned or wanted…hoped to do first."

"There is no use endeavouring to stop it, and what we want and hope for in life rarely matters. For us it is immaterial." Voices rose and fell on the other side of the heavy oak doors as if to prove his point. "It is not what I expected just before my departure, to end up with a wife." He clasped his hands behind his back and rocked forward and back on his heels, looking like his cousin, Mr Darcy, so remote and cold. "There is nothing to be done now." His face softened and he stepped towards me. "The truth is, I have never liked anyone half as much as you. Do you find me agreeable?"

"You know I do!" Thoughts of our walks and talks, as well as all the rest, flooded my mind and I could not help but smile a little.

"Well, then, we shall have a good start. Additionally, I shall be away so often that if we do not get on, you will not be overly troubled with my presence. If you do like me, you will spend beautiful hours pining like the heroines in your novels. Quite romantic."

My breath caught between a laugh and a gasp, and he stepped even closer, running a thumb along my cheek, making me melt.

He was decent and funny and wild and smart and attractive, and he loved to be out of doors as much as I. And as I had no choice in the matter, being matched with someone with all of those qualities made the prospect less terrifying.

A terrible thought crossed my mind. "James, I do not know much about being married."

"Nonsense. Why not?"

I shrugged with discomfort. He must have realised what I meant, for he ducked a bit so he could look into my lowered eyes, his expression one of uncharacteristic seriousness. "We will learn together. You shall see. We will be happy. I promise."

CHAPTER SIX

I t was decided that a rushed marriage without even the reading of the banns could breed suspicion, and— after we assured our families there was no reason to fear a child had been conceived—it seemed acceptable and prudent to delay until his first leave from the Dragoons. Since he would have to engage in training before six months of active duty and travel back, the time would allow me to learn the art of running a household. I would have preferred following James to enduring the ongoing fury and mistrust of our relations, but that was not an option with which I was presented.

As we were engaged, we were permitted to say a somewhat private goodbye (preceded by stern warnings regarding appropriate behaviour) when James departed a week later. I did not weep as I thought I might, and wondered if our feelings might be stronger in the future, making the leave-taking more painful. Quelling my emotion, in part, was his anger at his own family and general rage.

Margaret had suggested James and I walk in the garden.

I thought we might stroll arm in arm, but James stalked ahead. He stopped short to reach down for a stick, snapped it in half, and hurled the pieces at a rose bush, knocking yellow petals off the blossoms. "My family will give me nothing!"

My eyes widened; I had been hoping for sweet words and perhaps a caress, but not this news.

I endeavoured to gather myself. "Nothing?"

He shook his head. "As a second son, I was to have very little. Now, beyond the commission they purchased, they are prepared to give nothing more than a piece of their land on which I may build a home and that gift, they believe, is more than I deserve." He sank onto a marble bench, head in his hands. "With no money, however, I cannot afford a house."

I dropped next to him, my legs weak. "B-but how will we live?" Officers were expected to have at least some income, which was why their salaries were so paltry.

He shrugged, staring into the distance.

"I should come with you, then."

"The army will not transport but a few wives overseas, and those women have already been chosen."

"I could travel separately."

"With what money would you gain passage or survive? It is the same dilemma, Lizzy, as we have here. It is impossible."

The dark purple under his eyes made me long for the carefree James of before. His thin frame appeared even slimmer, and I wondered if he had been eating at all. Their cook was fine, but he once told me he could not eat when he worried.

"And even if it were not," he continued, "encampments can be rough places, I hear, and the towns around—without a man to protect you... No. Remain with your family and we will wed upon my return. Perhaps my parents will feel differently, and your father will have found something— anything—for a dowry."

I had known that Jane's and my financial prospects were grim, but I had not understood the full situation. "There is nothing?"

"If there ever was, there is nothing being made available." He bit at his bottom lip, which was cracked and peeling. "I was to marry for money, but…"

"I hate money," I said, which somehow made him laugh, and the loveliness of his features returned.

"We will find a way. Our passions led us to this impasse, but those same passions shall sustain us." James kissed my forehead, taking a moment to breathe me in.

We separated at the sound of my uncle calling to us, but I took his hands in mine. "I will do all I can to make you a good wife."

A smile softened his face. "Goodbye," he said, moving towards his home, "and be sensible while I am abroad."

"I should worry more about you, I suspect."

"We are equally foolish, I fear," he said, with a laugh and a wave.

In those months, I endeavoured to become more domesticated. Gone were the constant walks and endless reading, save for letters. Had we not been engaged, I could not have exchanged missives with him, and considered that one more bit of luck in an otherwise unfortunate situation. The happiest letter was the news that Mr Darcy would provide the funds for a modest house. I did not ask the details of their arrangement, but felt overwhelmed with relief. The second most joyful letter was from Jane declaring that she was, at last, planning her return.

Given that my financial future looked grim, it was clear I was in need of skills for keeping house. More than keeping it, I was to do much of the work. Hill and Ruthie tried to teach me. Hill hovered as she led me through the steps of cooking that went beyond peeling and cutting, but lost patience with my speed—too slow with the cutting, too quick and careless with the measuring. Ruthie brought me out to do work in the vegetable garden, but I kept wandering away, attracted by some plant or animal or good weather, anything more interesting than the task at hand. Our mutual dislike led to fits of fury from both of us.

What sent me into despair was the wash. Ruthie walked me outside before sunrise to a large tub filled with water and clothes. "These have been soaking since Saturday." I tried to imagine how long it was going to take to clean them. "To be clear," she said, "this is just the heavily-soiled clothing. The rest is over there." An overflowing basket rested behind me. I sighed, and she looked at me, but said nothing. "Let's start a fire. We've got to boil the linen and cotton in that copper pot to remove the soap and improve the colour. But before that, we must scrub each piece, rinse it, and wring it."

Pumping and hauling pail after pail of the water made my arms ache, and Ruthie took over after a time. Lighting the fire was my one success of the day, and I appreciated the pile of already-cut wood in the yard behind the kitchen. I was unsure if James would chop enough wood between deployments or if I would have to add that to my list of tasks. While the water heated, we peeled potatoes to make the starch water, and by the time the sun had peeked past the roof, it was time to agitate the clothes.

Ruthie handed me the stick which I attempted to turn

one way and then the other without splashing myself, but within minutes, my boots and skirt were a sopping, muddy mess. Blisters had formed on my hands and broken open before the first pile of laundry was even finished, but I kept churning. On the washboard, I cut my fingers, and after the third time I stopped to check for blood that might smear on the cloth, Ruthie had me step away. "Take a moment in the shade," she said.

As soon as I escaped the beating sun, tears welled up and spilled past my lids. I brushed them away and looked up to the hills, longing to walk in the shade of the trees and have nothing more pressing to accomplish than to identify the source of the birdsong.

Ruthie joined me in the shade. "You will have to get faster. That was not nearly the amount of linen you and Mr Fitzwilliam are sure to dirty in a week."

I stared at my swollen, red hands and inspected my raw fingertips. I hoped this was the worst job. If not, what had I agreed to? Everything hurt. Agreement or not, perhaps I needed to break off the engagement.

"Come, Miss Elizabeth. We must wring out the clothes and hang them. The day is warm and dry, at least."

I did not reply that I could not go on, though that was how I felt; nor could I say that I was ready to continue the labour, for I was not. However, it was expected of me. I could not be weak and I had to learn.

Ruthie filled the silence with a statement that only made matters worse. "Tomorrow we iron."

By the end of the first week, I had cuts and bruises in numerous places, and was sore everywhere else. I was an active girl, but ill-prepared for this sort of labour. I ruined a tablecloth, my butter never solidified, and I forgot to milk the cow one afternoon. Ruthie and Hill expressed their concern as the unsuccessful weeks passed, and I was at a near panic. What had I agreed to? Was this soul-crushing, body-breaking work my future? I could run away. I could accept that this work would consume my life forever. Or I could refuse the marriage and face my father's wrath, existing as a pariah. Which was the worst fate, I did not know.

CHAPTER SEVEN

At last, Jane arrived home. Before the Philipses' landau had come to a full stop, I was rushing through the door. I expected Jane to come bounding towards me, but she waited for a hand to help her down; even once the servant had moved on to assist our aunt, Jane remained perfectly still. Her regal bearing belied her youth, and her new gown shimmered in the autumn sunshine.

"Jane," I said, "how grand you are!"

She smiled sweetly and swept towards me. Gone was her girlish lope and confident stride, replaced by a grace I admired and a timidity I could not understand. "Oh, Lizzy, how I have missed you," she said just above a hush, folding me into her arms. Even her scent was different, at least at first. Under the perfumes and floral powders, however, I still noted her true sweetness.

"We must go for a walk in the woods and share everything that has happened—" I practically shouted.

"Tea is waiting. And there shall be no more walks." My

father glared at me. I had hoped with Jane's return, he would soften. I had been housebound for an eternity and thought I might run mad.

We all went in. At the table, I could hardly keep my eyes off Jane, having missed the sight of her dear face for so long. She kept her hand on mine whenever the use of two utensils was not required, as if I might vanish like an apparition.

We ate and the adults talked, and I noticed the conversation stayed away from controversial topics. My father drank more than usual, and his eyes were swimming by the time Aunt Philips said she was in great need of air. "The garden looks positively inviting. Would it not be lovely for the ladies to have some time alone?"

After a moment's hesitation, my father nodded his assent. The gentlemen rose, and so we three followed suit.

Once outside, my aunt said, "You might as well begin, dear Lizzy. How on earth did you become engaged to Mr James Fitzwilliam, and why is your father so especially angered over it?"

When I reached the end of my story, Jane, to whom I had not relayed the details in a letter lest it was intercepted, looked stricken, and my aunt's face was grave. "My dear, you are fortunate that your indiscretion matched you to someone with land."

"The land, I am afraid, is his family's. They have loaned a piece at the far reaches of their property so as to minimise interaction once we are wed. I cannot say the distance troubles me in the least."

"Lizzy!" Jane's eyes flew wide.

"Jane, they hate me. They always have, and you know that to be a fact."

Jane looked behind her in the direction of the Fitzwilliams' estate, though it could not be seen past our garden wall. She rose as if drawn towards it and then faced me. "How might you describe the house that is being built?"

"I could not. James asked me not to look until our wedding, and I will comply."

My aunt nodded in approval. For once I was heeding a request.

"I do not expect finery. It will match our station, which I know is low. It was generous of Mr Darcy to see to its construction."

My aunt crossed her arms. "Quite generous."

"I am learning to keep house. Soon I will be responsible for so much." My stomach churned at the thought of it.

My aunt's brows drew together. "You have snared a man of importance from a family of renown. You are lucky, my dear."

I wanted to feel lucky, but all I felt was an ache in my arms and back.

"OH LIZZY!" JANE AND I WERE IN OUR NIGHTGOWNS, ribbons tied in our hair to bring out the curls. We snuggled together in her small bed, the light from the candles making her face glow in the otherwise dim room. I had so missed her affection and these secret conversations. "How do you feel about your engagement?"

"I…" I shifted so I could see her face more clearly. "It was all so unexpected and then he departed. It hardly seems real."

"It is very real, indeed. It was the talk of all London."

"No."

"Yes!"

"What was said?"

Her forehead wrinkled. "Many suggested wrong-doing on both sides, I am afraid to say."

I sat up. "It was a mutual attraction gone too far, spotted at an inopportune moment. It ought to have ended when he went abroad but now we are to be bound for all eternity!"

"You make it sound so grim, Lizzy. I would have thought you pleased to be engaged, and to a man of such fine standing."

"The man in question has little personal means and his family hates me. He is even sillier and more lacking in control than I, which I fear bodes ill. And we are to have nothing. I shall be lonely and penniless!"

"Do you truly believe that?"

"I do." I flopped onto my pillow. "And yet not. Reports are that he shall make a fine soldier, and I know him to be a pleasing conversationalist. He is a great lover of the outdoors, and is endlessly amusing. In truth, I find I laugh more with him than anyone in the world, and his smile—oh, Jane, his smile. His entire face seems taken up by the broadness of it, and his eyes warm even further."

"You like him." At my nod, she said, "Then I need not worry?"

"No." I let out a small sigh. "I hope not."

JANE RAN INTO THE LAUNDRY WHERE RUTHIE WAS attempting to show me once again how to remove a stain. She held up a letter. "We have been invited to a ball at Netherfield!"

I had to laugh at the idea of prancing about with fine ladies and gentlemen whilst currently standing elbows deep in soiled linen. I wiped my hands on an apron. "The Mr

Bingley you spoke of in your letter lets Netherfield, is not that so?"

Jane eyed Ruthie. Ruthie, who had worked at our home for years and knew Jane well, gave a subtle nod excusing me from this odious chore—one that would be mine all too soon.

Once Jane and I were alone in the garden, she sat, her face bright, letter pressed to her chest. "It is indeed Mr Bingley who lets Netherfield. He is..." She paused to choose just the right words, as she was wont to do. "He is just what a young man ought to be. Sensible, good-humoured, lively, and I never saw such happy manners! So much ease, with such perfect good breeding!"

"And handsome?"

She dropped her gaze and nodded.

"You said you found him pleasant when first you met at a ball and that you danced two dances?"

"Yes," she said, looking up at me again. "And Aunt and Uncle and I had the great pleasure of dining with him and his party, if you recall. His sisters are quite fine, and treated me so kindly. Mr Darcy was there as well, for he and Mr Bingley are very dear friends."

I stiffened. "And will Mr Darcy be at Netherfield?" When Jane said he would, I pursed my lips. "Given your description of Mr Bingley, I wonder at Mr Darcy's friendship with him. Mr Darcy seemed neither lively nor kind when we have met him in the past. Have subsequent encounters altered your opinion of him?"

"He is distant, but I would not characterise him as unkind. Could a man building you a house be unkind?"

Rather than correcting her and pointing out the myriad selfish reasons he might be doing so, I merely said, "Jane, you are unable to see the ill in anyone."

"And you are too apt to see it in everyone."

"Not true." I threw back my shoulders, attempting not to smile. "And if I did, it would not be undeserved, for most human beings are intolerable."

"But not I."

"Not you." I kissed her cheek before returning to my work, promising we would discuss it again in the evening.

JANE DECLARED, "THE BALL AT NETHERFIELD IS UPON US," as Hill raced about with Jane's last trimmings in hand, and that phrase seemed to capture how I felt: put upon by the prospect of these particular festivities. I could not share in Jane's enthusiasm for the event, as I was not looking for a husband and anticipated the judgment of others whom I had avoided even more strenuously since James's departure. All our lives we had been stared at and gossiped about, and I feared this time would be no different. My only source of excitement was the opportunity to borrow a lovely new gown of Jane's. I could not help running my fingers along its length and noting the way it shimmered in the light.

Father would have insisted, as he often did, that we stay home but for a visit from Aunt and Uncle Philips. At tea following their arrival, they demanded arrangements be made for our attendance. When my father began to argue, my aunt's saucer clattered to the table. "The very future of this family and Jane's best hope of happiness and fortune depend upon it." This sounded dramatic, and yet I supposed she spoke in earnest and was quite accurate. Snaring Mr Bingley would set her up for life, as well as their children and generations to come. His fortune was indeed sizeable, and though his family had come into this money through trade, Jane's status as the daughter of a gentleman could be the very enticement he needed beyond her looks. Then again, our family was not entirely respectable. My recent behaviour could not have improved our standing.

Jane was asked to dance immediately upon arrival while I attempted to hide behind my aunt and uncle near the refreshment. I was successful at keeping out of view for a goodly time; however, I was eventually spotted by Mr Collins, an obsequious vicar to whom I had been introduced sometime prior, and made an excuse about why I could not dance. My uncle went along with my lie, adding embellishments about the twisted ankle, disparaging a footman he declared foolish and careless. I did hope Mr Collins would not seek out the identity of the young man and have him unfairly dismissed. My concerns were assuaged when he seized upon Charlotte Lucas, one of Jane's friends from Meryton.

"You must accept someone!" my dear aunt said to me when they were out of range of hearing. "It is unseemly for a young woman to stand about."

"I thought the purpose of dancing was to secure a husband. I have done so, making dancing entirely unnecessary. Is it not so?"

My uncle looked as if he might argue when I excused myself with the claim of needing air.

I stepped out onto the balcony and, not seeing a stair, stumbled into a man coming inside.

"Mr Darcy!" I said, marvelling that his tea merely sloshed into the saucer and not onto his shoes, as mine most assuredly would have done.

"Miss Elizabeth, do you make a habit of throwing yourself bodily into every interaction?" My laugh caught in my throat as I wondered if there was an untoward meaning in what might be an accusation. At that moment he seemed to realise the error in his choice of words, adding, "I mean to say, we seem never to meet without near injury."

"I have been accused of a degree of spirit not often found in ladies, yet I am unable to alter myself entirely."

"Have you truly tried?" he asked, somewhere between amusement and disapproval.

I was thankful that the balcony was otherwise deserted, for the thoughts spilling from my unchecked mouth were too unguarded, and his last comment cut me to the quick. "In truth, I have not endeavoured in the way I should for fear that if I bend too far, I shall break."

He cocked his head, his eyes piercing. "Do you believe that marriage shall break your spirit?"

I pondered this, stepping towards the carved rail to gaze at the pond encircled by torches, which flickered and sparkled on the black water. "I hope not, sir, though it is 'the undiscovered country from whose bourn'—"

"—'No man returns,'" he finished.

My head snapped towards him. "You know *Hamlet?*" I brightened. Perhaps this man was not so intolerable.

"I was forced to memorise its soliloquies by a tutor in my youth." He set his cup and saucer upon the stone rail, giving me a moment to imagine anyone attempting to teach him the love of great words, and also finding it impossible to picture Mr Darcy as a child.

I nearly laughed at the thought. Though only twenty-two, he seemed far older.

Mr Darcy asked, "It is grim for you to compare marriage to death, is it not?'

Now I did laugh. "Grim, but perhaps accurate."

A smile played at his lips, making his face suddenly kinder, more handsome. Mr Darcy was attractive, to be sure. Like James, his cheekbones were high and his jaw narrow, though Mr Darcy's chin was more pointed. His features were relatively delicate, though his general air of superiority hardened them beyond femininity.

He asked, "You are a great lover of the Bard, are you?"

"I am. And you?"

He shrugged. "His work entails too much irrational passion for my taste, I am afraid. If Hamlet would have simply accepted his father's death and returned to university, many lives would have been saved."

"A unique interpretation." I laughed once more, and his brow furrowed, perhaps in censure of my ongoing merriment. Undeterred, I asked, "To follow your logic, would you believe that Macbeth ought to have ignored the witches' prophecies?"

"Indeed," he said gravely, fiddling with a shiny button on his deep green coat. "Setting aside the murder—"

"The murdered king would find that a challenge, but go on."

His brow lowered. "Dishonouring his friendship for greed and position was ruinous. He could have done with less money and the title he earned."

"An easy condemnation from a man with unmatched resources and unshakeable status."

"All status is shakeable." He took a sip of what was left of his tea. With anyone else, the gesture would have simply been a moment to take in refreshment, but the deliberateness with which he moved seemed as if he was preparing himself—I feared for what. He set the cup down again with hardly a clatter. "I confess to being somewhat surprised at your engagement to my cousin."

I did not dare look him in the eyes. "Were you?" I attempted to sound aloof. "James—er, Mr Fitzwilliam and I have been friends all our lives."

He straightened, allowing him to look down his nose at me—a nose I was pleased to find fault with, for it had a small bump on the bridge, taking away from his perfection just that much more. "To find a friend is not the object of marriage, Miss Elizabeth. Your lack of money and your family's disgraceful past have hurt his status immeasurably."

At this I turned and glanced about to be sure that we were, indeed, alone. I realised it was not proper for us to be out here in such a fashion, and I feared worsening my reputation. As a woman engaged to this man's relation, I thought it might be acceptable, but I was always unsure of the rules, having no one to teach them to me. "Perhaps you would care to insult me in more company than a deserted balcony?"

"It would be prudent for you to hear what I have to say out of earshot of others." He cleared his throat. "Were you seeking to destroy James or were you as unthinking as he?"

I sucked in a breath. "How dare you, sir?"

"How dare I?" His voice sent a chill through me. "I will help you and my cousin out of familial obligation, rather than joy." His face was stone but for the anger playing around his now-cold eyes. "His parents view the matter differently and sought to punish you both by withholding a respectable roof from over your heads. I would not do such a thing, for whatever you might think of me, I do care for him and take familial ties seriously. However, the recklessness both of you showed lowers my esteem, and my good opinion once lost, is lost forever."

There were many insults and bits of unwelcome news in his tirade, but I did not wish for him to think he had bested me. "What a shame that we shall never be friends, for James admires and enjoys your company." I swallowed hard, finding it difficult to catch my breath. "Pray, allow me to leave you." At his nod I swept away, determined to keep my steps steady.

Once back in the overheated ballroom, I desired to run for home immediately, but the sight of Jane dancing with Mr Bingley convinced me to endure my pain in the hopes of her happiness.

Mr Darcy, unfortunately, followed me in just as Lady Lydia, James's sister, approached. "Miss Elizabeth!" Her face was flushed from dancing or excitement. Possibly both. "We have not seen you at the house since James departed!"

"Yes." I stole a glance at Mr Darcy who stood to my side, his high cheekbones flushed. "I am not welcome there, as I am sure you are aware."

"Oh, Lizzy—" This was the first time she had called me by this familiarity, and I found it disconcerting. "We are to be family! You must not let my parents' temper impede your visits." The music changed and she bounced on the balls of her feet, clapping, which made her appear even younger than her fifteen years. "The next dance is my favourite!" She spun in place, tittering. "If only Kitty were here. She and I never miss a step when she is my partner."

"Is Lady Kitty at home?" I enquired.

"Why, of course! She was not feeling well. And besides, my mother says I am more foolish when she is near." She giggled, perhaps proving the point.

A young man I did not recognise approached with a bow and said she had promised him this dance. She beamed and they took their place.

Mr Darcy scowled. "It would seem self-control is not especially valued in Meryton."

"Perhaps we value other things more, such as kindness."

"Would you call the Fitzwilliams kind?"

I had no response polite enough or retort clever enough, so I held my tongue.

"Why do you not dance?"

I knew my answer would vex him. "Because, sir, I do not know the dances."

"How can that be?"

I watched as the bows and curtseys began, caught between shame and amusement. "No one ever taught me."

"Yet your sister knows them," he said, eyeing Jane's joyful face and graceful figure moving through the intricate patterns required.

"She learned many in London these past months. My aunt and uncle hired a dance instructor."

"What did you learn from your tutor in your youth?"

"The Bard," I said, and with a curtsey skirted away.

CHAPTER EIGHT

I spotted a figure coming down the lane in a dashing red coat with gold embellishments. The swagger told me right away it was James. I shouted his name and we both raced for one another. In moments, we were a tangle of limbs and hair, not behaviour becoming anyone of our station, neither of us caring.

"I did not expect you so soon!" His last letter claimed he would not arrive for another week.

"When I told them my wedding was in a month, I was put on an early coach home."

"Less than three weeks now," I said, trying to keep a quaver from my voice.

He pressed his lips into a line, an expression that took the light out of his eyes, so I pulled him into a stand of trees, a place we had hidden before. In the shadows, he moved closer, cradling my face in his rough palms. Before his training, his hands had always been smooth, and he had never had such pronounced muscles. "You look older, Lizzy."

"It is the hard work." I laughed. "It is ageing me."

"No," he said, his voice gravelly. "I mean, more mature. Grown. It seems less like robbing a cradle."

"Is that how you felt before?"

"No." He traced my bottom lip with his thumb. "Perhaps." He let his hands drift to my hair, then down the small of my back. "But now less so." He pulled me closer and eased us to the ground. James had a new confidence about him, for he did not hesitate or fumble.

A shiver ran through me as he traced my body with his fingers. He kissed me harder and I was floating. I wrapped one leg around him and my entire body burned. His lips whispered down my neck and he groaned. "Lizzy, no one kisses as well as you."

I froze. "No one? How— Whom have you been kissing?"

His eyes widened. He blinked a few times, but remained silent.

"Whom have you been kissing?" I prayed he meant some girl he knew before our lives were entwined.

"The thing you must understand, Lizzy, is that the months are very long when a soldier is away from home."

I sat up, knocking his hands to the ground. "The months were long here as well, but I was not kissing anyone."

"It is not the same."

"How?"

"You are a woman."

"And women do not feel desire?"

"Not the same."

I did not know whether to laugh or shout. "How would you know?"

He sat up. "I do not, but— Let us drop the matter."

"Whom were you kissing?" He shifted but did not answer, so I asked, "Was it more than kissing?" He looked

68

away and my stomach dropped. "Exactly how much did you do with this-this mystery woman? Or women? God knows how many you have been with these eleven months?"

He swallowed hard and worked his mouth around as if searching for an answer.

"Have you been with a woman…entirely, James?"

He reached out for me but I pulled back, scrambling to my feet. "I wanted to wait," he said, rising. "I thought it could be the first for both of us on our wedding night, but then the men were all going into town—the battle—you see, we all felt…I'm sorry, Lizzy. Truly."

"Sorry?" I felt my bottom lip quiver, hot tears threatening to spill out despite my best efforts. "It was not an accident, James. You made a decision. You—" I wiped at my cheek roughly with the back of my hand. "If our marriage was not compelled, I would not marry you! I do not wish to see you until the wedding day."

"Our families will expect a visit."

"Then I shall sit and listen, but will not speak to you next until the church." I began walking to the lane, dodging branches and trunks.

"I could leave you, Lizzy," he called out.

I froze.

"I could cry out on this marriage and still find another wife. In fact, my family would be pleased if I did."

I sucked in a short breath, still unable to face him.

"There would be talk, of course, but the matter of you would be forgotten. I could secure a woman with more money and a better reputation, but you would be ruined. I would never do that to you." The weight of this truth was so heavy that I could hardly remain standing. He came closer, leaves crunching under his feet. "But you see, I do not want that. I care for you, Lizzy. I want you," he said, much more gently.

I brushed away more tears and ran into the light.

PERHAPS I SHOULD NOT HAVE BEEN SURPRISED WHEN MY father announced that my mother would be present at my wedding. Nevertheless, I ran to my room, slammed the door, and smashed my washbasin on the floor. Truth be told, I had always hated the garish pink roses painted inside and out, so it was not difficult to locate an object to ruin. I brooded until the skies darkened and then decided to try another tactic. Imagining how Jane might comport herself, I made my way down the stairs and into the sitting room, offering a curtsey as I entered. Sitting carefully at the edge of the sofa, I folded my hands in my lap in as great a show of ladylike grace as I could manage. My father stared at his book, and I kept my voice hushed. "I do not understand why she should be invited."

After a drawn-out silence, he looked up. "Because she is your mother."

"I do not want her here."

"I. Do not. Care." His tone was even, though his words were slurred with drink. "You will greet her with warmth or you will say nothing, but there shall be no more outbursts from you." He closed his book with deliberation. "Do you understand? If you hurt her feelings with so much as a cross look, there shall be consequences. Mark my words." And still holding his book, he left the room.

I stared at the door through which he had passed, and comforted myself with the thought that once I was married, I would never have to do anything I did not want to do or be spoken to harshly again. Or would I? I could predict less about James than I thought, and my fury at him had not entirely abated. He had come to the house asking to visit, but I had refused. Jane and Margaret declared it pre-wedding nerves, but I knew better. As did James. He returned a second time and the ladies insisted I speak to him, even closing the door to the parlour. Their concern that my coldness might ruin the wedding plans must have outweighed any constraints of propriety.

Once alone, I stared at my hands, still folded primly in my lap. "I will marry you, James," I said, wanting very much not to allow any emotion into my words. "I still care for you despite myself." I took a slow breath and looked up. I saw lines on his face that had not been there eleven months ago, and his downturned mouth and sunken eyes gave me pause. We had not spoken of his time with the Dragoons, and I wondered what his life had been these past months. "I am angry, but I will get past it. Even so, I think it prudent that we not be together until the wedding. I do not trust myself to be civil or wise with my words."

He nodded, brows pinched together in a frown. His bow, so oddly formal, almost cracked through my defences. "As you wish, Miss Elizabeth. Be well until we meet at the church." This turn of phrase made me smile, and his head tilted in confusion. "Have I amused you?"

"You always amuse me, James, which is why I am unable to refuse you." Images of him in a room full of partially-clothed women filled my mind, and heat flashed in my cheeks. No, I could not forgive so quickly. I straightened. "Until next week." I offered a perfunctory curtsey.

He began to walk away but turned back, opening his mouth as if to say something, but clapped it shut and strode out.

After my father left, I sat in the parlour while Uncle Gardiner read and Margaret did needlework. I was lost in a foul mood. Margaret quietly asked me to confide in her but I said nothing, staring instead at their son, sleeping in the cradle Father had made for his children—or, rather, had made for Matthew, dead and buried as it turns out. I pictured my mother walking away from me as I slept in this same cradle. I was not enough to keep her here.

I turned to my uncle, the small flame casting a youthful glow over his features. "Uncle, may I ask a question?"

"Of course." He set down *The Woodworker's Guide to Tables*. I had to smile at his choice of material: as dry as he. But he was a good man; a good father, warm when he thought no one could see—tickling his son's belly, smelling the top of the baby's head and grinning. A husband Margaret loved, his gentle side coming out in her presence, though she did have to force him away from his work and remind him to converse with her some nights. "Lizzy?"

"Yes?"

"You have a question?"

"Oh, yes." I perched on the edge of the chair. "Why would Father ask Mother to be at my wedding?"

My uncle jumped to his feet, as if to leave the room. Instead, he shut the door, took three measured steps to the mantel and stared at me, clenching his teeth. He turned and sat back in his chair. He crossed his right leg over his left, then uncrossed it and crossed his left over his right. Then he stood and walked back to the mantel. He turned a porcelain figurine exactly one-quarter turn and walked to the window. I began to fear he would continue in this way and forget my question, but then, still looking out at the darkness, he asked in his deep voice, "Why do you desire such information?"

I let out an indignant snort.

Margaret rose with her embroidery basket. "I shall leave you."

He snapped his head to her, his wide eyes shouting unspoken desperation, but she set a little smile on her lips and nodded, pecking his cheek. She murmured something I could not hear, and he watched her go.

"I…" He stared at the closed door as if hoping she might return and rescue him from this conversation. "Why do you ask this now?"

"She is returning in a matter of days!" I silenced myself, wondering if my father was near enough to hear.

"I am aware. I was responsible for the invitation. Both times."

I gasped and stood to leave, but sat again with a thud, deciding not to depart without learning what I had come to find out.

"I suppose— It was not right, her leaving, but I remember her love for her children." He turned, his eyes locking with mine. "It was real. I wanted her at my wedding because she was such an integral part of my childhood, and I wanted to remind her how much of my life she had missed. And I invited her to yours…for the same reason, I suppose. The missing, not the being integral." Beads of sweat lined his upper lip. "I ought to have asked, but you would have said no."

I considered his words. My uncle never asked for anything, and I never considered the hurt her absence might have caused him.

"Margaret says I should talk more to people," he said, rubbing the back of his neck. "I know she is correct. I-I have a difficult time—"

I crossed to him and pecked his cheek. "It is all right, Uncle. I know you try."

THIS TIME, AS MY MOTHER APPROACHED THE HOUSE IN HER carriage, I was more interested in my father. His look was impenetrable. Was he embarrassed? Excited? Angry? He took her hand and helped her to the ground. I could not believe she trusted him to take his hand at all.

I desired to speak to her alone, so I rushed past Hill and brought her up to a guest room. As she climbed the stairs, I arranged myself on the bed, thrumming with excitement, ready for a mother-daughter talk. She gave me an expectant look, and then I remembered that she was still the woman who left. She was still the woman who refused to exchange letters with me. I could not welcome her into my life. I bid her good day and walked out, shoulders slumped.

CHAPTER NINE

On my wedding day, I awoke before sunrise and decided to go for a walk. I considered climbing my hill, but without Jane, it simply did not feel the same. Jane was sleeping, and I had opted for tranquillity rather than a scolding, not wanting to waste time by waking her before she was ready.

I did not wish to think about James and other women, what our house might look like or if it was even complete, the debt we owed to Mr Darcy for it, who might say cutting things about me at or after the wedding, or what attention my mother might attract just for being present. I did not want to think of dirty clothes or meals to plan or cleaning floors. I wanted a few moments of blissful lack of duty and expectation.

I strolled through a pasture, snapping off blades of waist-high grass as I went. Steam was rising off the brook, and the birds were just beginning to sing their mad morning songs. I sat down at the water's edge and watched tiny fish float by and the bugs skating above them, improbably clutching the surface. I pulled my shawl tighter around my shoulders and looked up at the treetops, noticing that on some of the highest branches, the leaves were already lemon yellow. Each morning as I awoke for the next few weeks, more blotches of colour would mark those woods until all the green had been wiped away. Geese honked overhead and a chipmunk skittered in the underbrush.

I would have to go home soon and become a bride, but I tarried a few moments more, wondering if married life allowed time for appreciating nature.

When I arrived home, everyone was frantic. They assumed I had run off to escape the wedding.

"How can you be so irresponsible?" my father shouted.

"I was just—"

"Do not offer an excuse. The ladies have been worried sick about you. Sick!" he growled. "Make yourself presentable and do not embarrass us, today of all days." He stormed off, pulling a flask from his coat.

I saw my mother watching, and wondered if this was the sort of treatment she had received after bearing no heir.

Margaret walked in from the hallway wearing the yellow dress from the first day we met. Her normally serene expression had been replaced by pinched impatience. "We must leave for the church in half an hour."

"How can that be? I was only out walking for…" I realised I had lost track of the time. I had to wash, fix my hair, put on my corset, fasten the complicated dress, and locate my formal shoes. I would never be ready in time. I turned to Margaret, unable to breathe.

"We will have you ready." And with that, she relaxed and took control. "Start by getting the dirt out from under your nails."

I spotted my mother, still standing in the doorway, and

my cheeks burned. It was bad enough to be frantic and scolded, but to have the woman who abandoned me witness it made my heart race faster. I followed Margaret's directions, and even let my mother help. I said little and chose not to complain about the too-tight corset and impractical shoes.

I walked down the aisle on time and saw James's crooked smile, his expression one of pride or discomfort—I was not sure which, at the moment. His typically wild hair was slicked down and shiny, and he fiddled with the buttons of his tail-coat, all of which were distressingly charming. Even so, my chest tightened with uncertainty as I moved towards him, drawn by his dark eyes and handsome confidence.

At the beginning of the ceremony, I had difficulty focusing on the vicar's words. I could not quite believe that I was actually getting married, and to James: so strong, so tall, so very nervous just then. He wiped his brow a few times and appeared pale. Was he struggling to listen to the words as I was? Part of his worry had to be me. Over the past few weeks, I had wrestled with my anger over his experiences while abroad. Men had different latitudes than women, and as a soldier away for long periods of time he would have temptations. He had failed to deny himself pleasure. That wounded me, yet I understood. It was, however, something we would need to address as a married couple that would spend many years apart.

I looked over my shoulder at the crowd. My father scowled, a perfect echo of Lord and Lady Broxbourne. Uncle Gardiner looked perturbed, and Margaret was preoccupied with their son. The older guests looked on with approval except for Miss Taylor. Our last conversation had been an argument about why a smart girl would want to marry, and she had despaired that my days of reading and exploring out of doors were at an end. Despite my wariness over marrying at such a young age, I was not as certain as she that a life lived alone could be as fulfilling, or that it could be accomplished without great material or spiritual deprivation.

The vicar's words caught my attention as he described marriage. "Secondly, it was ordained for a remedy against sin, and to avoid fornication; that such persons as have not the gift of restraint might marry, and keep themselves undefiled members of Christ's body."

I dared not look at the congregation, knowing some who knew our secret would judge me as more sinful than I was, and judge James as less than he was. My eyes locked with James's and he cocked his head ever so slightly. Another apology? Yes, the minute twitches around his eyes told me he was, indeed, deeply sorry. I would have to forgive him.

"Thirdly, it was ordained for the mutual society, help, and comfort, that the one ought to have of the other, both in prosperity and adversity. Into which holy estate these two persons present come now to be joined."

The vicar continued speaking as I pondered the last. Would we be prosperous? Face adversity? Perhaps both, or neither. There were too many unknowns. For a couple born into families such as ours, there ought to have been more security, yet I felt upended. Adrift. The future was too shrouded in mysterious possibility.

"James," the vicar asked, "wilt thou have this Woman to thy wedded Wife, to live together after God's ordinance in the holy estate of Matrimony? Wilt thou love her, comfort her, honour, and keep her in sickness and in health; and, forsaking all other, keep thee only unto her, so long as ye both shall live?"

James made these promises, but would he keep them? He had already failed to forsake others, yet we had not exchanged vows when he did so. Would words and promises change him?

"Elizabeth, wilt thou have this Man to thy wedded Husband, to live together after God's ordinance in the holy estate of Matrimony? Wilt thou obey him, and serve him, love, honour, and keep him in sickness and in health; and, forsaking all other, keep thee only unto him, so long as ye both shall live?"

Obey and serve. It was my duty, if not my talent to do both. I would endeavour to be a good wife. I felt confident that I could keep only unto him, as I had never desired any other. Would he do the same?

"I will." I forced the words out, my throat thick with misgivings and concerns.

When the vicar placed our hands together, James squeezed mine. Still looking forward, he whispered, "I do love you, Lizzy."

I squeezed his hand back.

There was no escape. We were bound to one another.

THE WEDDING BREAKFAST WAS TEEMING WITH PEOPLE FOR whom I cared little, save Margaret and my dear Jane. Mr Bingley was present, which set Jane aflutter, and she spent much time in conversation with him and Mr Darcy. I had hoped he might take ill or find our little ceremony unworthy of his attendance, but I suppose he came to ensure that the wicked girl from the ball followed through on her promise.

Guests stared as James and I moved about, and I was unsure if they did so with envy or approval. Their gazes made me think about childhood walks through Meryton with Jane, causing me to shrink in on myself so thoroughly that James asked if I felt quite well. I said I had not slept enough nor eaten yet, so he ran off to retrieve sipping chocolate.

As I waited, I heard my mother speaking loudly enough that people turned to stare, some even hiding laughter. "We were surprised that Elizabeth landed so well. We had hopes for Jane, the more handsome and accomplished of the girls, never expecting our youngest to marry first. I have it on good authority that there might be another wedding in our family's future, and a connexion with a man of far greater fortune. But I say too much!"

My eyes darted to Jane, but she was happily oblivious to our mother's misstep, sharing a moment with Charlotte Lucas.

James returned with my refreshment, only to excuse himself with a kiss and a promise to return presently.

I escaped for a moment's solace to my childhood bedchamber, wishing to say a little goodbye to the place I both loved and loathed. When I descended the stairs again, I meant to quickly pass the sitting room, but then I heard, "What do you think of your cousin's bride?" I peeked and saw Mr Darcy standing with Mr Bingley. Mr Darcy's arms were crossed, and he wore his perennial scowl. Realising they were speaking of me, I pressed against the hallway wall and listened.

"She is tolerable." It was Mr Darcy, whose tone was more reserved than the bright and welcoming voice of Mr Bingley. "She is sharp-witted, to be certain, but too young. How could my cousin be foolish enough to marry a mere child with no fortune when he himself has no money to speak of? His family has all but disowned him for the misstep of becoming entangled with such a one as her, and I cannot disagree."

"Upon my honour, Darcy, you are too harsh a judge all around. She is delightful." A pause. "Darcy, I hate to see you standing about by yourself in this stupid manner."

"You know how I detest speaking unless I am particularly acquainted with the person. At such a gathering as this it would be insupportable. There is not a woman or man whom it would not be a punishment to me to speak with."

"I would not be so fastidious as you are! I never met with so many pleasant girls in my life as I have this day; and there are several of them you see uncommonly pretty."

"The only handsome girl is Miss Bennet."

"Oh! She is the most beautiful creature I ever beheld!"

A pause. "I know that look," Mr Darcy said, his voice filled with unspoken warning. "Bingley, you cannot seriously be thinking of linking yourself to this family. My cousin was foolish enough. You have no need to compound the problem. The mother not only abandoned her children—leaving them to learn no manners, nothing of society—but she is brash and without manners. The father is a drunk and has nothing but luck keeping him from losing his estate. There is no reason for you to mix yourself with one such as Miss Bennet."

"I like her. And she likes me."

"How can you tell? The wan smile she offers is no indication of affection."

"Darcy, I—"

"No, Bingley. I cannot hear of it. It would be a misstep of the highest degree."

"Lizzy!" James called as he came through the door, ending both the conversation and my eavesdropping.

Perhaps they were aware I had heard their scathing

conversation, but I did not care. I had no very cordial feelings towards James's cousin, house or no house.

James asked, "Have you your things? It is time for our departure."

I took the elbow he offered.

As we stepped into the carriage, my mother's voice rose over the din of the crowd. "Jane, perhaps you will be next!"

Jane turned shades of scarlet I did not know were possible on a human face.

THE HOUSE MR DARCY HAD BUILT FOR US WAS A SIMPLE cottage painted yellow, at my request, with black shutters. At James's instruction, it had been furnished more like a farmhouse than a manor, much to his family's horror. James opened the door and insisted on carrying me in, which I thought was foolish, but smiled despite myself.

We unpacked with haste and stood in the darkening house staring at one another, not certain what to do next. Now…now we were supposed to…be together. Completely. In ways I had not allowed. And I knew it would hurt, at least the first time. Margaret had been sure to warn me. I wanted to know what it was all about, but I was afraid. What if I did not like it? What if, now that we were married, James was rough with me? What if my inexperienced performance was so poor that James preferred the whores he had been with and never wanted to share a bed again? More than that, though, the reality of the situation, of a lifetime of looking at the same person in the same house, made my heart sink a little. It was not him or this house, but the idea of it all.

James might have had similar concerns, for he suggested we take a walk. The stream, which ran within view of our new house, was the same one I had visited that morning. He put an arm around my waist and his warmth began to melt away the fear gripping my insides.

"Why do we not sleep out here tonight?" I suggested, and though he regarded me with some surprise, he agreed.

There was no one to tell us that it would get cold or that sleeping outside on a wedding night was improper. It was liberating. We ran back to the house, changed into plainer clothes, grabbed blankets and ran towards the stream again, laughing the entire time.

Tree branches created a canopy over us, yet we could still see stars twinkling through the leaves.

Once our blanket was spread out, we sat and James reached for my hand. My heart pounded so hard it made me dizzy.

"We've touched before," he murmured, though no one was near enough to hear us. "The next step is not so great."

I tucked my lips between my teeth and swallowed hard.

"I will be gentle."

Perhaps he was waiting for my reply, but I could not speak.

"Lizzy, the first time for a woman can be——"

"I know. Margaret…"

He nodded.

I took hold of his cheeks and pulled him to me, kissing him hard and pressing my hips to his. "No need to stop anymore."

"We are free. We belong to each other."

"In every way."

It was a deeper vow than any we had spoken earlier in the day.

CHAPTER TEN

T he next few weeks were tumultuous. Each morning, James would meet with Mr Davis, a man he hired in the hopes of turning this small bit of land into an orchard and a self-sustaining farm. I had hoped the funds would be spent on a servant for the household. A maid-of-all-work, if nothing better, could be hired for a pittance, but James decided that as there were only two of us with nowhere to go and no fancy foods needed, we could save the money by having me do all the housework.

With him out and about, and Jane back to London with our aunt and uncle, I was left quite alone. Unaccustomed to running a household, I did not have a schedule, so the first night after the wedding when James returned, there was no food on the table. I had caught fish, but assumed James would cook it—as Hill had done. Eyebrows raised, James suggested that I take care of it while he went back out to measure a pen for animals we did not yet have the money to purchase. I knew how to clean and scale the fish, but overcooked them. James did not complain, for which I was grateful.

By the end of the first week, we finished the bread Hill had sent as a gift, and our clothes needed washing. A choking wave of anger filled me as I stood over his dirty shirts and trousers boiling in the large tub. With each chore that day, my anger grew until James came home. I threw a pail at him and locked him out of the house. No sooner had I set the latch than I regretted it and opened the door.

He was standing wide-eyed and wet, but did not speak first.

"I—" How to explain without making myself seem as stupid as I now felt? "My day was frustrating."

"Heavens, Lizzy, you cannot bar me from the house every time you are peevish!"

I blinked back tears. "I know. I know, but…I hate housework. I cannot imagine doing this for the rest of my life!"

He rocked back on his heels before reaching down to right the pail. I feared he might argue or yell, but he lowered himself to the front steps and patted the empty space at his side. "Sit with me."

I sat, still bracing myself for a fight.

"You knew that this would be the way of things, did you not?"

I looked out at the hills where I wished to roam and nodded. Still unable to look at him, I said, "The reality is so much…harder."

"What is the worst chore?"

"Washing clothes. The smoke burns my eyes. My hands crack from the boiling water. My arms ache from wringing out the cloth. I cannot do it. I truly cannot!" I knew how childish I sounded, but once I began admitting the truth, I could not stop.

James picked up a few rocks near his feet, then skipped them along the path. "What if we did it together?"

My mouth fell open. "Sincerely?"

"Why not?"

The *why not* was James's mother. She declared it horrifying that her son was working like a peasant and doing women's work, claiming his doings could be viewed from the sitting room of her house, which was a lie. The distance was too vast and there was a hill between our properties, so I suspected she had ventured close on foot or, more likely, paid a servant or tenant to spy on us. I did not say as much to James. I did argue with him about why he cared what she thought of our actions, but he did and that was that.

"Do not think of the rest of your life," he said, holding my hand that evening as we stood in front of our house watching the sun set. "Just one task, just that moment." He kissed the bridge of my nose, and I melted into him.

We remained there talking, trying to make the other person happier, even just a little. That, it seemed, was marriage.

The drudgery of my tasks became a routine and my fury subsided. James told me of his worries about earning enough money as well as his work around the land, and he shared details of life in the military. He described the travail of marches and the fear before an attack, and it made my complaints about stubborn stains and butter that would not solidify seem small in comparison. It did not make the chores more enjoyable, but I knew I was lucky to have a man who listened to me and hoped that when he returned to the house, he would find a contented wife.

Knowing he would leave for the Dragoons soon, and growing accustomed to doing the household tasks alone, I endeavoured to put on a cheery face. I had to accept that the work needed to be done, and no one could rescue me from it. Disappointment settled in my heart, but I tried to ignore it.

Just as I grew used to our life, it all changed.

"BUT MARGARET, HOW CAN I BE INCREASING?"

"I explained it all before the wedding."

"I know how, but *how*?"

"Did you rinse with vinegar?"

"Yes, every time."

"Well, it does not always work."

"Apparently!" It seemed so unfair. I did not want children at that moment. I simply desired to become accustomed to married life and to have relations with my new husband before he disappeared back to the military. I felt wholly unprepared to give of myself and my time the way Margaret did. She was never alone, and I loved being alone. She was always fussing over her new baby—a girl this time. I wanted to undo it, to go back to being free, but I would never be free again. I hated Margaret for being happy for me. She assured me that my feelings would change, but I could not imagine how, or how growing up without a mother would impair my ability to be a decent one.

SITTING AT THE KITCHEN TABLE THAT NIGHT, I TOLD JAMES and he nearly dropped his glass of port.

"Already?" he sputtered.

"Do not say another word, James!" I shouted. "If you blame me for this, I swear I will find something in this kitchen to kill you with!" My proclamation stopped us both short and we laughed. I kicked him half-heartedly under the table. "Do not make me laugh. I am angry at you."

"Me? I did not do this alone." Wiping tears of laughter from his eyes, he added, "This is good news, you know."

"I suppose." I rose and crossed to the fireplace. "But we are young and everything is changing so quickly. I thought we would have time together."

As I was stoking the fire, James approached. "We still have time…together." He pinched my bottom and I swatted his hand away, darting across the room. He gave chase and pinned me against the front door. "At least we can be freer since you are already carrying my child." He smiled.

"You are impossible," I said, before letting him kiss me.

ALONE IN THE HOUSE DURING THE DAY, I WOULD SOMETIMES marvel at my changing body and thrill at the idea of a child; other times I was overtaken by exhaustion, and more clothes to wash and cleaning to do. Then I was back to elated, only to feel a twinge and wish the baby away again. Some nights James and I would dream of our child, speculating about what he (always a boy for James) or she would look and act like. On other nights, I retreated into myself, responding sullenly or with great irritation to every comment and movement James made. James probably thought this was a normal way to act, and perhaps it was, though I never saw Margaret behave in such a fashion. Needless to say, it was a challenging time for both of us.

As evidence of the life inside my body was too clear to be ignored, my anger dissipated and my excitement and fear increased. I endeavoured to tell James everything I was feeling. When I was excited, he would smile and stroke my stomach and plan for the baby's future. Those were joyful times. In fact, the first time he felt the baby move, he wept and made me promise to tell no one. But when my thoughts turned to the pain I would endure, or to the many women I had known or heard of who died in childbirth, James dismissed my concerns with a simple, "But not you." It was not pessimism that drove my fears, but reality.

I had to confide in someone, so I attempted to speak to Margaret. On a number of occasions, I told her about my worries, but she shook her head and said, "Think of the baby that will come from it." I asked her about women who died and she refused to answer.

Focusing on the negative was not lessening the danger, so I decided to enjoy my life and hope that all would be well. I tried not to see my body as being pushed and forced to change, but as a miraculous transformation. Once I did, I could not help but touch my stomach all the time. I would pull my skirts tight against myself and look at my reflection in the windows.

Experiencing this without my sister was quite distressing. Jane and I exchanged letters, but it was hardly the same. Besides, she was miserable, so I dared not express my worries too thoroughly. Mere weeks after the wedding, James shared a rumour he had heard while drinking with some men from the militia: Mr Bingley had been dissuaded from a union with an unsuitable match. The men did not know it was James's relation of whom they spoke, and so speculated on what might be amiss with the lady. James had remained quiet, saving his outrage for our conversation— unaware that it was his cousin who had done the dissuading. Or so I suspected. For reasons beyond comprehension, I did not tell him. Mr Darcy, though loathsome to me, was somehow James's favoured relative and we owed him a great debt. Instead, I let my anger fester. James casually spoke of

Jane's need to find another man sooner rather than later—and one with a fortune—though, he was careful to add, she ought not reach so high in the future.

Jane wrote of her confusion as to why the Bingleys (for his sisters had joined forces against dear Jane) would no longer entertain her, and why the gentleman in question had forsaken her, but I had not the heart to tell her. Instead, I offered assurances that he was a fool and she could find someone better. Jane wholeheartedly disagreed on both counts.

Too soon, it was time for James to depart. I had known he would be away for most of each year, but somehow had not considered the fact that he would be away for the birth. I had grown accustomed to our new routines and found his company a joy, so being utterly isolated—more than ever in my life—at a time when I felt the need for both company and care, seemed unthinkable. James's departure and Jane's ongoing despair hit me equally hard and, as he rode off this time, I wept.

CHAPTER ELEVEN

A month before we thought the baby due, Margaret suggested I move back to Longbourn for my confinement. Sequestered in my old room, I listened to the crickets and the sporadic, muffled, jovial conversation from below and, to my surprise, I realised how deeply lonely I had been and how much I needed those people. They had always infuriated me, and I never felt they knew or cared about my thoughts and dreams. Even so, they were my family, and I wanted to be with them. It felt good to be home, and that shocked me the most.

My family had changed, or perhaps I had. My father still had little to say, but seemed to disapprove of me less. Perhaps it was his sense that I was maturing; perhaps he was relieved that I no longer lived with him. Regardless of the reason, he smiled every so often at me.

My uncle and I finally had something in common, so we were able to have brief conversations about child-rearing. Uncle Gardiner offered to build a cradle, as the one from my childhood was being used by his second. Upon its completion, my uncle said, "For your many children." I rolled my eyes at the thought, but gave him a rare embrace in thanks.

"Did you know," Margaret said, "that Mr Darcy is set to marry Miss Anne de Bourgh?"

"Lady Catherine's daughter?" Uncle Gardiner asked with undisguised distaste.

Margaret slapped his knee. "Yes, Edward, the very one. They have been promised since they were babes." When I asked what she was like, Margaret shrugged. "No one sees her at assemblies or dinners. She has been sickly all her life."

My uncle paused the lighting of his pipe. "Not very clever, either."

"Edward!" Margaret shot him a disapproving look, to which he shrugged and attended to his pipe once more.

It struck me as odd that the dashing Mr Darcy would agree to such a match. Despite my fury over his meddling with Jane and Mr Bingley and, for that matter, nearly every encounter we had had, Mr Darcy appeared to be a man of good health and a sharp mind. He was in no need of a fortune, having inherited a tremendous amount of money and land; if he chose to give up his biting tongue and judgmental nature, he could have any woman he desired. Truth be told, he need not even change his ways, for his fortune rendered him attractive to nearly any woman. I myself would never sink so low as to sell my peace of mind for his estates and riches, but most would.

"When is the blessed event?" I asked.

"Next week, if my calculations are correct," my uncle said. "Few were invited."

I had passed by James's family home and seen less activity than usual, and wondered if they had travelled for the affair. I also wondered if James knew. I would write him about it if I could remain awake long enough after I dragged myself up the stairs.

NOT LONG AFTER THAT NIGHT, MY LABOUR COMMENCED. Mild discomfort lasted the better part of a day, and then the real pain arrived. I was petrified, unsure how long I could endure it. Hill showed a sudden kindness and Margaret was her usual supportive self, while Ruthie and a housemaid scampered around readying water and stoking fires. I was given whisky periodically to dull the pain, but it was not enough.

During some of the difficult moments, I thought of Unity, a friend of Jane's who had died of fever mere days after giving birth, and Tabitha, the miller's daughter who had died before the baby made it out. I wondered if I would meet an end like theirs. "Do not bring bad luck at this time," warned Hill. "Do not speak of such things." Margaret held my hand and merely told me to push.

In the end, we had a healthy boy named Thomas—a name decided upon before James's departure. Everyone assured me that his squished head of light brown hair would look normal and round in no time; however, I did not believe them and prepared myself for a lifetime of explanation and insisting he wear a hat.

Many nights, I would take Thomas out to look at the stars—so many that one felt diminished and empty at the sight, but also connected to something greater than the earth and the day-to-day drudgery of life. Only loosely aware of the constellations, I borrowed a book about the stars from my father's library, studying the patterns and myths. I pondered the lives of those who thought up the names and images of the constellations, amazed that their creations had lasted so long. It was, of course, the blink of an eye in the life of the stars they had named, but an eternity for us mortals. Did a woman sit with her newborn baby, feeling lost in the light of the stars, and try to put some order into her world by telling a story about them? Did it help her to sleep at night knowing that she had put order to a piece of the sky?

A CHILL WAS IN THE AIR ONCE AGAIN WHEN JAMES BURST through the unlocked door late one afternoon.

"You're back!" I cried, my heart pounding, for I thought that it had been an intruder. "Why did you not write?" His letters had stopped so abruptly that I feared the worst, until a brief missive arrived saying he was pleased to hear of Thomas's ongoing health and my joy of him.

He approached and drew me into an embrace, nuzzling my neck and breathing me in. "I could not think what to say."

I stepped back to look at him. He had lost weight and there were dark circles under his eyes. "James, what has happened?"

He wrapped his arms around me again. "All is well now that I am here." A whimper from across the room caused James to startle. "Is that…Thomas?"

I laughed. "Who else would it be? Come meet your son."

James approached with caution, standing over the cradle with an expression of wonder that made him look like the boy who once walked with me through the woods, skinning rabbits and stealing kisses.

"You may touch him," I said, but James remained still, arms at his sides. I lifted the child and held him out, but

James took a step back. "James! You go to battle, but fear a baby?"

"Do not speak of battles!" he snapped, and I clutched Thomas against me, breathless. James's face softened. "I apologise. The ways of the men I have been with are rough." He chewed his bottom lip. "I have dreamed of this moment for months. I can scarce believe it is real."

Just then, Thomas passed gas noisily, and I said, "I assure you he is quite real, and likely in need of a change," which made James chuckle. "I shall do the honours presently, but you will learn and assist. With nary a servant, I will appreciate more hands about."

When I returned, James was studying the sitting room as if seeing it for the first time. "It is a fine house you are keeping," he said. "It has warmth. You have truly made it a home."

I walked towards him with a smile, holding Thomas out in invitation.

James hesitated, "I fear breaking him."

"He is tougher than he appears." I rested the babe in his arms, and Thomas's face crumpled as he readied himself to cry. James moved to hand him back, but I shook my head. "Try bouncing him gently, and say something."

"What would I say? He does not understand."

"Say what you will. He needs to become accustomed to your voice." James sat and began to bounce the baby, but his brow furrowed so I asked, "Do you know any songs? Singing would do."

"All that come to mind are drinking songs."

"Sing them. At three months of age, Thomas will not know the difference." James smiled and I kissed his cheek. "You must be starved. I shall fix some food while you two grow acquainted."

THAT NIGHT, I WAS AWAKENED BY THRASHING, JAMES moaning like a scream was unable to escape his throat. I shook his shoulder and he snatched my wrist like a striking snake, his eyes wild. I gasped in alarm and he rose to consciousness.

His panic evaporated as he realised what he had done. He lifted my wrist to his lips. "I am sorry, Lizzy. I—" He shook his head.

"James," I asked, "was the fighting worse? Was there a disaster of some sort?"

He sat up and pulled on his trousers, slipping out the door.

THE NEXT MORNING I FOUND HIM SITTING ON THE CUTTING stump. "Please do not ask," he said without turning from the sunrise, which bathed him in golden light. "I cannot remain long this time, and dare not ruin our fleeting moments together with tales of war." He reached for me and I stepped close, letting him press his face to my dressing gown. He slid a hand under, up past my knee and onto my thigh.

My breath caught. "Perhaps we ought to go inside." My body burned.

"Who will see us?"

"Mr Davis is unpredictable, but often arrives early."

"Then let him see," James said, pulling me onto his lap. "Let him see, but I cannot stop. You are too beautiful." He kissed my neck and drew his lips across my clavicle, then lifted me, my legs wrapped around him, and carried me into the house…where Thomas was wailing.

The moment was broken for me, but James moved

towards our bed undeterred. "James, I must—" I attempted to wriggle out of his grasp, but he would not stop. "James, Thomas needs me!"

James's face darkened but he released me. "My time home will be short. I do hope Thomas will allow us to be together now and then."

The impatience in his voice wiped away my remaining traces of desire.

I gathered up Thomas and pressed him to my breast where he soothed himself, eyes closed again. What did James think of my nursing Thomas myself? We had no money for a wet-nurse and I would not have wanted to give up these moments together anyhow (despite my family's offering to pay rather than be barbaric, as my father declared to Margaret). Mercifully, James did not comment.

"Why will your time home be short?" I asked.

"Another action."

"As an officer, can you not choose when to come and go?"

"Yes and no." He came behind me and kissed my shoulder, stroking Thomas's face, which plumped more with each passing week. "I am needed in Spain, and a request was made for our speedy return. I cannot let the men down."

"What about me?"

"What about you?"

I turned to face him. "*I* need you."

He chewed at his bottom lip, a habit that always filled me with concern as the gesture emerged when he was most uneasy. "All I wanted when I was there was to be here, and now that I am here, I feel a pull to return." He walked away and grabbed the bread I had baked the day before, slicing it. "I feel changed and unsettled, Lizzy. The thought of parties and assemblies and card games...none of it seems to matter."

"I've never cared a fig for any of those activities, but I do dream of sitting with you in our house, making a home together."

His eyes darted around the room, landing on Thomas and me. "I fear I will not be the husband you had hoped for."

"You are, James."

He shook his head. "I am not the man I was. I— This last action..."

"Tell me."

He shook his head again and reached for his coat, walking into the crisp morning. He busied himself in the fledgling orchard until tea, at which time he asked about Jane and my relations, making it clear he was in no mood to share. His silence about his service and his agitation, even while going about the motions of a normal life, left me worried. Something had gone wrong, something that, as he said, altered him. My wrist still stung where he had grabbed me, and I feared he would wake from his dreams and be out of sorts again. Or worse. How much worse I could not have predicted.

CHAPTER TWELVE

Two months later, having hardly returned to a routine of life without James, I once again realised I was expecting. Dread filled me. I did not want another child so soon. James and I had been too free, too careless, and I was left to face the consequences alone. I cursed his name while I did the baking, and kicked at the dirt when I should have been churning butter. Unable to fall back asleep when Thomas woke me in the night, I mulled and fretted. I had heard rumours of women attempting to end their pregnancies by rolling on the floor, jumping off tables, throwing themselves from roofs or worse. Could I? Should I? No. I was not that desperate, but I was unsure how I could manage carrying another child while Thomas, just six months old, needed so much of my attention. Where would I find more time? More energy?

The worst part was calculating my years of potential fertility. I wrote to James that I was sure we would have thirty children, which he assured me was an impossibility. In his letter, he suggested I hire a maid-of-all-work, which was a great relief, and assured me we would love as many children as God gave us. Neither of us went to church, so I found his sudden invocation of a deity vexing, but I decided to accept this child. And be more careful in the future.

Whether it was brought on by frustration or bad luck, carrying my second child was harder. I was ill and exhausted, and at six months I went back to Longbourn. Jane returned to keep me company. I could not help but notice her envy as she took in my altered body, and while I spoke of its misshapen lines and my discomfort, she shared her dream of children with such longing it pained me. At twenty she still had time, but I feared after another season in London with no marital prospects she was losing hope.

Contrary to what often occurs, bringing my second baby into the world was more difficult than the first. My labour came earlier than anticipated and lasted longer. I was in great need of consolation and distraction, and Jane sat at my side to soothe.

Jane said, "You must not fret. You know women go through this every day. I know you will say, 'This must be the worst,' but it cannot be."

She paused as a wave of pain swept over me and I trembled. She took my hand in hers and sat for a time quietly. She mopped my brow, which was sweating in the sweltering summer heat.

The next wave of pain was so strong that tears streamed down my cheeks despite my best effort to hold them back. I gritted my teeth and prayed that I should not die like this, in agony, trying to bring new life into this world.

I could not help but think at that moment of Mr Darcy, who had just lost his wife after an agonising three days of labour. Everyone tried to keep it from me. My father and uncle were too good at keeping secrets, but Jane was transparent. Her ashen face as she picked at dinner one night alarmed me, and later that evening she told me what had occurred once we were alone in her room. Mr Darcy, she explained, wished to remain at his own home for a while longer to ensure that his sister Georgiana was settled, but would travel for a time come autumn. With both mother and child buried on the property, it pained him to be at Pemberley.

I spotted the sun coming up on this second dawn of labour as another pain ripped through me from middle to ends. I was trying so hard not to wail, but I was not sure I could take another moment—let alone another hour or two or ten of this—and cried out. Jane, who had gone to rest, ran into the room, alarmed and at her wit's end. I looked at my sister and thanked God for her. She took my hands and pressed her forehead to mine and whispered how much she loved me and how I could not leave her.

"Jane, enough!" Hill said, pulling our hands apart. "She will live. Get Margaret if you're so anxious to do something. Won't be much longer now, I suspect."

JAMES DID NOT RETURN AS EXPECTED IN OCTOBER AS I HAD hoped. He had been injured and was convalescing before the voyage. Two letters had arrived; first from a fellow Dragoon when the outcome was precarious, and the second from a nurse, who had assured me that while it would take time, he would recover. His side had been sliced, but worse, his right leg and arm had been crushed when his horse, mortally wounded, fell upon him. I exhausted myself with my efforts not to worry and felt caught in a state of eternal waiting, wondering if a letter might arrive with information either tragic or hopeful. I had considered going to his parents, but knew my visit would not be welcomed. I hoped they would at least send a servant with news should they receive any, though I was not confident they would, and so I used precious spare time to write to James's other friends and relations to learn if they had heard more. None had.

At any given moment, one of the children invariably needed tending or a meal needed making. I had had difficulty adjusting to one baby's demands for food and comfort while learning how to run a household, but two felt impossible. Laundry, which I had always abhorred, was now even more voluminous, and the stink was sickening. Patricia, the girl we hired, was a help, but even she could not keep up. When one child finally fell asleep, the other seemed to wake. I would often weep when Alice needed to nurse just after I had finally gotten back into bed from attending to Thomas or the other way around. The offer by Margaret to hire a wet-nurse was occasionally tempting, but I was stubborn and did not want their aid, nor did I want to lose these fleeting moments of connexion.

At times, I regretted marriage and wished my children away. But then they would be asleep in beautiful peace or sitting quietly learning about the world, or I would see James in Thomas's smile, or watch Alice learning to reach for things, and I would be filled with intense pleasure. In those moments, I was sure I could make it through these early years.

It both helped and hurt when Jane came calling. Her hands were smooth and her dresses were fine, and though I did not envy her loneliness, I did envy her sleep and rest, and pondered what she thought of my appearance. She brought tales of balls and visits to the Lucases and plans to go with the Philipses to the Lakes. I could not help but feel a pang of envy, imagining the glamorous gatherings and furnishings surrounding her while I was covered in baby spit, yet I knew she desired to be in my place. I did hope she would marry someone with more money, however, so she could have help with the children. I wondered if she would want to be like many of our class whose children were whisked away and only brought in when one was of a mind to be with the little ones. I suspected Jane, with her warm heart, would desire to be with her children as often as possible, given her endless desire to hold Alice, who was growing into a fair-haired beauty like Jane.

In the spring, with baby Alice often sleeping peacefully in a carrying basket nearby and Thomas walking and digging in the dirt, I tended to my garden. Mr Davis, whose work was largely finished now that the orchard was dotted with saplings that had taken root, had suggested planting a variety of vegetables among the saplings, explaining this would help both the trees and the vegetables to grow. It gave me an occupation, for I loathed needlework and we had no pianoforte due to lack of funds. I did not miss such a luxury in the least, my music education having been paltry. Reading—my true pleasure—was out of the question, for Thomas always sensed my distraction and would climb onto my lap or demand a story of his own, and I was too exhausted at the end of the day to think of reading before bed.

I heard a carriage approach. I rose to watch as it slowed and one of the coachmen opened the door. Mr Darcy, of all people, emerged.

"Mr Darcy!"

Before I could ask any questions, he said, "Pray forgive

me for sending no word, but I have brought your husband back to you."

The other coachman joined him at the carriage door and reached in. A bandaged leg emerged first, then an arm, then a head. James! I blinked to be sure he was, indeed, no apparition. I rushed forward as the men helped him down and held him until a crutch could be produced.

He smiled weakly. "I am alive."

I swooped in and hugged him, nearly knocking us both to the ground.

"I am not steady," he said with a weak laugh after the men helped right us.

I looked him over. He was even thinner than his last visit and his skin was sallow. One arm, I now saw, was bound against his ribs. Touching his cheek, my voice quavered as I said, "My darling, what—"

He turned to kiss my palm. "I will heal, love. Let me see my children. The thought of you three was what kept me alive."

As I moved to reveal them a few paces off, James was overcome and turned his face away from his cousin as tears spilled down his cheeks.

I noted the wince that flashed across Mr Darcy's face, but I was too preoccupied to address the source of his pain. "I shall leave you," Mr Darcy said. James nodded and Mr Darcy added, "Drake, Simmons, please escort Colonel Fitzwilliam to his bed."

The title startled me, but yes, James had written of a promotion in rank, earned by his most recent action.

The men sprang into action and I tarried a moment, rethinking the man for whom I had harboured such anger for so long. "Mr Darcy, would you call on us on the morrow? I wish to know how—and what—I…" I laughed at my own inability to find words. "Our offerings will not be much, but it would be wonderful to repay even a small part of your kindness."

"It was familial duty."

I shook my head. "It was more than that." I did not believe James's parents had done a single thing to bring him home, though I was willing to be proven wrong. "You will tell the tale and I will feed you"—I could not think what I had in the larder—"a cake of some sort. Please be kind enough to call on us?"

He gave a curt nod as the coachmen returned, one climbing to his post and the other standing by the door to ease Mr Darcy into the velvet interior.

I grabbed the children and hurried inside to James. Thomas bucked against me, wanting to walk, and I hissed reprimands at him, saying I would put him down in a moment.

Mr Darcy's men had undressed James and he was settled under the light quilt I used in warmer months.

"James! I can hardly believe you are here!"

He reached out his good arm and beamed, though even a smile could not bring colour to his wan face. "Is this my Alice? And Thomas so grown?" I settled her next to James and moved to lower Thomas, but Thomas clutched at my bodice.

"Who?" Thomas asked, unused to strangers in our home.

"Your father."

Thomas cocked his head, perhaps remembering my descriptions of him, and then reached out, allowing James to hold him on his lap. They studied each other with wonder for a few moments, and then Thomas bounced too hard, causing James to wince and gasp.

I pulled Thomas back and, attempting not to move the mattress too much, lowered myself with care to the edge of the bed. "Tell me how it came to pass that you are here, and what happened in Spain."

He launched into a tale of a battle and a field hospital, then a real hospital and a ship home. I suspected he was leaving out details, but he offered enough for me to know that his survival had not been guaranteed and his healing had been a painful process thus far. "Had the bones not punctured my skin," he said matter-of-factly, "I would have been back on the battlefield within a month. This was...I lost weeks to the pain, and the infection nearly ended me."

"Do the doctors believe you will recover fully?"

He shrugged. "The original surgeon did not, but Darcy's physician treated me with new methods. He surmises I shall walk on my own and regain most of my strength, if not all."

"Darcy's physician?"

"Yes. Your letter about my injury prompted him to send assistance immediately. I thought I owed Darcy before. Now I owe him my health, possibly my life."

"He has promised to come tomorrow and we can begin to thank him with refreshments. Until then, you are all mine." I went around to the other side of the bed, set Thomas down, and scooted as close as I could with the children between us. James took my hand and smiled as he slipped into sleep.

CHAPTER THIRTEEN

The next day, as I removed the cake out from the oven, I saw James collapse outside and land face down in the dirt. I gasped and ran out the door. I had told him not to go to the orchard unaccompanied, as I saw how unsteady he still was. He did not pick himself up or even move. When I touched his face, he was cold, sweaty, and pale. I could hear Alice crying but there was no way I could go back to her. I patted James's cheeks and fanned his face. I did not know what else to do. After a few pats, he was still not revived, and I began to tremble.

"James. James. Wake up. Please. James!" My voice was escalating to a shriek. "Patricia!" I called, but I had sent her to the market in Meryton. I thought James might need water, but the pump was so far away. My heart began to pound. I loosened his shirt collar, fumbling with the buttons. Alice was screaming by now and part of me was furious that she chose this moment for a tantrum. The other part of me felt helpless in my desire to take care of my entire family at once. I sat in the dirt and stroked his hand and whispered, "Wake up before I kill you!"

"That is the sweet girl I married," he said, his voice a dry rasp. His eyes fluttered but his body remained still. "Could you help me to my feet?"

I stood, grabbed his good arm with both my hands and pulled, accomplishing nothing but landing on my knees in the dirt again. At last, I handed him his crutch, which helped, and with him leaning heavily on my shoulder, we made our way back to the house. I realised Alice had ceased her screaming. When we entered the house, I was amazed to see Thomas sitting with his sister, rubbing her head. Her eyes were locked on his, and she was calm. A lump grew in my throat as I gazed at them and thought of my own protector, my Jane, who had cared for me for so long. I missed her terribly and wished she found more joy in Longbourn rather than seeking pleasure elsewhere.

I was suddenly aware again of James's weight. We walked together toward the sofa and, although I attempted to ease him down, he hit the firm cushions with a thud. "I assume you put our children down more gently," he croaked through a smile.

"No. Roughness builds character." I pinched his cheek. "Your mother taught me that."

"You are wicked, Lizzy. Water?"

I turned for the pump and as I entered the yard, saw Mr Darcy approaching.

I called out, "James fell in the orchard! Go in and I shall be with you presently." I was so flustered I ended up running to the pump without my bucket. I rushed back for it, gave a few hurried pumps of water, and spilled a good amount on my skirt and boots.

I found Mr Darcy in the sitting room, offered a curtsey,

and brought a cup to James. After he had had a good long drink, I put my hand to his forehead. "James, are you hurt? Feverish?"

"No." He pulled my hand from his face and kissed my knuckles. "I do not know what happened. One minute I was taking a step, the next I had a mouth full of dirt and a hysterical wife standing over me."

"Do you wish for me to call the doctor?" I asked, ignoring his description of me as hysterical.

"And waste what little money we have? No. I simply must remember my limitations." I tensed at speaking of money in front of Mr Darcy. James squeezed my hand. "I am well. Please bring me the children."

"Heavens!" Mr Darcy's eyes went wide as I returned with the little ones. "I saw them fleetingly yesterday, but I cannot believe these are yours, James."

"Why not?"

"They are too fine looking to be your offspring." For a moment I worried at the implication, but the most unexpectedly brilliant smile cracked across Mr Darcy's face.

Had Mr Darcy made a joke?

The men laughed. Mr Darcy was so much more handsome when he smiled.

"This is Thomas," I said, relaxing and pointing at our son who toddled over to James. James scooped him into his lap, only wincing a little at the effort, and Thomas squealed with delight. "And this is Alice. Do you wish to hold her?" I asked, lifting Alice towards Mr Darcy.

"No, I—" Before his protest registered, I had placed the baby in his arms, and she stared into his eyes. He looked so nervous I thought to take her back, but after a moment he settled down, touching her hand and stroking the fine crown of her head. He looked like Jane watching a deer drink from the brook: awestruck. He put a finger in Alice's palm and she clasped it. "Heavens," he whispered, as much to himself as to anyone else.

"Who?" Thomas asked, pointing to Mr Darcy.

James stroked his little face. "This is my cousin."

Thomas seemed satisfied with that, breaking free of James to toddle over and kiss Mr Darcy's knee, making us all laugh.

I served gingerbread cake and tea. Depleting our reserves of brown sugar for the cake was worth doing to receive such a generous compliment on its taste. It stung, however, when Mr Darcy added, "Not one of our cooks could have done better." He caught himself in the accidental slight, and offered more compliments on the perfect balance of spice as well as the needlework on the pillows upon which we leaned—my only such project. At least that was acceptable employment for a lady of my background and so necessitated no apology.

"The house is quite warm," Mr Darcy said. "Nothing foreboding, unlike Pemberley or your parents' home, is that not true, James?"

"We thank you for it," James said, his expression pinched.

Realisation swept across Mr Darcy's face. "N-no. I meant— Well, you told me what you desired, and while I doubted the simplicity of it at the time, I now see its beauty. Exposed wood, light paint, nothing engraved or adorned. It is a perfect cottage for a perfect family." He searched James's face and James nodded, battling self-consciousness, I could see.

"The house suits our lives," I said, hoping to break the accidental tension. Mr Darcy held out Alice, who had begun fussing, and I took her, swaying. "Having stepped away from society, we are able to enjoy simplicity. When James is not abroad, at least."

James shifted in his chair, wincing as he adjusted his bad leg. "I shall be about the house for the near future, I am afraid. Or perhaps forever, depending on how I heal."

The news ought not to have surprised me, but it did. What would he do if not in the regulars, and how different might it be to have him home permanently? Despite my initial misgivings about married life and then his constant departures, I enjoyed being separate from all I had known. I had developed routines and habits, and each of his returns prompted a period of adjustment. I did grow accustomed to sharing my days after a time, though I despaired when he was distant or haunted or restless, then mourned his leave-taking, beginning the cycle anew. Would I relish his being here for good?

As if to assure myself, I reached for James's hand. "I would like you here forever." He took it with a smile, and I noticed Mr Darcy staring. The moment I did, he looked away, his colour high. Did our exchange remind him of the loss of his wife? Had he enjoyed simple moments of domestic joy? James and I had had few, but perhaps this was the beginning of a new era of calm. His terrible dream of the night before, however, said otherwise.

Thomas tugged on Mr Darcy's trousers and lifted his arms. Stiff and unsure of what to do with a child, Mr Darcy's shoulders slackened once Thomas sat on his lap, curled into him. Thomas pointed at Mr Darcy. "Story." Mr Darcy declared he had no stories to tell, to which little Thomas lisped, "Non–sense!" sending the adults into a fit of laughter.

At James's suggestion, Mr Darcy shared a tale of two boys on a wintertime fishing expedition that ended with frozen feet and ruined shoes, and a certain woman (whom I recognised as James's mother by the mimicked voice) forbidding future journeys out of doors until the weather improved.

Thomas's eyes were wide. "Sad." Perhaps he remembered our adventures in the snow, stomping about and packing freezing balls between our mittened hands.

"It certainly was!" James said. "Very sad. Boys are meant to play out of doors in all weather." He reached for a crutch. "I fear I tire too soon. You must excuse me."

"I shall depart then," Mr Darcy said, setting Thomas on the floor and smoothing his trousers.

The afternoon had been so pleasant I did not wish for him to feel rushed away. "Stay, sir. If it pleases you."

"I do not desire to disturb my cousin as he rests," he said. He hesitated, the corners of his mouth twitching as if searching for the right words or the courage to say something. "Though it would please me to walk about the orchard James spoke of so often during the journey."

I had never noticed the warmth in his eyes, always having seen him in the company of large crowds, which he seemed to abhor, or during an argument. "Of course."

I turned to Thomas and told him to sit with his toys a bit. When he objected, saying he wanted the man to play, Mr Darcy assured him he would return very soon. To my surprise, I hoped he would keep his promise.

As we walked, I cradled a sleepy Alice in my arms. He stole a few glances at her, and said, "I have been melancholy these past months. You will find I am poor company."

"Not to worry, sir. When I am peevish, there is little I wish to discuss."

He took hold of a delicate apple blossom, one of many

dotting each branch. His brow furrowed. "Mourning is more than peevishness."

I bit my lip and looked away. "Of course. Forgive my ill-chosen word."

We walked on and he enquired about Jane. I wished he had not, for I could have held my tongue on the subject otherwise.

"She is sad and lonely." I clenched my teeth, considering my next words. "I understand that is due to you."

He came to a stop, drawing himself up to his full height. The coldness was back in his eyes, making me feel quite small. "If you refer to a match with Bingley, I admit to offering my opinion. The financial situation of your family, though objectionable, was nothing in comparison to the total want of propriety by your mother, and occasionally by your father and even you. Pardon me. It pains me to offend. I will only say further that my purpose was to preserve my friend from what I esteemed a most unhappy connexion."

Despite the truth in his words, my vision shook as rage enveloped me, and I spoke in a tone I regretted even as the words left my lips. "You have ruined every hope of happiness for the most affectionate, generous heart in the world!"

His nostrils flared. "I have no wish of denying that I did everything in my power to separate my friend from your sister, or that I rejoice in my success. Towards him I have been kinder than towards myself, for I entered into an imprudent marriage and have paid for it dearly."

My mouth fell open, but I could not pity this man. He had ruined Jane's hopes!

"I daresay I am surprised by your assessment of her hopes for happiness resting on Mr Bingley when she showed no clear signs of affection."

"She shows as much as her nature will allow. If I can

perceive her regard for him, you must be a simpleton, indeed, not to discover it."

"You call me a simpleton?"

"Yes. No. I…" I gathered myself, my cheeks burning. "Jane is reserved, yes, but her affection was real."

"It did not seem so," he said, his jaw set.

Mr Darcy's expression and lack of apology sent me back to the house with the excuse of tending to the children. We would not see him again for some weeks, for which I was grateful.

CHAPTER FOURTEEN

Each day James grew stronger, though still nowhere near his former health. Some days we would all venture into the woods and James would hold different leaves to the children's faces and let them discover how each one smelled and felt. Other times we simply lay on our bed with the little ones. We laughed often, but under the laughter was the fear of what was next if he did not recover fully.

Night terrors plagued him, and upon waking he was generally short-tempered. Certain noises sent him into a rage, or he was crippled by pain. He often languished in discomfort and despair. When I asked if he wished to unburden himself by sharing stories of his battles, or the sensations that gripped him, he refused—falling into melancholy for longer stretches than ever.

Just before Easter, Jane wrote that she would be returning home, and asked us to Longbourn upon her arrival. Our walk to the house was slow due to James's aching leg, and he had shouted at me more than once to stop fussing over him. I would not have offered help after the first altercation had he not appeared to struggle carrying Thomas. When we finally arrived, we were surprised to find Jane out front in the company of Mr Darcy.

"Lizzy!" She met us on the path since James's walk was still laboured. Eyes sparkling, she reached out to grasp my hand. "You will never guess. Mr Bingley is here. He—he wishes to marry me, Lizzy! Can you believe he thought I was indifferent to him? But when he and Mr Darcy called on me in town, the matter was resolved. Everyone should know such happiness, Lizzy!"

My husband enquired, "Where is Bingley?"

"Inside asking Father for permission."

James said he could go no further just then, set Thomas down, and lowered himself to a tree stump a few paces away.

Jane said, "In all of my excitement, I neglected a proper greeting for you, Colonel Fitzwilliam. Welcome home."

They exchanged pleasantries and Alice began to fuss, so I excused myself to nurse her inside. As I approached, I stole a glance at Mr Darcy who stood in the shade by the door. His face was impassive, but he offered a little nod. I returned his nod, acknowledging that he had, indeed, orchestrated this happy event in response to my sharp words, adding a small smile which I hoped would convey all of the thanks I had within me.

Walking to my old room, I passed the slightly ajar door to Father's study and saw Mr Bingley, hunched with anticipation, patting sweat from his upper lip and then my father jutting out a hand in an agreement of some sort.

Jane and Mr Bingley were both kind and thoughtful, reserved and loving. Yes, their union would be a happy one.

WHEN ALICE WAS SATED AND SLEEPING, I JOINED THE FAMILY downstairs.

"Lizzy!" Jane said, aglow as never before, "we are to be wed in a month!"

Mr Bingley's clear blue eyes shone with equal excitement. "My sisters might be disappointed to change their plans to visit friends, but I hope they shall understand."

I remembered seeing Caroline, sour-faced and impatient at the ball, and doubted his assessment. It seemed he was as blindly generous as Jane.

"Your sisters," Mr Darcy said, acid in his tone, "might be improved by a modicum of disappointment."

Margaret looked scandalised, but I snickered, rather agreeing. He caught my laugh, his lips twitching as he worked to suppress his own.

Father suggested the men join him for cards. Although I knew he despised games, he hated women's conversation and the tumult of the children more.

Margaret, Jane, and I were only too pleased to be left alone, and we indulged Jane, endlessly discussing the flowers Jane hoped to have and the latest fashion for dresses. Being entirely removed from society, I feared not being smart enough for her event, and asked her to advise me so I did not embarrass her or myself. She shared that Mr Bingley had promised to send the best dressmaker from London— oh to have such funds!—and would be sure to have me measured and consulted as well. The gown would be a gift. I felt so peculiarly removed from the life Jane had chosen, and while I still loved Jane the sister, I struggled to understand Jane the lady.

A knock at the front door brought a message for James, Mr Darcy, and Mr Bingley. It seemed that James's parents wished to invite some of us to dinner. Uncle Gardiner,

Margaret, and my father were not included. James had not seen his family since his return, nor had he been in their house since our wedding. It was many years to live so close without interaction and, though I would not call it a loss, I did take offence at their lack of invitation.

That night, James's dreams were vicious. After the third time waking with a shout and having sweated through his bed shift, he changed and hobbled out so as not to disturb me further. When I rose to feed Alice, I spotted him through the kitchen window, his night shirt glowing in the moonlight. Seated on the cutting stump, his head was in his hands.

I started at the sound of Patricia clearing her throat behind me. Patricia said quietly, "I heard him weeping. I did not know what to do." I thanked her for the information and tended Alice first. Once she was asleep, I ventured to James.

As I shut the door, he put up a hand to stop me. When I continued my approach, he turned his head away. "Do not ask, Lizzy. I will not tell you of my dreams or why they come." I moved forward and rested a hand on his shoulder.

He tensed. "Do not ask," he said more strongly.

I squeezed his shoulder and kissed the top of his head. He rose and limped into the night.

LATE THE NEXT AFTERNOON, JAMES AND I DRESSED TO VISIT his family. He wore his dress uniform, though it now hung on him. His bad arm, happily, had healed enough that he wore both sleeves correctly. I donned a day dress of Jane's she had loaned me the day prior. Most of my dresses were not fine enough for this visit, and my pre-marriage dresses did not have enough fabric in the bodice since I was still nursing. Lady Broxbourne would have been horrified to know that the dress I had worn for much of the day had a scorch mark. In winter, I had been holding my own child (something I doubted she ever did) and stood too close to the fire (something I knew she had never been required to do given the size of her fireplaces and the endless supply of firewood chopped and kept alight by servants). A popping log had sent a spark flying, and in the time I had taken to set down Alice before slapping it out, the burn had grown sizeable.

We approached the grand Fitzwilliam home by foot, having no horse or carriage, which was challenging since the dark clouds indicating imminent rain made James's leg ache all the more. I noticed the sweat on his forehead and suspected it was not merely from the heavy wool of his uniform.

The immense door opened and we were escorted into the grand entry, our children whisked away by two servants. Lady Broxbourne's sharp look was enough to keep me in my place despite the cries of Alice and Thomas, who were unaccustomed to strangers. James offered his elbow to me and leaned down to whisper, "They should be well cared for." I wanted to believe him and allowed myself to be led to the sitting room where the other Fitzwilliams were waiting, along with Mr Darcy and Mr Bingley.

"Cousin," said Mr Darcy, rising, "how well you look back in your uniform!"

Mr Bingley said, "You seem to be regaining your strength. I noticed it yesterday."

"Oh yes, you were present for the engagement," Lady Broxbourne said, her lips curling. "Now Mr Bingley shall be linked with the Bennets as well. How fortunate to share the same pleasure as we." Sarcasm twisted her handsome face.

James glared at his mother while I begged my heart to stop racing.

Lady Lydia bounded over, followed by Lady Kitty, and both threw their arms around their brother while Lady Mary stood back with her hands clasped.

"Oh, how I missed you!" Lady Lydia said.

Lady Kitty squealed, "We were so worried!"

"Were you?" asked James with a hint of bitterness, appearing crushed by their embrace. "I received no letters."

Lady Lydia said, "Mother told us not to write to you—"

"Lest it encourage you to linger in your sickbed rather than healing and returning home," Lady Kitty said.

James's cheeks flushed with irritation.

"It is what she said!" said Lady Lydia, her eyes wide with innocence.

Lady Broxbourne glowered but did not deny it.

Mr Bingley interrupted the tense moment, asking the girls about the militia's return to Meryton.

Lady Lydia bounced on her toes as she had at the Netherfield ball. "They have gatherings every night, and when we are allowed to go—"

"Oh!" Lady Kitty said. "So many handsome men with such happy manners and a talent at whist."

"Kitty lost most of her monthly allowance," Lady Lydia said with a titter.

Lady Kitty crossed her arms, her colour high. "And your enthusiasm and telling tales has us banned from visiting after dark!"

"Girls!" the earl said. "You will behave with decorum or we shall send you to the nursery with James's children!"

They both tucked their lips between their teeth in a laughably similar manner.

Lady Mary looked at her sisters with distaste. "As it says

in Proverbs: 'The prudent sees danger and hides himself, but the simple go on and suffer for it'. "

The earl sniffed. "Let us go into the dining room."

We took our places. As it was mostly a family dinner, I was not sure if the arrangement would be wherever they pleased or by rank, or in the newer fashion of men alternating with women, although our numbers were uneven. Mr Darcy was seated to Lady Broxbourne's right and James to her left. I was seated between Mr Darcy and Lady Lydia.

Mr Darcy was reserved on the whole, speaking only when required by a question posed by his aunt or uncle. As they began discussing coal prices—my least favourite topic—I had the opportunity to study the cousins again. James and Mr Darcy had the same high cheekbones, thick brows, and full lips—though a smile more regularly played on James's mouth while Mr Darcy's turned down at the corners. Both had an air of assurance, but James was in constant movement while Mr Darcy held himself with a preternatural calm. Mr Darcy's eyes were deep brown, like the soil after it is tilled, while James's were pond water: green, grey, and brown all at once. Mr Darcy's blushes—from embarrassment and discomfort, as well as too much wine—were more apparent. In the past, I would have said James's expressions were warmer and more relaxed, but since his return, this was not true.

Mr Darcy turned to me when the conversations split. "You will forgive me, Mrs Fitzwilliam," he said, a title that took me aback given the few times I had been called that in the past few years. Without formal calls or assemblies, my interactions had been limited to family, and mine was rarely formal when alone. "It seems that Miss Bennet is pleased with the turn of events?"

I glanced at Mr Bingley, who was engaged in conversation with Lady Mary. Her dourness had faded, making me suspect that the antics of Lady Lydia and Lady Kitty brought out her moralistic and disapproving side. I wished Jane had been invited, for she and Mr Bingley had sworn they desired to spend every moment possible together now and forever. It was quite a thing to hear such expressions of affection. Had I ever felt that way towards James? Lustful, yes, especially before the children, before his injury. Over time, our love and trust had grown in some ways, it was true, but were we passionate for each other's company? I would need to meditate on the matter.

"She is, sir. And I thank you for your intervention."

He shook his head. "There is no need to discuss it. The error was mine and I felt it only correct to express my misunderstanding to Bingley. The rest was his decision."

"There was more than the matter of her feelings," I said quietly. "Your assessment of my—the rest—was not entirely incorrect." My cheeks burned and I twisted the napkin in my lap.

"Nonsense. It was unkind of me to have judged your family in such a fashion."

I was taken aback by his reversal and the pain I saw in his eyes as he spoke. It made my chest squeeze, and I wanted to explore the topic and my reaction to his altered expression, but I sensed Lady Broxbourne listening. "Do come to the house again. And bring Mr Bingley, for—"

"Mr Darcy ought not need an invitation, as he had the house built," Lady Broxbourne said.

James's head snapped towards his mother. "Mother, it is unnecessary and improper of you to bring up such matters."

"It was my wedding gift, Lady Broxbourne," Mr Darcy said calmly, though I noticed his knuckles were white as he gripped his spoon. "I was only too pleased to offer it."

My esteem for him in that moment rose immeasurably.

She lifted her chin as she turned back to her son. "It was not built so far away that we should never have been invited. Which we have not."

James's eyes hardened.

She smoothed her napkin in her lap. "And it is so near the church that I wonder why you are unable to attend, James. She does not attend when you are away, either." Lady Broxbourne seemed unable to even say my name. "The only time I have seen your children was for their christening, and there was not even a luncheon afterwards. She has been a bad influence on you, James. As I think on it, you have not been to church since your wedding."

"Are you implying," I said, my cheeks burning, "that I have taken your son from the church?"

She pressed her lips together as if considering how best to insult me when James leaned forward, his face murderous. "We would attend if we cared to do so, but I do not care to do so ever again. If the church is to teach kindness and love, Mother, perhaps you ought to attend more often." He shot upright, the chair scraping against the floor. He took hold of his crutch and said to me, "Let us gather the children and depart."

I rose, and thus the men stood, as well.

Mr Darcy said, "Cousin, let us endeavour to mend—"

"No!" shouted James. "You and Bingley are welcome to my home, but that is all!"

Lady Lydia pouted. "Not even us, James?"

James rounded on her. "Whilst you are silly enough to be swayed by the cruelty of this house, you may keep your distance."

I offered a small curtsey, my eyes meeting Mr Darcy's. He looked as lost and desperate as I felt. I hated the

Fitzwilliams, and found his mother's comments distasteful—nay, hateful—but I was shocked by James's outburst. Where was the man who laughed at the rules of society and its judgment? Where was the man who laughed at anything at all?

CHAPTER FIFTEEN

With no carriage or horse, the journey home was trying. Alice needed to be nursed, but Jane's gown was not easy to manoeuvre so we decided to make her wait—meaning she bellowed for the entire walk. James tried to hold Thomas, but the child squirmed, wishing to walk on his own. James made to release him, but the ground was muddy, the rain having passed during the meal. I begged him not to, knowing I would have to clean Thomas's clothes, for Thomas would inevitably stumble. James limped on, his rage bubbling.

Once inside, Patricia tended to Thomas after helping me undress, and I sat in my shift with Alice, who had turned purple with fury. Just as Alice had begun to quiet, James stomped in and slammed the bedroom door, startling her into wailing anew. He raised his hands in surrender at my glare before sitting at the foot of the bed. In a hushed voice, he asked, "Why would my mother invite us only to hurl insults? And in front of Darcy, not to mention Bingley!"

"Because she enjoys inflicting pain."

"How dare she? I could not stay a moment longer."

I stroked Alice's cheek and rocked her. "Do you really mean not to see your family again?"

James clenched his teeth and nodded.

"That is a rash decision, James. Perhaps—"

"It is not rash. I have doubted their affection and loyalty for years, but when Darcy was the one to rescue me from that infernal hospital, my suspicions were confirmed."

Alice's colour returned to its usual pink and I felt my shoulders relax at last.

"You are an extraordinary mother," he said, surprising me. "You once confessed concern that you knew not how to minister to the needs of children. How did you manage it?"

"I thought about my mother and yours. And did the opposite."

We smiled at each other, and it was fine to see his face relax, bathed in candlelight.

"Let them not vex you so, James."

He flopped back, staring at the ceiling. "Our troubles extend beyond the purchase of this house. I receive half-pay when I am on leave. That is part of the reason I always hurried back to service. Our bills are too high as it is, and earning half...Patricia is already overworked, as are you. Should I remain here, which it seems I must for the foreseeable future, how am I to occupy myself? I have no training, no purpose, and no way to earn. And there are so many things of which we are in need. A horse would be of help, and a cow rather than a goat could provide far better. Thomas will need proper shoes come winter, Alice will need dresses. And worst, Jane's wedding will cost us dearly."

I had not thought of my sister's happy event as a financial impediment. I rose and placed Alice in her cradle. "I could—"

He bolted upright. "Do not say ask for assistance. It is humiliating, and our families lord our poverty over us."

"Not everyone. And we are not impoverished." I sat next to him and kissed his cheek. "We must ignore our families' demands and commentary and find a way. I know we shall. We are strong and care for each other. All could be worse."

After a pause, he reached over and took my face in his hands, kissing me deeply. His hands drifted and he lifted my shift past my knees.

I clasped onto his hand to stop him.

"Elizabeth." Though it was a name he rarely called me, the coo of his voice made my heart quicken. "I want to be with you. I have been in too much pain, but I can wait no longer." His lids were heavy as he leaned in again.

I could not think of any more words as he whispered his lips along the length of my neck. My body burned.

He groaned. "It has been too long."

"Yes, but we have not discussed—" I scooted away. "James, I do not want another baby."

He squinted, studying my face. "Ever?"

I paused, afraid to tell him that I thought not.

"We will have more children, you can be certain of that." The thought made my stomach sink, and he added more gently, "There are ways around it."

"How? We tried them once, and we were gifted with Thomas. We tried again and we conceived Alice."

"There must be methods."

"Nothing I know of is reliable!" I took a deep breath. "It was so difficult last time. You were not here, but I assure you, it was far worse than with Thomas—"

"But Alice is perfect and you are healthy."

"Who is to say I will be next time?"

"Who is to say you will not?" He brought both of my

hands to his lips and kissed my knuckles. "Lizzy, we cannot stay away from each other forever, and I am ready at last." He kissed me right behind my ear.

I jumped up. He grabbed hold of my wrist so hard it sent spikes of pain up my arm and made my knees buckle. I broke away, making for the door. He leapt up and caught me, digging his fingers into my upper arms and making me cry out.

"You would force me?"

"I should not have to!"

As he pulled me to him, I struggled and pushed, causing him to stumble and shout in pain, clutching his leg at the site of the break.

Steadying myself, I looked about for a place to run or an object to use in my defence. I was afraid of James, something I had never imagined possible. When I caught sight of his face still twisted in agony, I desired to help him. Yet I feared moving forward.

James sucked in a laboured breath, then walked to the door and opened it. "There are other options for me!" he shouted. With that, he slammed the door, waking the children.

THE NEXT MORNING, MR DARCY AND MR BINGLEY ARRIVED for a call, as we had discussed the evening prior.

Upon seeing my face, Mr Darcy frowned. "What is the matter? Is someone ill?"

"No." I felt foolish to have anyone know, but I had to confess. "James is…he is not here. He left last night and never returned."

Mr Bingley, blue eyes wide, countenance sweet as always, asked, "Shall we look for him?"

"No," I hastened to say. "Jane will arrive presently." Mr Bingley brightened, and I knew I was correct to allow them time to meet together. "I believe I know where he is. I had hoped he would return after a time, but I did not wish to leave the children alone with Patricia, as today is a baking day."

"Leave them with us," Mr Darcy said, and I nearly laughed. His snow-white cravat, crisply knotted as always, and his immaculate tail-coat would be ruined within moments if he attempted to care for the children. His brow furrowed. "I always seem to amuse you when I am not attempting humour."

"Indeed you do, sir, but forgive me. My little ones are a challenge, more so for gentlemen unfamiliar with the womanly arts."

Mr Bingley smiled and put his fists on his hips, jutting out his chin. "You believe we are not up for feats of strength and bravery?"

I smiled in return and suggested we wait until Jane arrived at the least, for she was Thomas's favourite and knew how to soothe Alice.

Jane arrived moments later, and happiness filled the sitting room like morning light.

Patricia brought in tea, and as I poured, Mr Darcy caught sight of the bruises on my wrist and arms. "Heavens! What— Did my cousin do that?"

The teapot hovered in mid-air as I calculated whether to set it down and attempt to somehow cover the evidence of the altercation, or finish pouring and attempt to explain. "It is nothing," I said, my tone even.

Mr Darcy leapt to his feet. "It is not nothing to hit one's wife!"

"He did not hit me, sir." My eyes flicked to Jane and Mr

Bingley, whose faces were both frozen with alarm. "We scuffled, yes, but the bruises were an accident. He has never raised a hand to me and never shall."

Mr Darcy sank down again and murmured, "It is barbaric."

I sat, wondering how to preserve James's honour. "Since his return, he is…altered, as you are aware. However, the aggravation with his family and the pain in his body, compounded with other worries—" I stopped short, for sharing our difficulties was bad form.

"We are family," Jane said, her eyes flicking to Mr Bingley. He gave a little nod, a smile playing at his lips. She beamed at his agreement before her smile faded. "You may tell us all."

I sipped my tea, studying my free wrist a moment. "He is a good man," I said, and noted with relief that all three nodded in agreement, "but last night's events pushed him beyond endurance. His intention was not harm. His emotions ran high and I was…in the way."

Mr Darcy's jaw clenched. "How can we be sure you will not be 'in the way' in the future?"

I set down my teacup. "There are no certainties in life, but I am not concerned." Their exchanged glances of doubt brought me to my feet. "If you will excuse me, I would like to locate my wayward husband."

I FOUND JAMES ON THE BANK OF THE STREAM WHERE WE spent our first night as a married couple, a place we often brought the children to let Thomas splash about. James's clothes were rumpled and dirty. Foolishly, my first thought was how difficult it would be to remove some of those stains from the fabric.

"Please sit with me," he said quietly, not looking up. I did. His eyes remained fixed on the babbling water. "Words cannot express how sorry I am for everything. From the moment I seduced you all those years ago—"

"You did no such thing!"

He looked at me and I could see a deep weariness pulling him under. "Near enough."

"No, James. I pursued you from the beginning. You neither trapped me nor disappointed me."

He chewed at his bottom lip, then took up a pebble and tossed it into the water. I reached out to rest my hand on his knee, and he saw the bruises. "I did this?" He clicked his tongue. "I ought to return to Spain."

"You will be of no use to them, and I wish for you to be here."

"Do you?"

"Of course."

We sat in silence for a moment before he covered my hand with his. "The words I said about other options. I…" My heart quickened as I feared the worst. "While I am sure there are such women near where the militia train, I did not even enquire. I came here directly and sat all night thinking." I squeezed his thigh and he rested his head on my shoulder. "Were you in earnest about not desiring more children?"

How to answer? "Not never, but not yet."

As he nodded, his unkempt hair tickled my cheek. "We will be careful, and I will leave after Jane's wedding. There must be something I can do with the Dragoons."

"Do not. Your health is still poor, and your mind not yet mended."

Using his crutch, he stood, taking up another small stone and throwing it into the water.

"Learn to be satisfied with us. Your children hardly know you. These years with them are irreplaceable." He did not turn around, so I rose. "I have been thinking. James, please do not reject this immediately. What if…you see, my Uncle Gardiner has a very dear friend with a respectable line of trade, and I imagine at my uncle's introduction he would be more than willing to bring you in—"

His head snapped to me. "Have you already made enquiries?"

"No." I braced myself, fearing he might bruise me again. "I would not betray you in such a fashion, but I have considered the possibilities and I—"

"Do not breathe a word of this scheme to anyone. There must be another way."

I fought back more arguments and contained my frustration. "We have guests, James. We ought to return to them."

He nodded to the brook and we returned to the house together.

CHAPTER SIXTEEN

The morning of Jane's wedding, a hired carriage arrived to bring my family to the church, then on to Netherfield and eventually back home. This, as well as arrangements for my gown, a room for Patricia at Netherfield in which she would entertain the children during the festivities, and a hamper of treats were Mr Bingley's gifts to us. Lest James fall into a fury over charity, Jane made clear that Mr Bingley had extended the same offer to Margaret and Uncle Gardiner, as well as some dear relatives on his side. All of this was unusual and overly generous, but we agreed. Margaret and Uncle Gardiner would leave their children home and take their own carriage, but it allowed us to accept the offer with more dignity, and preserved us from a time-consuming and lengthy walk that would have pained James.

The prior day, we had gone to visit Jane and discovered that my mother was at the house. I ought to have expected it, but instantly my mood soured. She was arranging flowers she had picked with Uncle Gardiner and Margaret's oldest children that morning, a point which stung when I learned of it. She was more of a grandmother to them than to her own.

I walked through the door with my writhing daughter, only for my mother to approach and lean in. "Are you Alice?"

She knew my daughter's name. I suspected Uncle Gardiner told her about my life in his letters—ones he exchanged with her regularly—and the thought stabbed at me.

"I am your grandmother." When Alice merely stuck a pudgy finger into her mouth, my mother straightened to address me. "She is welcome to remain with me for a while if you like."

I swallowed hard, unsure. "If it is not too much of a bother."

"Not at all. We will get acquainted," she said, smiling as she handed Alice a flower. Alice crushed it immediately, and my mother laughed, to my surprise. I wondered what sort of mother she had been before abandoning us. "You will make someone a beautiful bride, my darling," she said to the baby, stroking her cheek. "Though you had best find one with money!" My stomach squeezed. Not even able to walk, and already the pressure of matrimony mounted. I took Alice back.

Just then, James walked through the door carrying Thomas. "Mrs Bennet, it has been a long time."

"Indeed," she said. "Are you treating my daughter well?"

Her daughter?

His face was stony. "I believe I am, madam."

"Who is that?" Thomas asked. Each month his language and knowledge of the world improved at such a pace it stunned me.

"Your grandmother," James replied, irritation tinging the edges of his words.

"Oh," Thomas said, and, wriggling out of James's grasp, went to take her hand. "Greetings."

I felt repelled by the scene but did not wish to be rude. I should want Thomas to have a grandmother.

She locked eyes with me. "Thomas, let us go out and see the horses. Uncle Gardiner says you like horses."

I watched them go hand in hand, though in truth it felt like she was stealing a piece of my heart.

"I shall see to Jane," I said, and James went to find my uncle. Once upstairs, I knocked on Jane's door. At her invitation to enter, I was overcome by the sight of her room filled with flowers—on her dressing table, vases of wild-flowers picked, she said, by Mr Bingley himself; and on the windowsill and bedside table, vases of hothouse flowers, grown and selected by his staff. "Oh Jane, you shall be positively spoilt!" Her eyebrows rose with concern, to which I said, "And you will deserve every bit of it after what he put you through. And because you are the most perfect person heaven ever sent to Earth and he is lucky to have you." I kissed her temple and lowered Alice onto the bed where she kicked happily before I sat on the edge of the dressing table. "Have you readied yourself for tomorrow?"

She nodded, but one emotion after the next flickered across her face: joy, hesitation, fear, and excitement. "The event is much larger than I anticipated. I expected merely a small breakfast. I feel shy about it all." She stroked a flower petal with the tip of her finger. "And after…when we are alone. I am…quite nervous."

I reached out and took her hand. "You will grow accustomed to each other. Take your time and be sure you talk about it. You should enjoy being with him." Her face flushed and she looked away. "Jane, I am in earnest. Some women speak only of duty, but I assure you, there is happiness to be found on both sides."

She leapt to her feet and went to her bed, sinking to its edge and tickling Alice's belly. "And what if we do not? What if there is no joy in any aspect of our lives?"

I laughed. "Oh, Jane, I cannot think of two people better suited to one another. Your happiness is fairly preordained." Her shoulders loosened, but her face was still tight, so I asked her to show me the gown Mr Bingley had had made for her.

When she removed it from the wardrobe and held it against her body, I gasped, running my hand along the luxurious pale blue silk and fingering the fine lace at the sleeve. I marvelled at the delicate flowers embroidered near the hem. "You shall be magnificent in this, and make women jealous for years to come as you don it for balls and dinners. Every man in attendance will wish he had chosen you!"

She blushed, and asked if I liked mine. She had been with me when the dressmaker had produced the bolt of dove-grey satin. "It is so fine. I think I shall insist Patricia hold Alice all morning so it is not ruined. I cannot think on what occasion I would wear it next."

Jane touched my cheek. "You will come to Netherfield and enjoy many gatherings there. Mr Bingley does so love guests."

"And you?"

"And I...love him."

I left that afternoon confident my sister would make an impeccable bride and overcome her shyness to become a gracious hostess, the perfect partner to Mr Bingley in every way.

I FELT NO RESERVATIONS WHEN WE ARRIVED AT THE CHURCH for the ceremony other than the size of the crowd, which I knew would frighten Jane. Most of the village appeared to have come! As the church was open to all, it was not disallowed and I ought to have expected it. Perhaps she did, for she appeared serene. The guests also gawked at me as I accompanied her inside. What a relief for us to be stared at for the right reason after so many years of judgment and disapproval. Jane had chosen well and could at last live at peace.

The ceremony was followed by the wedding breakfast. Many guests were already at Netherfield when we arrived. Despite my claim that I wanted the children nowhere near my fine new clothes, I could not help but take Thomas for sipping chocolate. The thrill on his face was as pure as anything I have seen in my life and worth the risk of spots, which luckily did not appear on my gown. Patricia took him away soon after, wiping at the corners of his lips, and a Netherfield servant carried Alice after them.

I felt lighter—literally and metaphorically—than I had in years. James looked dashing in his uniform, newly tailored to fit his still-thin frame, and he looked at me with more contentment than I could remember. We walked in the garden and might have tarried longer had his presence not been requested by Bingley himself.

I was set to return to the house with him when I heard a voice call my name. It was my old tutor who had so loved books and plays.

"Miss Taylor!" I smiled, and motioned for James to walk ahead.

"It is a comfort to see you at long last." We embraced, and she asked, "Have you been reading much?"

"There never seems to be the time."

"There is always time for reading!"

"Not with two children and a household to run."

She sighed, and her disappointment pained me. "Do you enjoy this life you lead?"

I thought she might listen and understand in a way most others would not. "I meant to be so unique, so adventurous. I dreamed of leaving Meryton, of having a life worth remembering. I am not at all who I dreamed I would be."

"Ah," she said, bringing her gaze back to mine. " 'Oh, Hope! Thou soother sweet of human woes! How I shall lure thee to my haunts forlorn!' " She narrowed her eyes. "Alas, has it been too many years?"

I shook my head. "Charlotte Turner Smith. One of your favourite poets."

She smiled and touched my arm. "My dear, do not consider what might have been. I ought never to have criticised you, for I would have chosen your path had I the chance. Do you think I set out to be a spinster?" She chuckled as if the word did not pain her. "I dreamed of being a mother and a wife, of living in a magnificent house like the one into which I was born, and having an enormous library in which I would read all day. As you know, none of that came to pass. But my cottage is my library, I have read a good many books—more than my share, I am sure—and have been a good teacher, I hope."

I gave a vigorous nod. "But why did you not marry?"

She shrugged. "No one desired my hand. I was not wealthy enough or handsome enough to overcome either deficiency. I guarantee, Elizabeth, if you spoke to each person here"—she gestured at the crowd milling about the grounds—"most would admit, however grudgingly, that life has not been what they expected. Are you happy with your husband?"

"Most of the time."

"And motherhood?"

"Most of the time." We smiled. "It is simply that there are other paths I desired."

"As a woman, your choices were always limited." She took my hand. "Dear Elizabeth, I imagine there is not a thinking person on Earth who is completely satisfied with their life at the end of their days." It was not the most comforting thing she could have said, though probably the most accurate. "Let us return to the house. The sun is too strong for me."

Upon depositing her in a chair in the parlour, my attention was drawn by my mother chattering to Lady Lucas, and unfortunately, all could hear. "Nothing could exceed their income! Why, he has four or five thousand a year, and very likely more. I am so happy for my dearest Jane! I have not had a wink of sleep since I heard the news. Oh! He is the handsomest young man that ever was seen!"

At least her wagging tongue could no longer damage Jane's marriage prospects.

Just then, James entered and brought me to the music room where Mr Darcy was standing with a young woman of about fifteen. His dour expression faded as we approached. "I would like to introduce you to my sister, Miss Georgiana Darcy."

"Oh Mrs Fitzwilliam, what a joy to meet you at last!" She beamed.

"You may call me Elizabeth if you like." I added with a whisper, "Or Lizzy, if you are daring."

Her eyes lit up and she looked to Mr Darcy, who gave a slight nod in approval.

"I hope we shall be friends M—Lizzy!" she said, taking my hands in hers. "I understand that you are a great reader of Shakespeare. I do love his romances." She folded her hands across her heart, looked to the gold-trimmed ceiling, and said with breathless awe, " 'When love speaks, the voice of all the gods makes heaven drowsy with the harmony.' " She sighed. "Have you ever heard such words from another writer? Oh!" She fanned herself, the dream of the sentiment still hovering around her like a mist.

Mr Darcy looked on with an indulgent smile. It was a new view of him: permissive, kind, and paternal.

"Mr Darcy," I asked, "as I recall, you were not such a fan of his work?"

He fiddled with the ebony buttons on his perfectly cut coat and I detected the hint of a smile tugging at the corners of his mouth. "The two of you might bring my mind around."

"Perhaps more time together and we shall!" Georgiana said, bouncing on the balls of her feet. "I would so love visiting with you, Lizzy. My only company most days is the staff, who are naturally distant except for Mrs Reynolds, our housekeeper, and Mrs Younge, my governess. My brother travels too often and visits too rarely." Her enthusiasm, which tripped over social custom, and her need for companionship, especially that of a female peer, reminded me of myself upon meeting Margaret years ago.

"You always have me for company," said a man from over Georgiana's shoulder, and she spun around.

"George!" she squealed. "I did not think you would be in attendance."

The young man in well-fitting regimentals—red coat with gold trim and cream trousers—smiled at her with dazzling teeth, so straight they reminded me of keys on a pianoforte.

"Mr Wickham." The colour drained from Mr Darcy's

face, and Mr Wickham's smile faded ever so slightly. "I did not expect to see you here."

He brushed a lock of sandy hair from his forehead, his expression impassive. Was he as unconcerned as he appeared or was it pretence? "Mr Bingley invited me."

Mr Darcy's eyes were cold, but Georgiana seemed not to notice, and asked Mr Wickham question after question about his service and if they were treating him well and if the food was plentiful enough, hardly giving him time to answer each enquiry.

At last, Mr Wickham gestured towards the musicians. "Georgiana, would you care to join me for a dance?"

She eagerly took his elbow and they drifted to where the musicians played.

James said, "Darcy, you must not allow yourself to be so troubled by him. He now has a position and can be of no further bother to you."

"Nonsense," Mr Darcy snapped. "He will always find ways of causing me trouble, and I wish Georgiana would heed my warnings."

James leaned in, his voice pitched just loud enough to be heard over the sizeable crowd. "You have not shared with Georgiana the whole of his situation, or his public arguments with you—have you?"

Jaw clenched, Mr Darcy shook his head. "I ought to. She does not understand my warnings otherwise, yet I do not wish for her to hate him entirely nor to deprive her of one of the only relationships she had before our parents' dea—" He pressed his lips together.

I marvelled at the infrequency with which he allowed himself to express true emotion. I also wondered how much the care of his sister and the absence of his parents weighed on him. When I thought my mother deceased, I had ached at the loss daily; though I found little comfort in my father, I had to imagine being entirely without parental figures created an unfillable void.

As if conjured, my mother passed by as she spoke to a woman I knew not. "We always knew Jane's good looks could secure her a wealthy husband, but this exceeds all…" I was pleased not to hear the rest, and James looked at me with a mix of horror and amusement.

"Mr Darcy!" A woman approached and he bowed his head in greeting. She turned her falcon-like gaze upon us and I immediately recognised the woman I had once met as Caroline Bingley, though she had subsequently secured a husband. The blessed event occurred—not coincidentally, I thought—just after Mr Darcy married. "Mr Fitzwilliam, Mrs Fitzwilliam."

I gave a small curtsey.

"How is married life, Lady Snowley?" Mr Darcy asked.

An expression of boredom passed over her face as she sighed. Tipping her head to where Mr Bingley and my sister were sharing a laugh, she said in a droll voice, "My brother seems to take more pleasure in marriage, though the blush is still on that bloom, so who is to say? Her lack of culture might eventually wear on him."

I stiffened. Did she not recall that I was Jane's sister? No, I was certain she knew what she said and whom she offended. "Money cannot buy kindness, *Caroline*," I said, using her given name intentionally, "but I suppose it can buy a title."

She narrowed her eyes before slithering away.

"I know." I spoke before Mr Darcy or James could scold me. "But I find myself unable to hold my tongue at times."

"You are not the one who owes an apology," said Mr Darcy. "Pray excuse me. I must locate Georgiana."

When James and I gathered our children not long after, guests were still dancing and eating, making this an affair of uncommon length. But Jane seemed not to mind the lingering or our leave-taking. She and Mr Bingley were smiling as brightly as that morning when our father had escorted her down the aisle of the chapel, and looked at each other with a love I hoped would stay with them forever.

CHAPTER SEVENTEEN

S oon we were at a christening for the Bingleys' son and James departed once again. He limped when it rained, but said he could ride and fight as well as before his injury, claiming we could no longer afford to live on half-pay—though I thought we were managing.

His next leave brought Thomas and Alice more joy than his prior returns, for they were old enough to recognise him, and his subsequent departure brought more heartache. I adjusted more easily than the children to his absence, but soon I realised I was expecting once again.

Initially I had been pleased to discover I was to have another child, but by early summer it was apparent that my pregnancy was not ordinary. Five months in, I was nearly the same size I had been when I had had Alice and Thomas. I decided to consult a doctor. Dr Thrup was freshly trained and new to Meryton. He had red curly hair and apple-red cheeks, which grew redder when he spoke of *woman troubles*.

"Perhaps you would feel more comfortable speaking with my, eh, wife about such matters," he said, his words seeming to trip over themselves in his nervousness as he dabbed his glistening brow with an embroidered kerchief.

"Well," I said, considering how to respond, "you are, after all, the doctor. Would you not be the better trained person to consult?"

He chuckled as he wiped the back of his neck with the darkening handkerchief. "I suppose that would be true in most matters. Yet, in actuality, she has more experience in matters of, er, bringing new life into this world."

"Did they teach you about delivery in medical school or not?" I asked, anxious at paying for a visit in which the doctor did nothing but refer me to his wife. I had not wished to add to our expenses by traveling to a proper accoucheur in London, but I was beginning to think it might have been worth the cost. Then again, not living in town, this man might be a necessity as my time approached.

Dr Thrup's left eye began to twitch as he removed his spectacles and cleaned them. "No need to be testy. If you would like me to, eh, examine you, I will." He looked as if begging me to decline.

By this point I put no stock in his advice, but was interested in seeing how uncomfortable he would become and what new ticks he might develop should I accept, so I looked at him square in the eye. "I am in need of an examination."

His cheeks caught fire, as did his forehead, ears, and neck. Dr Thrup stood and escorted me into his examining room. He clasped his hands in front of him, shifting from one foot to the other.

"Shall I remove any article of clothing?" I asked.

I venture to say he might have gasped, but I cannot be

certain. He wiped his brow and put the kerchief in his pocket. "Your, em... Madam, I would feel better if my wife were here."

"Dr Thrup," I said, suppressing a laugh, "if you wish to avoid women's problems, it might be more prudent to join the military."

"Oh, my wife would not allow that," he replied. He looked down, squeezing his thumbs against his index fingers so hard they turned white. "I have had women patients. My professors said I ought not to think of it as indelicate, but like treating a cow or some such." My mouth dropped open. "I know I shall grow accustomed to it. Some doctors in the poorer wards had far more experience than I, a student constrained to higher-class ladies."

"Did they not allow themselves to be examined?"

"When they did, I was asked to leave the room. For propriety's sake." He looked up at me and added, "I assure you, madam, I have read the books and studied hard." He returned to wringing his hands, sure I would run out the door.

Sympathetic to his lack of experience and discomfort, I said, "Perhaps today you would find comfort in your wife's company. I have no objection."

He went out the door with a lighter step. After a few moments, Mrs Thrup walked through the door shaking her head. She had an apologetic look on her face, and stood to my side as a calmer Dr Thrup began to ask questions. After each question, he looked at her and she nodded.

"How many months have you been, er, with child?"

"Five months."

Look. Nod.

"Have you any other children?"

"Yes. Two."

Look. Nod.

"And you say this time is different. How?"

"I am tired more often. I vomit more. It has not stopped in all these months."

"Constant vomiting?"

"No." I wondered if he was listening to me. "Five months of constant vomiting and I would be dead. Daily, though. And my stomach is enormous."

"Ah. I see," he said, lifting an eyebrow. "Please excuse us." And with that, he and his wife stepped out of the room and had a whispered conference before they returned to their same positions. "My wi—my conclusion is, er"—he looked at her and, at her nod, he continued—"that you are expecting twins."

I had had my suspicions that might be the case, but I thought there would be some examination to confirm it. Mrs Thrup stepped forward. "Mrs Fitzwilliam, I assure you, when your time comes, Dr Thrup will have more experience. There are currently four other women in their confinement." She chuckled.

"Indeed." I smiled, relaxing somewhat. "Will you be accompanying him at the births?"

"It seems to make him more comfortable, so I believe I shall."

I felt even more relieved, for myself as well as the women who would go before me.

I WROTE TO JAMES BEGGING HIM TO RETURN. BY THE TIME he arrived, I found myself unable to do my daily tasks; even more frustrating, the need to care for my children grew stronger even as my body prevented it. Some days, despite my best efforts, I could only dress and feed them, and spent the rest the rest of the day sitting or lying down, hoping they would not run far or get hurt. I braced myself for what two more babies were likely to do to our family and our resources.

One evening, I sat on the sofa with James as he rubbed my sore feet and swollen ankles. "We should hire someone to help," he said. "Patricia cannot keep apace."

"With what money?"

"I could ask my mother and father."

"No!"

He smirked and I realised he was joking. He raked his fingers through his hair. "My cousin?"

I shook my head and stared at the ceiling, my heart sinking as I imagined the scowl on Mr Darcy's face if he received another request for assistance. "Please do not. My pride cannot withstand more charity, and I daresay neither can yours."

As if summoned (James later denying that he had done so), Mr Darcy arrived a fortnight later while James was out tending to the animals. I brought him in, my cheeks heating when I saw his eyes fix upon the laundry hanging across lines in the kitchen. I forced a smile. "With the rain yesterday, there was nowhere else for it to dry."

His gaze lingered on the stockings and shifts a moment too long for my taste, but at last he turned his attention to me. "You are looking well," he said.

I thanked him, adding light-heartedly, "Though I do not quite agree. I feel heavy and ridiculous."

His smile twitched into a fleeting expression of pain, and I wondered if he was thinking of his wife. He asked, "How are the children?"

"Resting, mercifully." Again, I felt guilty. Was it painful for him to see his cousin with all he himself had wanted? Perhaps not all, for I was fairly certain that Mr Darcy would not have wanted to be concerned with a goat's swollen udders.

"And James?"

"He is well. He is in the barn and shan't be long."

He nodded, and I offered him a chair in our sitting room, the one space not wholly taken over by our belongings. He sat and I picked up one of Alice's dolls from the sofa so I could face him. He was working his lips around as if searching for the words, a gesture that emphasised his high cheekbones and pensive demeanour. "I am concerned by your lack of assistance. I am aware that though another servant would be a pittance, James has refused to secure anyone."

My head spun. "Refused is a strong word, and how did you come to this knowledge of our need?" Could it have been Jane? I had not confided in her, though I am sure she quickly surmised the reason for our lack of a larger staff.

"Allow me to hire a girl—"

I shook my head.

"I thought you might listen to reason. The idea of your working like this when you could have comforts—"

"You have all the comforts one can purchase." My eyes narrowed. "Are you happy?"

He tugged at his waistcoat. "My happiness is of no consequence. You are carrying a child while acting as scullery maid, cook, governess, and housekeeper. It is unhealthy and an embarrassment."

"An embarrassment to whom?" I snapped, rising as quickly as I could given my girth. "We see no one socially because their condemnations are as petty and dull as their

149

company. I thought you might be different." I walked to the front door, taking hold of the handle. "You are not welcome here if you intend to judge us so harshly. Now good day, sir."

Mr Darcy, jaw set, strode towards me. Just as he stopped and opened his mouth, presumably to argue, James clomped in, having entered through the back.

"Darcy!" he cried. "How good to see you again. Has Lizzy made you comfortable?"

I was thankful that Mr Darcy did not say what I had made him, which was cross, defensive, and unwelcome.

Something in his look gave James pause. "Has something happened?" James looked to me, then Mr Darcy and back, while I only gawped.

"Your wife had a twinge, but it seems to have passed." Our eyes locked and, while I was grateful for his discretion, I was not yet ready to forgive him. "I would like to offer a servant to help her around the house, if it would please you."

"Yes," said James too quickly. His cheeks caught fire. "I confess it pains me to turn to you yet again for assistance, but my wife is overworked for her condition and I have no means of providing more resources."

"James!"

He shook his cousin's hand and threw me a look making it clear that I was not to say another word against the idea. "It will only be temporary, but I give my hearty thanks."

I was furious but kept my peace by departing to check on Thomas, and found him contentedly playing with Alice's blanket as if it were a cloak. I scooped him up and, since Alice was still sleeping, brought him out to the men.

My anger quieted upon seeing Mr Darcy's fists and rigid

spine relax as the cousins laughed together. Thomas reached out for Mr Darcy.

Mr Darcy's face brightened, which warmed my heart. "Would you like to hold him, Uncle Darcy?"

Mr Darcy froze. "Uncle?"

Why had I presumed that such a title would be acceptable to him? Why could I never follow rules of propriety or be more sensitive? His only child had passed at birth while James was creating a sizable brood with ease. "I am sorry, Mr Darcy. I ought to have asked before calling you that."

Mr Darcy pulled in a breath and his shoulders relaxed. "I would be honoured to have such magnificent children call me uncle, especially having no nieces or nephews of my own."

"Yet," said James.

Mr Darcy threw him a look of irritation. "At sixteen, Georgiana is still too young to make me an uncle."

I chose not to mention I had been only two years older when I had Thomas.

Smiling, Mr Darcy rose to take Thomas. "Well, well, young man, if you grow any more, you shall be carrying me!"

Thomas threw his arms around Mr Darcy's neck. "Uncle Darcy, I missed you."

I went to see about tea. Once in the kitchen, I avoided the temptation to pull down our washing, deciding that Mr Darcy would live through seeing our true existence for the duration of his visit. As I readied the kettle, everything hurt, and I hated to admit my relief that someone else would be baking and laundering and lifting Thomas, who had grown too large for me.

I heard Mr Darcy say to James, "You must warn her away from him!"

James said, "Lydia and I do not speak."

"Remedy that, James, or he shall charm her as he did Georgiana, and that nearly ended in disaster."

Alice awoke, preventing my hearing the rest, and I knew I would have to ask James about both matters. After changing Alice, I brought her out to the others. She squealed with delight the moment she saw James, reaching for him and kicking until he had her firmly in his grasp.

James invited Mr Darcy to the floor to play with the children. Mr Darcy looked like a giant being asked to squeeze into a walnut shell, and his expression of unease made me laugh, though I stifled it so as not to shame him.

"Take off your waistcoat and tails, Darcy," James said. "I know you would be more comfortable, especially in this heat."

Mr Darcy's eyes met mine and I nodded encouragement, adding, "Do not stand on ceremony here. The rules of society do not apply in our home."

With great hesitation, he removed his coat and folded it with careful motions, draping it over a chair. All the while Thomas was leaping in circles pretending to be a cyclone, a sort of weather he had heard about from one of his books. "I never was as unconstrained as that," Mr Darcy said, nodding at Thomas. "It is as though I was born with a weight around my neck."

James bounced Alice on his knee. "I cannot say if it was from birth, but you were always so serious."

"Mother and Father insisted upon it."

"Have you never been happy?" I asked, unable to help myself.

James glared at me. "What a question!"

Mr Darcy shook his head at his cousin. "No, James, it is natural to wonder." To my surprise, he pulled at the knot in his cravat until it was loose, then removed it completely. "I have had moments of joy. Visiting with Bingley and now Jane, riding in the country, acquiring horses and paintings, spending time with you two. Four." He watched the children a moment. "But sustained happiness? I daresay no. My entire existence has been obligation and requirement." Mr Darcy lowered himself to the floor.

"Darcy"—James handed Alice to him—"you have been constrained by everything miserable. With us, you may be free."

"You make it sound easy."

"It is!" he cried. "No one need know that you come here and forget about the rules as we do. Not only do we under-dress," James said, tugging at his bare shirtsleeves, "we often walk about barefooted." James laughed, and Mr Darcy's thick eyebrows lifted.

I said to James, "You will scandalise him. One step at a time, my dear." Alice began to fuss, so I handed her a doll. "Mr Darcy, what do you wish you could do that seems forbidden?"

"Walk...on the grass with bare feet." He said it like a child about to open Christmas presents. The thought of such a simple act lit up his face and made something inside of me melt. Gone was the judgmental furrowed brow, gone was the rigid bearing. Instead, I saw a man longing for freedom and opportunities for true joy, and I hoped to play a part in such a transformation.

James began pulling at his own boots and stockings, encouraging Mr Darcy to do the same. Reluctant at first, then caught up in the moment, Mr Darcy pulled off his shoes and stockings and charged out the door ahead of James, who had stopped to take hold of Thomas. The three of them ran about hollering and tagging each other. Their shouts of glee made me laugh, and when the men fell to the ground with exhaustion, faces upturned to the sun, breathing hard, I smiled wider than I had in months. I was enthralled to see them all so happy. If only such happiness could last.

CHAPTER EIGHTEEN

Nora, whom James hired to assist me, was a wonderful help to me during those last few months. The daughter of a Netherfield tenant, she slept on the floor of the kitchen, assuring us that it was the most sensible thing and that it was where she slept at home anyhow.

We did not wait long, as my labour began earlier than expected. I awoke with a back-ache that I ignored, assuming the twins had shifted, but by late morning I realised it was labour. Knowing it would take some time, I went about my work without telling Nora or James, pausing to breathe when my stomach squeezed. By the afternoon, I could not hide my discomfort from Nora, and when James returned from the orchard, he found me perched on the edge of our mattress panting. The pain was greater than with my other children…different.

James happened to be at the house. For the other births, he had been abroad, and both of us assumed that this time he would busy himself elsewhere like most men did. He was buttoning his coat to fetch Margaret and remain with my uncle, yet I was gripped with panic. "Do not leave me."

Sweat broke out on his upper lip. "Wh-what can I do?"

"Send Nora to get Margaret." He held me and paced and held me more, shaking when he saw the blood running down my legs and cursing when I cried out. I assured him this was perfectly normal, while doubting it myself.

Once Margaret arrived, she took in the situation, then turned to Nora. "Send for Dr Thrup. His wife, too."

Both James and I gasped. The thought of the apple-cheeked doctor was funny for a supper time laugh, but decidedly not amusing at the moment.

"Why?" demanded James.

I attempted to argue but let out a cry.

In her calmest voice, the one she used when there was trouble, Margaret said, "Just do as I ask."

"No, please, no," I said, my teeth clenched.

"Shhh. Do not worry. Shhh," she said, stroking my hair. The last 'shhh' had a tremble behind it. She excused herself, saying she needed to gather more linen, though I believe it was to gather herself.

"James," I gasped, holding out my hands to him. He assisted me to my feet, for I wished to walk, only for my knees to buckle as another wave of pain came over me. Our eyes locked as my arms encircled his neck for support. He staggered under my weight but held me still. I suddenly thought of Mr Darcy's wife. Could the cousins be destined to share the same fate? I reached up and touched his cheeks, tracing the freckles I so loved that dotted his nose and cheeks. "I will miss these."

"Stop it."

"You must listen." My time could be limited—I had to tell him all my thoughts before it was too late. My fingers dug into his shoulders as I struggled to hold myself up. "The children will not remember me. That is natural." The thought of it hurt my heart, but I had to continue. "You cannot wallow, though. You wallow too often." At this, we both smiled in acknowledgment through our tears. "You must marry again—"

"No. Liz—"

"Listen! You must listen to me!" I paused to take a deep breath, and allowed him to ease me back to the edge of the mattress. Fatigue pulled at my limbs, my eyelids. It might be easier to let myself slip away from this pain, from life, but I was not ready. Not yet. "James, you must. The children will need a mother and you shall need a wife."

"No!"

I squeezed his hands. "Do not pick someone silly, for you will hate her. Or someone simple or lazy. Pick—"

"No one. I chose you. You are my only."

I shook my head. "A sensible girl. And see to it that you find someone who will love Alice and Thomas as if they were her own. Growing up without maternal love is-is... unbearable." He kissed me and threw his arms around me, and I held him as he wept. I stroked his wild hair. "Love them with all of your heart. They will need you."

"This is my fault. You did not want more children, but I was selfish and—"

"Enough of this!" Margaret said as she stepped through the door, telling James I needed to concentrate on the task at hand and to stop being maudlin, though I wanted him right where he was. James paced, then held my hand, left the room and then came back, over and over. He tried to avoid

Margaret's gaze and the blood, but his eyes would dart to the sheets and to her, and he would flee the room.

Finally Dr Thrup, his wife, and Nora burst through the door. The lantern light reflected off Dr Thrup's sweaty but kind face. My pains were very close together, and I was losing strength and consciousness. When Dr Thrup finished examining me—he had obviously had much practice with women and births since last we met, as he hardly hesitated in kneeling to get closer—he met my gaze. His eyes had dread in them the likes of which I had not often seen. He stepped back and Mrs Thrup knelt where he had been and examined me. With pursed lips, she stood and walked towards the door, Dr Thrup and James in tow. They closed the door behind them. How could they leave me alone, and worse, hide the truth from me? However, I was too exhausted to speak, let alone protest. Instead, I fainted.

I awoke to feeling something cold reaching inside of me. I had heard of forceps, but never known anyone who experienced them during a birth and was not sure if Dr Thrup was employing them. I wanted to ask them to stop, but could not speak. I pried open my eyes and saw Margaret's worried face over mine as she put a cool compress on my forehead. I could only manage to suck in short breaths until I felt a tearing of my flesh. Blackness overtook me again and as I faded away, I heard a man's voice ask, "Is this much blood typical?"

I SHIVERED. THE SUN WAS BRIGHT ON MY LIDS, BUT I COULD not open my eyes. More shivering. No light. Light. No light. I wanted to open my eyes but I could not, and drifted away. More light. More darkness. Babies cried. I attempted to speak but my mouth felt like it was filled with sand. More shivering. Voices whispered. Someone pulled at my arms, my blanket. So cold.

"Open your eyes."

I mustered all of my strength to do so. Late afternoon light streamed in the window across the room. I blinked a few heavy times but my eyes fell shut again and no matter how hard I tried, I could not open them again.

It was dark when I found the strength to try again. Was it even the same day? I was able to focus on the lamp, then shifted my gaze next to the bed. James was slumped forward in the stiff chair, his head bobbing against his chest. I wanted to wake him, but could not speak. My body burned and my mouth felt thick from want of water. I spotted a mug next to my bed and endeavoured to reach it, but the few inches of movement sapped my strength.

The next time my eyes opened, Jane was there. "Thank God." She dropped to her knees and clutched my hands. "Thank God!" Feeling her hands on mine chased away some of the dread that I would never recover. "James!" she shouted as she started to cry. "James, come quickly!"

I heard his thundering steps come to an abrupt halt at the door. I wished to smile. I shivered and my eyes closed against my will. I was conscious, however, so I could hear him come closer. "Lizzy? Oh, Elizabeth, please be well. Can you hear me?" I attempted to move my head a bit, hoping he would see it. He must have, for he grasped my shoulders and fairly lifted me off the bed. I was dead weight, and he put me right back down. Dead weight. Not quite dead. I did not want to die. I wanted to be with James and my children, and to see them grow. I felt determined to hold them all but could move nary a muscle.

IT TOOK AGES FOR ME TO REGAIN MY STRENGTH, BUT IT DID happen. Dr Thrup had been forced to pull the babies out. They were alive and well, which I had feared might not be the case. Once the bleeding stopped—and neither the doctor nor his wife thought it would—I developed an infection that none thought I could survive. And yet I did. Why I lived through this while most in my situation did not, I cannot understand.

I asked to see my children as soon as I could speak. I wanted to see Thomas and Alice most, as they were more real to me than the babies—babies whom, I fleetingly thought with resentment, had nearly caused my death. And yet the moment I saw the tiny bundles, with their impossibly small faces peeking out from their blankets, I was entirely overcome with joy. Sarah, whom we called Sally, and Henry. Henry, with his thick head of brown hair, pensive eyes, and creased forehead; and Sally, her mouth screwed up like she had an argument to make, made my family say they were perfect reflections of James and myself. I had to agree.

I was overcome with guilt for having been sick, for their having to endure the first month of life without a mother. Yet with Margaret and Uncle Gardiner, James, Mr Darcy, Jane, Bingley, and all of the children, they had been surrounded by love.

RAISING FOUR CHILDREN UNDER THE AGE OF FIVE WAS NOT for the faint of heart or the recently ill. Nevertheless, day by day, I was on the mend and anxious to regain my strength so that I could begin facing the challenge on my own, in my own way.

Each time James looked at me, it was with relief, tinged

with apology. After a few days, I took him by the cheeks. "James, stop. I am alive and mending."

"I nearly killed you."

"No," I said. "No. It is a peril of being a woman. You bear no responsibility."

He buried his face in my lap and wept.

CHAPTER NINETEEN

Months passed and we saw many changes. Jane brought a daughter into the world, and Margaret gave my uncle another son.

My father fell ill and slipped away with little ceremony or heartache, and the house in which I had been raised belonged now to the Gardiners. My mother came for the funeral and left as quickly as she had arrived. After her departure, Jane confessed that she had asked our mother to visit when I was ill but that she refused. The news did not surprise me, though it had stung, much as I hated to admit it.

James claimed that he would return to the Dragoons, but he made no plans to depart, for which I was relieved. To my surprise and satisfaction, he did enquire after work with my uncle's friend. He spoke of it only once after receiving a letter explaining that the man would be pleased to speak further on the matter, and invited James to London to discuss the needs of the ever-growing business. James had not yet travelled, claiming the money was better spent on

Nora's salary, though I suspected that was an excuse to give himself time to think.

The most concerning event occurred in late spring. I was walking to Meryton on a rare outing when I spotted Mr Wickham on the road. We spoke for a few moments about our mutual health and the weather. He appeared anxious to bring our conversation to an end, looking past my shoulder multiple times. The last time he did so, I turned and caught sight of a young woman in the shadows. Lydia Fitzwilliam. She ducked behind a tree and when I looked back, Mr Wickham's face was scarlet.

"Lady Lydia!" I called, and she approached, eyes downcast. As a woman who had, in her youth, thrown aside customs concerning appropriate interactions, I was not scandalised by a man and a woman planning to meet in secret, but rather was alarmed at Lady Lydia being associated with this particular gentleman. Just after Jane's wedding, this same Mr Wickham had attempted to run off with Mr Darcy's sister, Georgiana! Mr Darcy had prevented that disaster, and I feared this charmer was attempting to turn scoundrel once again.

"Lady Lydia, would you do me the great favour of walking with me?" I asked. I did not feel at liberty to warn her, if she did not already know, of Mr Wickham's history. Simply having planned for an elopement could ruin Georgiana's reputation; however, I could hint at his prior entanglements and impart some of the wisdom Margaret had shared when first I had been discovered with James.

Lady Lydia emerged from the shadows, her usual effervescence replaced by wide-eyed concern. "I am afraid I cannot walk with you. Pray pardon me. I am due back at the house presently." And with that, she scampered away. Mr Wickham bowed and walked in the other direction.

I hoped that would be the last of the matter, though I shared the tale with James. He refused to speak to his parents about it, but did consult Mr Darcy, who advised an audience with Lady Lydia. She did not reply to the letter James sent asking for her to come to our home, and it was not certain if the missive was received and ignored, or never delivered. Either way, the events that followed could have been prevented, and many parties shared the blame.

ANOTHER SUMMER WAS UPON US, AND IT WAS THE WARMEST I could remember. The hills seemed constantly shrouded by the incredible humidity. Milk curdled so quickly we could not use it fast enough. Everything felt slow and thick. This necessitated daily swimming and the occasional sleeping out of doors. We must have been quite a sight, splashing one another and jumping about, holding the twins—now two years old—in the water. Thomas and Alice, who both felt very important as the older brother and sister, passed the little ones gently back and forth in the stream. I loved watching James lift them out of the water, their legs kicking, making their fat bottoms bounce.

In mid-July we went to the annual fair in Meryton. The day felt milder by comparison, and without the oppressive humidity I could breathe easier, my steps light as we made our way to the festivities. Flags and bunting hung from the shop windows, transporting me to the happy times when Jane and I would run with such excitement through these streets, anticipating a day of fun. As always, the stalls were filled with enticing foods and wares.

James and I had agreed upon how much money we would spend that day, deciding to be extravagant, wanting to give the children and ourselves some joy after so many months of privation and anxiety. The puppet show—Thomas's favourite—was free, as was the music Alice loved so dearly. We kept an extra close watch on her because, two years prior, I had lost her in the crowd when she toddled off to hear an organ grinder.

Today, in the sun-dappled shade near the village green, Thomas and Alice marched and twirled by turns to the sound of flutes and drums, and a troupe doing tricks on tightropes made us all gasp. We bought nuts at a stall and shared the bag as we watched Morris dancers leaping and knocking their sticks, which, unsurprisingly, inspired Thomas and Alice to pick up twigs and copy their motions. All was well until Thomas hit Alice's twig hard enough to snap it, causing her to wet James's coat with tears. Promises of sausages and puddings brought her out of her despair and allowed us to gather the food and move towards my family. The sounds of drums and flutes and laughter were everywhere as we walked with the twins in our arms. James reached out for my free hand and smiled.

We chose the same picnic spot—under a weeping willow at the edge of the green—that Jane and I had settled into every year since we were children. The spot had been ideal for keeping away from the eyes of judgmental townspeople. I had always wanted to sit where we could hear the music best, and would have been happy to stay and fight with the rest of the children, but Jane always took the picnic basket in one hand and led us to a safe distance. Our father had rarely attended the fair; if he did, he did not sit for a meal with us, preferring to inspect the stalls or speak to an acquaintance.

On this day, we watched our children play in the shade of the willow tree. Jane put her arm around me and we sat, smiling with contentment. Our group had grown so large we hardly fit under the shade, even though the tree had grown as well. Uncle Gardiner watched Margaret manage their brood, their servants having been given the opportunity to enjoy the festivities. James was rocking both of our sleeping twins, his face untroubled, the tune he hummed wistful. I would never take for granted his moments of joy and the continued fading of his injuries and troubles of the mind. Bingley joked with the older children, tickling and teasing them.

Mr Darcy and Georgiana joined us this year. Georgiana had complained of being bored and lonely, left too often at Pemberley. He had promised her more entertainment, and they were staying a fortnight with the Bingleys after passing the Season in London and Brighton before that. Georgiana had grown into a composed young woman, kind and serene, who had met an equally charming young man while in Brighton, though no offer had yet been made.

Her eyes were bright as she explained, "We met while shelling on the beach. I was going to make a picture from them—it is the fashion with many ladies, you see—and he came up and handed me the most perfect, pure white shell I have ever seen!" She beamed and her gaze flicked from me to Jane as if asking for confirmation that this did, in fact, make him the perfect suitor.

I was sure that when I looked at Mr Darcy, his face would be twisted in judgment. Instead, a smile played at his lips. "Was it as romantic as she describes?" I asked him.

He arched a brow. "The wind was blowing his hair rather perfectly." Georgiana swatted at him, and he winked at her. "I concede he was a gentleman and quite thoughtful, and his conversation at tea the next day was entertaining."

Georgiana detailed the topics the young man had discussed while I considered how Mr Darcy had changed in the years since I met him. Had his rigidity and grimness been due to grief over losing his parents and then his wife, or had his growing comfort with James's and Bingley's circles made him more enjoyable company?

I turned at a shout. Thomas was wrestling with the two eldest Gardiner boys while Alice looked on in disdain. She hated to be dirty, so she sat with one arm tucked through her father's, leaned on his shoulder, and smoothed her frilly skirt.

We passed the afternoon listening to music and talking in different clusters, waiting in vain for the older children to tire. As the shadows grew long, we decided to pack our belongings. Thomas pulled at my skirt. "Mummy, you promised I could have a toy, the wooden horse. You promised."

"I did not forget," I said, though I had. "We shall get it on our way out."

"No, now. I can see the man putting them away."

"Thomas—" I was about to chastise him, but recalled my promise that if he did his chores all month without arguing he could pick out one toy, and knew I had to go.

James said there was one more stall he wished to visit, and Georgiana asked Mr Darcy if they might look at some ribbons before our departure.

James looped his arm through mine as we walked towards the stalls, Georgiana and Mr Darcy strolling at James's side.

"The one with a black mane," Thomas called after us.

I turned around. "Yes, a pink mane."

His nose wrinkled. "Black!"

"Yellow?" asked James over his shoulder.

"Blaaaack!" Thomas stamped his feet, then fell to the

ground giggling as only a six-year-old can do over a silly, simple joke.

The walk to the stalls was brief, but we decided to split off for our purchases as we each desired something different. The toys were the closest to where my family sat, while fabrics and trimmings were further on, near the permanent shops. James wanted to investigate the livestock offerings despite our discussion of finances that morning. We had concluded that we had not the funds for anything so extravagant, but he wanted a moment to see who had the best animals in case our fortunes changed.

I paid for the toy horse and waited, marvelling at a passing performer able to juggle while singing and doing a jig. Soon James returned, telling me of a pig farmer he thought might cut him a deal at the end of the week if the entire litter was not sold at the fair.

Georgiana raced towards us. "Come quickly! My brother is in need of assistance." My breath caught at her haunted eyes and pale face. We hurried after her.

CHAPTER TWENTY

James and I followed Georgiana as she ran past the stalls towards the town's permanent buildings. The crowd thinned and, as we approached the back of the milliner's, we all stopped short. Mr Darcy was squared off against Mr Wickham, who was accompanied by…Lady Lydia! Both Mr Wickham and Lady Lydia were in travel clothes, and I noticed a satchel on the ground near her feet.

I could not see Mr Darcy's face, but his shoulders were tense and his hands balled into fists. Mr Wickham, on the other hand, appeared more relaxed with one hand pressed against the wall of the shop. His other hand was on Lady Lydia's shoulder.

"Lydia!" James called out, his voice barely containing his rage.

Mr Darcy spun around and once he spotted her, ordered Georgiana to return to the group. Gone was the civility and caution he typically used with his sister, replaced by a panic and fury I had never seen. She scurried off, glancing back once at the man who had nearly ruined her life.

"Lydia," James repeated, and what was left of the colour in her face drained away.

Mr Wickham leaned in and said something in her ear that made her blush.

Mr Darcy's nails bit into the palms of his hands, as if willing himself not to strike Mr Wickham. "Wickham, I shall ask once again: what business have you with my cousin?"

Mr Wickham merely glared in response and James, with a jerk of his head, motioned for Mr Darcy to step aside. Eyes ablaze, Mr Darcy stormed to where I stood.

Lady Lydia shifted, causing Mr Wickham's hand to fall to his side. "W-well, we—you see, we are— He came to find me because he wishes to m-marry me."

My eyes darted from James and Mr Darcy to Mr Wickham, who—to my astonishment—returned his hand to her shoulder.

James's jaw clenched. "Are our parents aware that you are here?"

She shook her head. "You know they do not approve of such events, nor of our mixing with those not in our circle."

"Let me return you home," James said, his fierce gaze fixed on Mr Wickham.

No one moved.

"Lydia, come along!" When she did not move, James stepped toward her, hand outstretched.

Mr Wickham slapped James's hand away. Everyone froze, and in that moment I became aware of the distant sounds of drums and laughter.

James bared his teeth. "Remove your hands from my sister at once."

Whereas the rest of us were balled nerves and tense muscles, Mr Wickham appeared relaxed, leaning back on his heels. I could not tell if his calm was feigned or if he was truly unconcerned, sure he would win this argument and whisk Lady Lydia away as he desired. As if speaking of the weather, he said, "Lydia shall depart with me."

"An elopement?" Mr Darcy bellowed, stepping to James's side. "You attempted that once! You would bring another lady into disrepute?"

Lady Lydia jutted her chin at us, seemingly emboldened. "Wickham told me all about playing at eloping with Georgiana. What a laugh! He promised to marry me the moment we reach London. No harm will come of it. Wickham is dashing and strong and exciting. Mother and Father would have me marry someone old or disgusting just for money, but I shall not sell myself to please them."

She did have a point.

"Do not be a fool!" James flung his arms wide. "He is taking advantage of you, Lydia, for your money. I will not allow it!"

"You have no say in the matter. When did last I see you? It has been years."

"Because—" He checked himself, perhaps not wishing to air family grievances in front of one such as Mr Wickham. "You shall ruin our family reputation."

"Any worse than you did by marrying her?" She pointed in my direction, her eyes narrowed. "Our eldest brother would not even come to your wedding for the shame of it. None of us are to speak of you. Who is the embarrassment, truly, James?"

I was not certain what was worse, James's mortification or Mr Wickham's expression of triumph.

She lifted her chin, a smug smile pulling at her lips, and Mr Wickham took her hand.

"Unhand her at once!" Mr Darcy rushed forward, grabbing Lady Lydia by the arm.

Mr Wickham locked eyes with Mr Darcy. "She wishes to leave with me, Darcy. She will be a better choice in every way than your simpering sister."

I sucked in a breath.

Mr Darcy released Lady Lydia and punched Mr Wickham in the face. I gasped as he fell against the wall. Mr Wickham shook his head, as if his ears were ringing, and touched his fingertips to his cheek with a glare as Mr Darcy rubbed his knuckles. Mr Wickham removed his coat and tossed it to the ground.

Lady Lydia stepped to his side. "No, Wickham. Let us depart and—"

Mr Wickham did not even acknowledge her, but raised his fists, aiming several quick jabs at Mr Darcy's face. Mr Darcy bobbed and weaved out of the way, then advanced, forcing Mr Wickham back several steps before he unleashed a flurry of blows in return, one striking Mr Darcy's side. Mr Darcy let out a grunt of pain, then responded with a punch of his own, causing Mr Wickham to double over.

As Mr Wickham panted, hands on his knees, Mr Darcy stepped behind Mr Wickham. "Will you forget Lady Lydia and vanish once and for all?"

In a flash, Mr Wickham straightened, smashing the back of his head into Mr Darcy's nose hard enough that Mr Darcy collapsed. Mr Wickham kicked him across the face, opening a bloody gash across his cheek.

Throwing aside Thomas's toy horse, I rushed into the fray, shoving Mr Wickham's chest as hard as I could, hard enough for him to stumble.

James held Mr Darcy under his arms and attempted to drag his cousin away. Mr Wickham spat to the side, a sneer twisting his features, before he launched himself towards us again. He shoved me aside and I looked about in desperation, hoping someone from the fair might see the conflict and come to assist us. Unfortunately, we were just removed enough that no one seemed to notice.

I turned back to see Mr Wickham kicking at Mr Darcy and James, a grunt escaping as he raised a booted foot to stomp on Mr Darcy's ribs. A nauseating crack filled the air. I gasped and Lady Lydia screamed. James set Mr Darcy on the ground, then with a growl charged Mr Wickham and a shocking volley of punches and jabs ensued. Lady Lydia screamed again when Mr Wickham caught a hard blow to the face.

By now, Lady Lydia's shrieks had attracted the attention of a few people.

"Someone stop them!" I yelled, but the crowd kept its distance, several men elbowing each other in glee. How could they enjoy the pain of men I cared for?

Blood streamed from James's nose and Mr Wickham's bottom lip was cut, filling his mouth with blood like a beast after a kill. A cheer from the crowd when James landed a punch in Mr Wickham's gut filled me with rage, as did Lady Lydia's cry of, "James, do not hurt him!"

Mr Darcy was still too close to the brawl, sprawled on the ground moaning, eyes pinched shut. I ran to pull him out from under their feet, but though I dug my heels into the dusty ground to brace myself, I could not move him far enough. With a curse, Mr Wickham attempted to kick Mr Darcy again. I knelt over Mr Darcy's bloodied head, hoping to shield him, and James punched Mr Wickham's side, only to receive a fist to the jaw in return.

"James, stop! James, please!" I did not want our children to see his bruises and have to explain their cause. And I was terrified at the thought of his arm or leg, both of which still pained him, being broken once again.

Lady Lydia stood, hands covering her mouth, shoulders shaking with sobs. I rose, disgusted, anger giving me the strength to move Mr Darcy further from the fight.

At the sound of Mr Wickham's roar, I whirled around only to see James drop to his knees, clutching his throat where Mr Wickham had clearly struck him. Mr Wickham backed away as James fell with a thud onto his chest, dust caking the blood streaming from cuts across his face. My legs buckled as his face turned from deep red to dark purple. I ran to turn him onto his back. He gripped his throat, gasping for breath, his legs kicking sporadically. I could see knuckle marks on his neck. Blood from his cut lips seeped into his mouth.

I thought he might choke, so I took my hem and tried to wipe away the blood. James swatted at my hands and shook his head. He pointed to his throat and writhed. My stomach churned as he gurgled. "Help!" I clutched his shoulders, looking to the crowd. "Help! He cannot breathe!"

He grabbed my hands, his eyes frantic, a bubble of blood forming between his lips but no more sounds.

"James! No! Nooo! Please! No!" I screamed for him not to let go. I looked up. Lady Lydia stood without speaking or moving or crying. She just stared at us. James's eyes squeezed shut before opening wide and fluttering closed. His hands dropped to the ground at his side. Blood trickled down his face until it mixed with the dirt beneath his body. His chest was still, yet the blood continued to flow, turning the dry summer earth underneath his body a deep wine.

"Get help!" I screamed, but no one moved. "Go for help." My mouth was dry, my tongue thick.

There was nothing that could be done and everyone knew it.

I shook him, tears falling onto my blood-covered hands until Dr Thrup rushed to my side. He checked James for only a moment and whispered, "He is gone." I collapsed onto James, feeling his warmth and his blood soak my skin.

Several men grabbed Mr Wickham and led him away, alternately calling for Lady Lydia and protesting that it was an accident. Dr Thrup had someone else bring water while he checked Mr Darcy.

Soon, my uncle pushed his way through the crowd. "Oh God!" He crouched at my side and said my name. I forced myself to sit up and allowed him to see James's face. "Oh God!"

The crowd began to disperse, leaving us to our grief.

I clutched James harder and sobbed. I felt removed from my body, numb, as if I was floating above myself. "It cannot be. He cannot be dead!" I wailed. "Get another doctor. A good doctor!" Dr Thrup flinched, but continued his work on Mr Darcy.

Uncle Gardiner touched my shoulder and I pushed his hand off, unable to look away from James. "Wake up. James, stand up!" His nose had been broken, as had two of his teeth, and my stomach churned. I could not bear to see his wrecked mouth, and covered it with my palm. When no breath came, though oddly I expected it to, I began weeping again. A crowd was re-forming, only closer. My skin prickled and rage peaked within me. I hated all of them. I wanted to rise and kick every one of them to the ground, watch them gasp for breath. Instead, I closed my eyes and recalled the day James and I were married, how young he was, how hopeful and kind.

An eerie calm washed over me. I sat, eyes closed, unwilling to hear or see anything for a time. Finally, I opened my eyes and said to my uncle, "I will tell them."

"Who?"

"His mother and father." My voice sounded detached, as if someone else was speaking. "I shall...I shall tell them."

Uncle Gardiner was squatting, and pressed his fingertips to his temples. "No, you do not have to."

"Yes, I do." I was not sure why I wanted to be the one, but I knew I had to be. "I need a conveyance."

"My wife will bring you," said Dr Thrup, who had finished binding Mr Darcy's arm against his chest to stabilise the ribs.

Mr Darcy attempted to get to his feet but winced and slumped back to the ground. "No, Mrs Fitzwilliam. Remain here."

I stood. My legs and back ached. "Make sure, make sure our children—" my voice caught—"the children are looked after. Do not—do not tell them yet."

"Of course," replied Uncle Gardiner, his eyes drifting to James's still form.

I spotted the wooden horse in the dust where I had thrown it, and snatched it up. That toy. That blessed toy! If only we had not gone back to the stalls. If only Thomas had forgotten my promise. If only.

After checking that there was no blood on the body or mane, I handed it to my uncle. Swallowing the lump in my throat, I said, "Please give this to Thomas."

He nodded, his face pained.

I could not have my children see me covered in their father's blood, and I could not face their beautiful, innocent faces and tell them their father was dead. Not yet. I was led away by Mrs Thrup and attempted not to think of anything at all. People were staring at me. A few even asked if I needed help. *Where were you before?* I thought bitterly, and walked on without reply. My gait was stiff as I endeavoured to keep my arms away from my blood-soaked dress. We reached the Thrups' gig and I hoisted myself inside. *I must tell them. I must tell them. I must tell them* were the only words I allowed in my head.

Eventually we came up and over the last hill and I could see the Fitzwilliam house. *I must tell them.* I dismounted as a servant opened the door. His bland expression disappeared and he hurried back inside.

Within moments, the earl joined me outside. Evidently I was too coarse to be shown to the parlour like a proper guest. "What on earth?" he said, his eyes flying wide.

Lady Broxbourne emerged. "Who is there? Whatever is the matter?"

I swallowed hard. "James—" I choked on the rest as James had choked, and felt my lower lip quiver. No. No! I could not fall to pieces. Not yet. Not here, in front of these people.

Lady Broxbourne sank to her knees with a shriek. Her husband stumbled and leaned on the wall. After some time, he held Lady Broxbourne by the elbow and helped her withdraw. She wailed up the stairs and as I stood dazed, unable to move, I heard her again through the widow above. My legs buckled and I sat on their steps, covering my ears, trying to block out her voice, ignoring Mrs Thrup and the servants assembling around me. Even so, their murmurs and chatter scratched at me: 'James', 'dead', 'tragedy'. I sat still, listening to the rush of blood surging through my ears. I was breathing fast despite my efforts to slow down. Every time I managed it, the livid purple of James's face came to my mind and I felt panic, as if my own breath was being squeezed out of me.

I stumbled home, collapsing against the front door. As the first star appeared in the dimming sky, a carriage approached. Mr Darcy was helped to the ground, wincing. He hobbled closer. I did not say a word for fear of what might come out. Screaming? Crying? Cursing?

After a few moments he said, "I stopped at my aunt and uncle's. The doctor will be coming for Lady Broxbourne." He paused, his wary gaze on me.

I did not respond. I did not care. I felt nothing.

"Your children are with the Gardiners."

I wished he would stop talking. My eyes fixed on the cuts on his knuckles; his hands were likewise scraped.

"Oh, Mrs Fitzwilliam, I cannot express—" He looked away, stifling a whimper.

I tried not to think about why. I tried not to think about my children. I tried not to think.

Eventually he cleared his throat, bringing my attention back to his face and the angry slash on his cheek which had been stitched at some point. He was looking at me with such pity that it made my chest squeeze. No. I could not allow myself to feel! I closed my eyes, hoping to shut the world away.

"Do you want to wash?" Mr Darcy asked. "You ought to." The silence stretched out. "You need to wash yourself," he insisted. I looked at my blood-stained hands and arms and dress and began to shake.

He ducked his head to look into my eyes. "Come inside. The servants are not here this evening. You gave them the day and night off due to the fair, if you recall. I shall bring water for you."

I shook my head, but he took me by the elbow and led me in. We stopped in the sitting room. He let go and took a step back. "Mrs Fitzwilliam——"

"Elizabeth," I said dully. "Please call me Elizabeth. You might have done so long ago."

His eyes ran the length of me, lingering on my hemline. "Elizabeth, you will need to change your clothes as well."

I nodded, trying to stop my teeth from chattering. It was sweltering—why was I so cold? I swayed, staring at Mr Darcy, not able to move or feel anything as he hurried around the kitchen.

"And you ought to call me Darcy, as my true friends do."

I gave a vague nod. It seemed an absurd time to discuss such things, but what else could be said?

"The others were occupied with the children. I apologise that I am here alone. Dr Thrup should be by soon."

I sank to the floor and put my head in my hands again.

Darcy squatted down. "Elizabeth?"

"You did not tell my children, did you? Alice and Thomas. They…"

"No. No." He patted my arm. His hands were cold, too. "We told them their parents had to come here and that you would see them in the morning."

"You lied to them? How am I to explain——"

"We could not think what else to——"

"It does not matter," I said, closing my eyes. James's bloodied face was all I could see. I worked to catch my breath. My eyes flew open. "Did Thomas get his toy horse?" I asked, another wave of panic crashing over me.

"Yes, your uncle gave it to him before we left the——" Darcy's voice broke. He stood, swiping at a tear. "He was excited to receive it."

"Oh, good," I said, unable to feel any joy.

He continued studying me as if any moment I would explode, and pressed a handkerchief, already soiled, to the cut across his cheek. "They know something is the matter, though. No one is telling them, but they are asking. They know…something is amiss."

I winced and an odd squeak came out of my mouth. I struggled to contain myself and held my breath. Darcy limped into the kitchen. From across the house, I heard a sob and then silence. He had his back to me, but I imagined he was covering his mouth to stifle the sound. Tears streamed down my own cheeks and I had no strength to wipe them away.

A few minutes later, Darcy approached holding a pitcher, and sweat was visible across his forehead. His injuries were too severe for such exertion, but I could not find my voice to tell him to stop. At his suggestion, I rose and trailed him to my bedroom. He set the pitcher on the dressing table and handed me a cloth. "I shall be just on the other side of the door. Call if you require anything."

I looked at myself for the first time in the mirror. Dark stains covered the front of my dress, dried blood on my neck and cheeks. My hair was askew and my eyes had a wild look to them. I was terrified by my own reflection. I turned away and dipped the cloth into the basin. The water darkened and I realised that this was the last bit of James I had, the last contact I would have with him, the last proof of his final moments. I sat down at the dressing table, put my head on my arms and sobbed.

After a while, Darcy spoke from the other side of the closed door. "Elizabeth, can I get you anything?"

"Dar—" My breath caught. "I cannot—I cannot do it."

He cracked open the door. "Oh," he said softly. "I ought to have insisted that Jane accompany me, but she…"

After a moment's hesitation, he entered and knelt by my side, lips tightening in pain. He took one of my hands in his and used the other to dip the cloth. Slowly, gingerly he wiped away the blood. At times, I could only close my eyes and weep. Tears streamed down his face too, but he worked with methodical strokes to clean my face, my arms, and my neck of my husband's blood.

Then he hesitated. "I believe you will have to do the rest on your own. Let me get you some fresh water."

I lowered my head. "Thank you." After he returned with the water and left the room, I removed my dress and looked again at my reflection, continuing to wipe away the signs of my husband's struggle and his death.

I put on a new dress, balling the soiled one—a favourite of James's with delicate flowers scattered across the filmy cotton—and tossing it in the corner. I walked out as Dr Thrup entered the front door, only for him to stop short, as did I. "I am so sorry," he said and bowed his head. "Lady Broxbourne has been given a draught to help her rest."

The men nodded at each other before Dr Thrup turned back to me. "Mrs Fitzwilliam, shall I examine you for injury?"

I shook my head.

"Darcy, your ribs—"

"Are of no consequence."

"They are. You must not exert yourself overmuch, nor lift anything extremely heavy. Will the lady's family attend to her this evening?"

Darcy shrugged. "Mr Gardiner suggested he might, but with the children and—it is not certain."

"Do not leave her if they do not arrive. I know you would be alone together, but as her husband's cousin, no one would think twice. She needs watching, I am certain."

Dr Thrup excused himself. "A damnable shame," he muttered, shaking his head.

I followed Dr Thrup, as if sleepwalking, through the front door to one of the chairs that James had set out for us to watch the sunrise. Darcy followed a few moments later, and sat next to me holding up a bottle of brandy and a glass. When I shook my head, his lips pursed. "It will do your nerves good."

I allowed him to pour me a dram. I choked on my first sip and it made me think of James struggling for breath, but I wanted to feel what he felt, to lose my breath as if I could experience his last moments as he did.

I asked for more, tipped my head back and drank another glass. Warmth spread through my body, and I drank still more.

"Not too quickly," Darcy warned. My eyes were heavy and I leaned my head back, the pull of drink and sleep dragging me into unconsciousness.

CHAPTER TWENTY-ONE

I awoke in the early hours with a start, wondering why I was not in my bed. My neck hurt. The owls and frogs were making a terrible ruckus. No breeze blew to cool the night and a blue mist hung low on the land. As if surfacing from a dive, memory slowly returned. I covered my face, a whimper escaping my lips. I had not cried so much in my life and knew I had not yet exhausted the tears.

I found Darcy asleep on the ground near my feet, beginning to stir. Nausea welled up as I took in his bruised jaw and left eye, and the gash on his cheek which was still seeping. He squinted and propped himself up on one elbow. "Are you quite well?"

It was an absurd question, but I had no voice to tell him so. I looked at the horizon. He sat up and leaned against his vacant chair.

"Thank you," I said.

"For what?"

"For caring for me last night. I do not know what I should have done without your assistance."

He shook his head, unrolling the tail-coat he had used as a pillow. "It was nothing."

"It was not nothing."

Our eyes met and he offered a small smile that was exactly like James's. That was enough to make the tears come again, and I buried my face in my hands, relieved that Darcy said nothing.

"How long—" I blinked rapidly, willing away more tears.

"How long what?" He put on the tail-coat, smoothing down the collar.

"How long until you ceased thinking of Mrs Darcy and the child?"

"Jove, Elizabeth, I know not." The question seemed to exhaust him. "I never—I mean to say, I still do. All the time."

"Oh." My shoulders slumped. I had wanted to believe this pain would end soon.

"Well," he said, perhaps searching for a better answer, something to soothe me. "Do you mean 'think of' or 'grieve for'?" At my shrug, he ran his fingertips along the light stubble on his jawline searching for an answer. "I do not still weep over them. It takes time, but it…it becomes less, well, consuming."

I nodded.

"It is different, I suppose, for everyone. I wish I had something helpful to say on the matter. I once thought about her and the baby every second and could do nothing without considering what had happened and feeling emptiness. And now…I do not do so very often. It has been many years, however, and my feelings for her were never as strong as yours for J—" We both froze. He rose, his face pale, and went inside.

I bit at my lips, much as James once did. What was I going to say to my children? Were they too young to understand? What if they cried? I dreaded facing them, but I had already waited too long.

I WALKED TO MY CHILDHOOD HOME ALONE, HAVING REFUSED Darcy's offer to accompany me. He said he would return to Netherfield, and promised whatever assistance I required that day and in the future. The sadness and pity in his eyes had pushed me to make a hasty departure. By the time I arrived at Longbourn I was dripping with sweat and covered in dust, so I stopped at the pump to wash off and to collect my thoughts. After a few minutes, I heard the metallic click of the back door opening.

"Lizzy?" called out Jane.

It was the first time I had seen her since I had walked arm-in-arm with James to get the toy horse. I turned to her, hands dripping with frigid water. The moment I saw her pained, beautiful, comforting face, my legs grew weak and I fell to my knees, unable to cry or speak or move. I wanted her to come to me like a mother might and carry me to my room and tuck me into bed.

As if she knew, Jane knelt down and hugged me. "Dearest."

The perfection of her kindness broke me and I wept into my hands. I cried until I could stop, and still she held me.

The distant laughter of children pierced the quiet of our breathing. "Your children are playing by the stream with most of Margaret's."

"The little ones?"

"They are there, as well. They are safe," she added.

Nothing felt safe anymore.

I dragged myself to my feet and into the house. My steps sounded louder on the hardwood floor than I wanted them to. The entrance hall seemed darker than it should have been on a summer's day, the air more still.

Through the doorway of the parlour I saw my uncle, who hovered at the mantel, twisting a handkerchief in his hands. We nodded at one another and then he looked down. The way everyone looked at me now—the pity and the worry—was a hideous reminder of what had happened and my nausea returned.

I heard tentative footsteps on the stairs and Lady Lydia came into view. I stiffened and would have charged towards her in a rage had Jane not grasped my arm.

"Elizabeth," Lady Lydia said, her hands shaking even though she clutched them together. "I am sorry for what happened."

"Why is she here?" I hissed to my family.

Jane stepped closer. "Her mother was undone and her father in a rage. We thought it safer for her with us."

Everyone was frozen as if waiting to see what I might do next. I spun on my heels and walked into the parlour, unable to catch my breath. The tingling that had started in my fingers when I first saw her worked its way up my arms and down my legs.

"Lizzy," said Jane, trailing me, "she came to apologise. It could not have been easy."

"Not easy for her?" Jane blanched, but I could not stop. "I hate her! She is worthless and snivelling and the reason I must raise four children by myself! That shall not be easy, I promise you."

"Shhh. She will hear you."

"I do not care! Let her hear me! Let my words haunt her for all of her days!" I pressed on, feeling terrified and

186

thrilled as I became increasingly undone. "Can you hear me, Lady Lydia?" I screamed at the doorway. "Do you hear me? Leave! Leave now!!"

My uncle rushed nearer. "What on Earth? Have you lost your senses?"

"My husband is dead and it is her fault. I will not be tamed by you, Uncle. Not today! Depart if you do not wish to hear me speak my piece!"

He shook his head and left the room.

"Dearest." Jane stepped forward, her pale cheeks and taut mouth belying the calm in her voice, and reached out for me.

I stepped out of her grasp. "Do not attempt to silence me."

"No. Of course not," said Jane, holding her palms out as if facing a wild beast. "I simply thought you might wish to see your children." My children. My face went numb and my legs felt weak. How could I tell them? What could I say? My bottom lip quivered and I searched Jane's face as if an answer might lie there. "You do not have to tell them anything now," she said, her voice soothing. "Just see them. Let them see you."

I nodded. I was tired...so very tired. And sad. Such a small word for such an all-consuming feeling.

I walked outside, concentrating to stay steady on my feet.

BEFORE REACHING THE CLEARING, I HEARD THE HAPPY splashing and playing of a large group of children. I hated to disturb their peace—forever, I feared. I listened to their joy another moment before approaching. A governess was watching over them, standing tall at the water's edge. Her smile was serene, and she held Henry in her arms as comfortably as if he were her own. Alice held Sally in her lap as I had shown her, and dribbled water onto Sally's round belly, to squeals of delight. Thomas was with some of Margaret and Uncle Gardiner's children. I moved closer.

"Mother!" screamed Alice, struggling to lift Sally. I moved to her and squeezed both girls. "Oh, Mother, I am so glad you have returned. We missed you and Father!"

"It was only one night," I said, gathering my strength to sound normal.

"I know, but you have never been away before. And, well, everyone was acting so strangely. They gave us cake before bed!"

"Well, I have returned, so no more cake." I forced a cheery expression.

"And Father. Has he returned?"

"Sweetheart, dry off now." Sweat broke out across my back. "Thomas! Thomas, come out of the water, please." He pouted but galloped out. The governess started towards me, but I was afraid that she might say something in front of Alice and Thomas I was not ready for them to hear, so I shook my head.

"I am dry, Mother!" cried Alice. "Now bring me to Father!" Did she have a sense of what had happened, or somehow know something?

"Come, darling," I said, taking her hand. "Thomas, take Sally's hand." I moved away from the creek towards the clearing where Jane and I had passed the hours together under a tree when our father was raging. I trembled, unable to catch my breath. "I have something very difficult to tell you."

Sally began to fuss, wanting to break free of Thomas's

embrace. I held my arms out to her and she came running, bouncing up and down to play. "No, sweetheart," I said gently, but she kept bouncing, bending her knees and springing up. I felt my temper rising, for I wanted to tell them, to finally tell them, and had not expected this. I held her arm in my hand and squeezed a bit. "Stop, Sally. Sit down." She giggled and leapt again. "Stay there!" I took hold of her with both hands and plopped her onto her bottom, only for her to begin crying. I ought to have left the twins with the governess. They were too young to understand anyhow. "I am sorry, Sally," I said, picking her up as she squirmed in protest, and Henry bellowed for me to hold him.

I imagined having to drag four crying children back to the house on my own and reconsidered. "Let us take them to the house and then we can talk." Better to have only two while alone.

Alone. I was alone and would be forever. How could I manage them and the house alone? I felt sick as I started to stand.

"Mother, I am tired," said Alice. "Let us stay here."

"Alice, please help me get them all moving again."

"But we have already been walking!" she whined.

"Alice, take Sally."

"She is too heavy!"

"You carry her all the time!"

Her lip quivered and I bent down to her. "Please be a big girl and help Mother. I count on you." I endeavoured to be patient, knowing that she was reacting to me and how oddly the adults had been behaving. Additionally, she was five and difficult when she chose to be. "Please," I whispered.

We approached the house, somewhat bedraggled.

"How fare you all?" my uncle asked, hovering at the threshold of the front door.

"The twins were making it difficult to talk," I called out in warning, my voice more panicked than I desired.

Out rushed Margaret and Hill. "Here we go, sweet girl," exclaimed Margaret as she took Sally from Alice. Hill locked eyes with me as she took Henry. I looked away first.

"We shall be in the garden, I suppose," I said, and took Thomas and Alice by the hands. We walked in silence to the back porch. I settled them onto seats around the table where Margaret preferred her tea when the weather permitted, and sat across from them.

"I wish—" I cleared my throat. "I wish I did not have to tell you what I am about to tell you." I looked to the sky and felt my clothes sticking to my body. Even a summer dress was not light enough. I hitched it above my knees and took in their little faces, patient and wide-eyed. I could not make them wait any longer. "I..." How to say it? I had practiced so many different ways in my mind and could not remember any of them. "Your father...he... There was an accident." Alice's face began to crumple, more from fear at my tone, perhaps, than a real understanding of my words. Thomas stared at me blankly, his face so like James's it made me ache. I swallowed hard. "Your father was hurt. And he is... not alive anymore." I winced a little at my poor phrasing and the bluntness of it.

"He is dead?" Thomas asked, his eyes like saucers.

"Yes."

"Like Grandfather?" he asked slowly. I nodded. He kicked the dirt with his foot and made swirling patterns with his toe.

"Things get dead," said Alice matter-of-factly. "Like Persephone." Persephone had been our goat. I nodded.

"Then we should just go get Father back." We had bought another goat and she had insisted on calling it Persephone, as well.

"No, darling." I reached across the table and took her hand. "There is no getting him back. Remember, when Persephone died, she was gone forever."

"But I want Father now."

"I know, sweetheart." I sniffed. "But he is gone forever."

Thomas's face squished up and tears began to stream down his cheeks. It was so pitiful. Drool came out of his mouth and dripped onto his already wet shirt. I rose and reached out, and he flung himself against me, sobbing. Alice leapt to her feet and pressed her face to my other thigh. I knelt and they rested their heads on my shoulders, wailing.

I could not do this. I could not help them or watch them grieve. I had my own sadness and no way to stop theirs. I could not watch their lives fall to pieces.

I patted them and murmured reassurance. Empty words.

Thomas stepped back, drying his face on his sleeve. "How did he die?" His tone was so oddly mature coming from such a little boy.

"Your father was caught in the middle of a fight."

"Why was he fighting?"

"He was trying to help...someone." I could not bring myself to say Darcy's name, to make him a part of this terrible moment for my son. "He was hit very hard a-and —" A wave of nausea ran through me as the sound of Mr Wickham's fist hitting James's throat echoed through my mind. James's purple, desperate face pleaded with me.

Alice buried her head against my neck, and the feel of her heated skin against my scorching body was too much.

My skin prickled and a roar of protest rose up from within, but I could not let it out. I had to be calm for my children.

"That is not right!" cried Thomas. "Father says 'no hitting'."

"I know."

"So why did he fight?"

Alice stepped back, wiping her eyes with the back of her hand. "Did the person who hit him say he was sorry?"

I recalled Mr Wickham's smirk as he stood insinuatingly close to Lady Lydia.

"If he says he is sorry it will be better," Alice said, sounding like Margaret giving instructions on comportment. I ached at her sincerity.

"No, it will not, idiot!" shouted Thomas. "He is dead! I wish the man who hit him died, too!"

"Thomas, stop that," I said as Alice began to cry. I took hold of him and smoothed down his hair, as unruly as his father's. I kissed his head, which I always did to calm him.

Alice sniffed. "You should always say you are sorry. Then everything is mended."

Nothing was mended, and if I had had the chance to kill Mr Wickham or Lady Lydia myself, I just might have done it. And I would not have been sorry.

CHAPTER TWENTY-TWO

That day dragged on and on. I sat and stood with members of my family, as well as people who arrived to offer condolences, the feeling of desolation and loneliness and dread constant.

Darcy arrived late in the afternoon, standing nearby as though the gesture could protect me. He smelled of grief. I swear it has a smell.

Over tea, Darcy shared what he knew of the final arrangements. "He will be buried with the family in the churchyard."

My anger flared. "Church? No. It should be at our home."

Darcy let out a huff. "It is where our family is always buried. Darcys and Fitzwilliams are not buried in fields."

"But the *church*yard? James did not go to church."

"It is expected."

"Your family is denying who he was at every turn! This is not what he would have desired."

"You do not know that." Darcy smoothed his pristine

cravat, and I recalled the lazy wonderful afternoons he spent at our house without the trappings of formal society. His posture had also returned to its previous stiffness, making me sadder than I already was. "The ladies will be sitting vigil over the body and gathering funeral favours. None of the women will attend the service, as is customary."

"I will attend."

Jane winced.

Darcy lowered his chin, and I saw more clearly the bruise surrounding the gash on his cheek. "It would be unseemly, especially if you are overcome with emotion."

"I will attend," I repeated.

Darcy's hands balled into fists. "Your stubbornness arises from effeminate indulgence!"

"I beg your pardon!"

Jaw clenched, he excused himself for a walk.

Jane opened her mouth but I held up a finger. "Do not say a word." I jumped to my feet and left the room.

I AWOKE TO HENRY'S CRYING. WE HAD AGREED TO REMAIN at Longbourn, but doing so unsettled all of us. My sleep had been filled with horrors. I changed Henry and lay in bed listening to the crickets. Thomas cried out with a bad dream, causing Alice to wake. I brought them to the kitchen to heat milk, but a servant heard me and insisted on performing the task herself. The milk helped Alice, but Thomas would not talk and could not settle. At last, I suggested we go outside and look at the stars. The beauty distracted us for a time, but then the stars began to fade as the first fingerlings of dawn spread across the sky. We returned to the still-sleeping house and Thomas curled up in my arms as I sat in the drawing room.

My uncle was the first to rise. He shuffled in and sat with me wordlessly. Margaret entered and kissed him on the head and he patted her hip. How many of these exchanges had James and I had? I could not remember. Did we have routines of kindness? Exchanges of pleasantries, demonstrations of love we thought nothing of? Love? There had been so much tension, so many months apart, so many arguments, illnesses and sleepless nights, but we had a life together. Did I love him? Yes. Not, I suppose, in the way I had hoped, like some romance in one of my books or plays where the heroine is overcome with emotion at each departure or arrival of the beloved. No swooning at the thought of him. No longing. I never expected more. I never imagined a marriage as good as the one I had, given the poor examples of those around me. And yet, I had longed for more. The days moved so quickly and our responsibilities and burdens had grown each year, yet affection had been there. Two people cannot appreciate every moment together, but did we appreciate enough?

"You are up early," Margaret said gently.

"I could not sleep," I replied, and she lowered her eyes.

It was odd. It felt like I had a disease, and people were afraid to look at me for fear that the unpleasantness was contagious. I supposed they were discomfited by the inability to help, by knowing not what to say. Nevertheless, it was unsettling to have so many people looking away from me mid-conversation.

Ironically, during my young life I had complained of being stared at. The curiosity and judgment of others had been my torture. Would I attract that sort of attention again outside of my home? Would my children? I feared the worst.

My uncle set aside his book. "The doctor will be by to attend you and Lady Lydia later in the morning."

"To see Lady Lydia?"

"Her nerves."

"Her nerves?" My volume roused Thomas, who squirmed in my arms and closed his eyes again. I told myself to lower my voice, but it came out as a hiss. "She is the cause of this! Her selfishness."

Margaret and Uncle Gardiner exchanged glances before she said, "She has endured a shock."

"She deserves to suffer."

My uncle rose. "Cease being childish!"

I glared at him. "You have accused me of that for my entire life! Cease being so mature!" I was losing control and as a result, Thomas sat up. I pinched my lips together and lifted him to his feet, whispering in his ear that he had to leave. To my relief, after only a brief hesitation, he obeyed and departed. Once the door shut, I leaned forward. "I am not some chair or table you can glue together, or some uncooperative tenant you can bend to suit your will. I shall not forgive to soothe everyone else!"

He shook his head and left the room muttering under his breath. I wanted him to stay and fight and he wanted me to be quiet. I had tried. Over the years, I had endeavoured to be silent when I was not sure what to say or to avoid a confrontation. I had endeavoured to be calm and polite, more feminine, more like Margaret. But he never saw it. He seemed to see only my flaws and never my efforts. I desired his patience and indulgence for one day, but he could not give that to me.

I banged out to the garden and sat alone until my children came to find me, which was sooner than I would have liked.

The morning of the service, Alice would not leave my side, even as I readied myself. "I miss Father," she said with a sigh.

Jane kissed the top of Alice's head. She would not come to the funeral, remaining instead with Lady Broxbourne and the other ladies. We glanced at each other, acknowledging that we knew the children would bring up their father over and over, and it would cause all of us pain, but there was nothing Jane or I or anyone could do but kiss or reassure them. Nothing would fill his place.

I wore a gown of Jane's, made of fine fabric and trimmings, as my furnishings were not yet ready and the one black dress I had was too plain. She had offered to buy me a mourning wardrobe, and though I feared impoverishing myself, I would not hear of it. I had gone into the jar where I kept our scant savings and gathered enough money to purchase a new dress of crepe and to have a few others dyed and adjusted with black overlays. My bonnet, which sat on my childhood dressing table, was covered in crepe, and black ribbons replaced the colourful ones. I picked it up and looked in the mirror to tie it, noticing how it exaggerated my already-grey pallor. I turned away, thinking that the custom of covering mirrors in a mourning home had more than one advantage, and planned to turn mine around to face the wall the moment I returned to my house. I would not spend the money on black fabric when removing the mirrors or facing the silver to the wall would have the same effect.

When our father passed, I had chosen not to go into full mourning because I disliked him. One regular dress dyed black and worn on the rare occasions I saw others in the shops or at a family dinner was enough to make it seem to

197

the world as if I were a dutiful child for the expected six months. This time, I would wear my black for the entire year.

Jane and I met Bingley in the entry and were soon settled into his carriage, leaving the children and the Gardiners at the house. After a short ride, the driver stopped at the Fitzwilliam house.

"Do not go to the church," Jane implored as a servant opened the carriage door. At my sigh, she allowed the man to help her out.

Bingley looked as if he was about to say something when Darcy appeared. He stepped back from the door as if awaiting my exit, but when I looked out the opposite window, after a pause, he stepped in, taking the seat vacated by Jane next to Bingley.

I turned back and noticed his lips were pressed tight. Was he fighting off the urge to tell me that I ought not be on this journey? "How are you feeling, Darcy?" I asked, hoping to prevent such a discussion. He was pale, his eyes ringed with red, leading me to wonder when he had last slept. "Do your ribs trouble you?" I asked, a wave of nausea crashing over me as I recalled Mr Wickham stomping on Darcy as he lay in the dust.

Darcy shifted on the velvet cushion. "I am healing. Thank you." His face was haunted as if he, too, was reliving the fight. He pulled a kerchief from his pocket and coughed into it, perhaps stifling a sob.

Bingley cleared his throat. "Jane tells me that she communicated our desire to have you and your children stay with us at Netherfield for a time."

"Yes," I said, fiddling with the bow under my chin. "However, I have declined, at least for the foreseeable

future. We must return home and"—my voice caught—
"grow accustomed to our new situation."

"Why not stave off the inevitable?" Bingley pressed, his
kind, clear eyes sparkling.

"Because as you say, it is inevitable," I said. "It must be
faced, and I would rather do so sooner than later."

Darcy regarded me. "How changed you are," he said,
his tone one of gentle admiration. "When first we met, you
were a silly little thing who sought pleasure at all times."

"Not entirely." It was as close to a smile as I had experienced in days, though I had to admit that James and my
pleasure-seeking had led to our union, and my foolishness
had been on display too often in front of this gentleman.

"First impressions do leave their mark."

"Happily," I said, thinking of how rude I had once
found him, "they fade and are often replaced by better
ones."

"Indeed." He folded his kerchief. "I daresay you and
James altered my world view."

"Pardon?"

Pushing the cloth into its designated pocket, he said, "Your
ease with one another. I had not thought such a relationship
possible. When I entered your home, I felt…transformed."

I blinked a few times, searching for the scenes of
domestic bliss that he referenced and only recalled hanging
laundry and bruised wrists. But, no, there was more. James
and I had been playful, and we both cared for our children,
showing affection towards them and a desire for their happiness and peace. I recalled the day Darcy even removed his
shoes and stockings, though I would not speak of the
memory in front of Bingley lest it embarrass Darcy.

Bingley leaned in. "Do Jane and I transform you, as

well?" One who did not know Bingley might have thought his expression gave him out to be haughty or hurt, but in truth, he was teasing. What a relief from the constant sadness and careful interactions of late.

Darcy's eyes twinkled. "Bingley, you have been transforming me since the moment we met."

"And are you not the luckier for it?"

Darcy smiled, but all joy slid away as the church's bell-tower came into view. "Elizabeth, have you steeled yourself for the service?"

I nodded, my laced fingers tightening in my lap.

Bingley asked, "How are the earl and Lady Broxbourne faring, Darcy?"

"They are beside themselves. That the cause of their heartbreak is their own daughter's indiscretion has nearly broken them."

I cared little for the Fitzwilliams, though I had to imagine that this was intolerable. Lady Lydia had not yet returned to their estate. She had made herself mercifully scarce at Longbourn, yet simply knowing she was in the house made me uneasy. I wanted her to leave. Charity had its limits. And yet, where was she to go?

The carriage stopped and Bingley offered his elbow to me. People were gathered in the road, and though I knew they were likely staring, I chose to keep my eyes down. Whether they disapproved of my attendance or desired to show with their long faces that they were saddened by James's passing, I desired none of it.

As we passed through the heavy doors of the church, much of the light was eclipsed. A refreshing chill enveloped us. We stepped forward once our eyes adjusted, but I stopped short when I saw the black lacquered coffin at the altar. Lord Broxbourne was standing at the front with the vicar, Mr Cless, the same man who officiated at my wedding. As Bingley escorted me towards the altar, the doors opened again, and my uncle entered.

Mr Cless greeted us and the earl slid away with only a small scowl. The vicar told me how sorry he was for my loss, what a tragedy it was to see such a good man pass. Mr Cless had the good grace not to mention that James's presence while on leave had been sorely lacking.

I could hear men entering, their hushed voices echoing around me. Darcy suggested we sit and Bingley brought me to a seat that was on the opposite side from the earl and James's older brother, Edmund Fitzwilliam, the Viscount Pulham.

Viscount Pulham had come for James's funeral, but not his wedding. James would have wanted him to stay away from this as well, for James despised pretence based on obligation rather than desire. Perhaps his brother had soft feelings for James, but knowledge of the impropriety associated with our wedding dissuaded him from showing his face at such a potentially shameful event. Then again, when I had written of James's injury, he had not replied at all. Darcy—a cousin rather than a brother—had intervened and assisted.

I knew the congregation was looking at me, the woman in this space, the widow. I could not lift my head at that moment. Widow. *I am a widow.*

Studying my clasped hands, I noticed the skin around my fingernails was torn. I had been picking at them for days and would need to stop lest an infection set in, especially with the return of my duties. Patricia had announced her engagement a week ago—or was it two? I had no sense of time anymore—and would be leaving at the end of the month. Would I have the money to replace her?

Music commenced and the sound was so beautiful and mournful that I had to lift my head. I watched the young man who was playing, entranced by how he closed his eyes and swayed, fully lost in the tune. The way his hair fell reminded me of James, and a bubble of joy rose in me. But were the marks of Mr Wickham's knuckles still on James's throat as he lay in the casket? My head spun.

A hush fell as the kind vicar stepped forward and began to pray, his voice soothing. My mind drifted over the past, to James chasing me through the woods as we laughed, to embraces at the bank of the stream, to arguing over having children or how to raise them and how to provide for them. I thought of his smile and the mischief that played endlessly in his eyes, and well as the anger and battle memories that clouded them.

"Colonel James Fitzwilliam," Mr Cless said, glancing at the casket to his side, "was a passionate young man who loved his family and served his country. He was a defender, a protector. He gave his life to protect one of God's children."

Darcy shifted in his seat, and I wondered at the burden he felt over this.

"He will, no doubt, be rewarded in Heaven for his deeds."

The congregation joined together to say, "Amen."

"Amen," I whispered.

More prayers were said, a speech was given, more music, more prayers. I was not quite in my own skin, floating above myself. Everything was at a distance and I willed myself not to faint. All expected such swooning from a woman, and I would not give anyone the satisfaction of this or even many tears. Some were flowing, yes, but I would not make a spectacle of myself.

When the service ended, there was no question of my

attendance at the interment. While my presence in the church was frowned upon, it was not expressly forbidden. However, I could not be present as James's casket was placed in the Fitzwilliam family tomb, a lovely structure that I would not be buried in. The Fitzwilliams would succeed in death where they had failed in life by keeping us apart.

I was meant to wait out on the lane for the men, yet I could not move. Bingley offered to help me to the door, but I remained where I was. I simply needed a moment alone. A quiet moment in this quiet place to say a quiet goodbye.

My uncle said, "Elizabeth, you must depart."

"Leave her," Darcy said, his voice low and commanding.

I offered him a small grateful smile before lowering my head to the pew. A pause followed during which the men might have gestured or mouthed words. I did not know. I did not care. The footsteps faded as they exited.

I breathed in the echoing silence of the sanctuary, straining to hear the service in the churchyard but unable to catch more than a few murmurs now and again.

"Oh, James," I whispered, pressing my fingers to my eyelids. "James, how could you leave me like this? What am I to do?"

CHAPTER TWENTY-THREE

O n our return to the Fitzwilliam estate, Darcy
presented me with a mourning ring the
Fitzwilliams had given to guests. It was black
enamel and twisted gold, with a delicate plait of James's hair
worked into the design. It was the last piece of him I would
have. I saw that both Bingley and Darcy wore their rings,
though Bingley's would likely go to my sister. Dearest Jane
might wear hers for a bit, but I suspected it would go into a
box along with others she would gather over the years.

At the house, a great many people spoke with me, most
of whom I had not seen in ages. I attempted to smile when
they praised James for being a good man and frowned when
they spoke of the tragedy. Some conversations I felt, and
others I merely attempted to make look correct.

Darcy threaded his way through the crowd and gave a
curt bow. "Mrs Fitzwilliam, pray, follow. You are needed."
Anxious that it was news of one of the children, I was
surprised to find myself in an empty parlour. "I suspected
you might desire some time alone."

His thoughtfulness was a given, as was his generosity, but I appreciated them both immensely at that moment.

"Thank you. I suspect you need a moment's quiet as well."

He nodded.

I closed my eyes for a moment, breathing deeply. "I do not even know what the people are saying. I simply repeat 'thank you' to whatever comes out of their mouths."

He nodded sombrely, clasping his hands behind his back. "Understandable."

"Except they could be saying, 'Your hair is on fire,' and I would say, 'Thank you.' "

A slight smile tugged at his lips. "Your horse is chasing the cat."

"Thank you."

"Who is also on fire." We laughed more loudly than the joke warranted, letting go of tension, but aware that we ought not be laughing, which made us laugh all the more. Footsteps passed near the door, which sobered us.

"What will you do now, Elizabeth?" he asked.

"I do not know. I truly do not know." I rubbed my forehead. Everything ached and no matter how I stretched, I could not get the pain to ease.

"Might I be of assistance?"

"No. I— Perhaps. I am not certain," I said. I could not allow myself to think too much about anything. Every time I did, I was overwhelmed by the impossibility of it all.

Darcy absently touched the bruise on his cheek, and James's desperate face swam through my mind. Oh, how I wished that fight was not the last I had seen of him. Blood oozing from his mouth, his eyes wide. What must he have been thinking? Just that he wanted to breathe? Or did he know he was dying and realise all he would miss of his life?

Of our children's lives? I gasped. How could I face each birthday, each holiday, each of our children's milestones, their troubles, without him? I did not want Darcy to see me weep. I went for the door, but fumbled with the handle and slid to the floor.

"Oh, Elizabeth. I am sorry. I did not mean to upset you."

"It wa-was not y-you." That was all I could manage before a soft keening escaped. I sat with my back against the door. I covered my mouth but could not muffle everything. I wanted to run screaming from the room, but could not face one more person offering their condolences, so I remained where I was, eyes screwed shut, trying, *trying* to calm myself.

Voices came through the door. "At the church. Unheard of!"

"Those Bennets never did anything by the rules."

My eyes flew open and, from Darcy's frown, it appeared he could hear the insults, as well.

"Nothing those Bennets ever did was correct."

"Married under such circumstances and given no money."

"She does the work of a scullery maid, I hear."

"The children ought to be taken. She cannot be trusted to raise Fitzwilliams properly."

My heart hammered and Darcy's eyes were ablaze, but I would not allow him into the hall.

"People will talk." Anger gave me the necessary energy to gain my feet. I smoothed my dress, determined to stand tall. Darcy held out a handkerchief, which I took with a grateful nod.

He said, "There was a time you would have run out and argued with them."

I nodded, offering him a faint smile, which was all I

could muster. "I am not the child I once was, and I am determined to control my temper, amongst my other poor qualities."

"You have no poor qualities," he said. As our eyes met, his face flushed.

"We can both concede that is not the truth." What a strange comment from a man who had looked at me with regular consternation when first we met. But perhaps I had changed more than I realised. Or he had. "Fear not, Darcy. No one will take my children."

"They will want for nothing. You know that." His jaw was set with determination, his warm brown eyes now steely with resolve.

I nodded. Confident the gossips had passed, I stepped aside so he could let himself out. I followed a while later and found Jane with Georgiana in a drawing room I had never seen. It occurred to me how little time I had spent inside James's ancestral home. The tall windows with heavy striped curtains, the ornately carved gold frames surrounding massive family portraits, the intricately patterned carpets, and the dark, heavy furniture were all so different from the simplicity of our home. The design had been done to James's specifications before we were wed, and I realised how thoroughly he had rejected all that his family valued.

Georgiana's face brightened as I approached, and she enquired as to my well-being. I shrugged, and Jane threaded an arm around my waist, pulling me close. Jane's presence was a balm, and Georgiana's was equally soothing.

"How was it here at the house with the ladies?" I asked.

"When at last we finished procuring the rings and meats, and wrapping the rosemary, there was time to mourn," Jane said, reminding me how beautifully the black silk ribbons had been tied around each rosemary sprig. I touched the mourning ring on my forefinger once more. "Lady Mary prays often and Lady Broxbourne weeps and carries on."

"For a son she never spoke to."

Jane pressed her lips together, unable to argue that point but unwilling to be unkind.

Lady Kitty approached, looking more sombre than ever I had seen her. "Elizabeth, if I tell you something, do you promise not to cause a commotion?"

I looked to Jane, bracing myself.

Lady Kitty said, "My parents said that James's commission will be sold, but the money will not go to you." Her voice was full of excited outrage.

I blinked. "That cannot be correct."

"It is what they said."

Jane's eyes widened slightly, but her face remained otherwise passive, while Georgiana went pale.

Attempting to find strength in Jane's calm, I took a moment before asking, "Where, pray, are your parents now?"

"In Father's library."

"Cautiously," Jane said, her voice barely a murmur.

"Accompany me, dear Jane?" I asked.

She shook her head. "Best to approach with my husband. Or Mr Darcy. Perhaps both."

My heart pounded so hard that it caused my vision to shake. Still, I needed to find the men. Mercifully, Jane held my elbow as we searched, trailed by Lady Kitty and Georgiana, for I would likely have stumbled more than once as unsteady as I was. When at last we found Bingley, I attempted to force out the words, but my voice had evaporated like water on hot stones.

Jane leaned to his ear and shared her message, and he reared back. When he whispered to Darcy, his outrage was far more explosive. Before Bingley could concoct a plan or hold him back, Darcy had charged ahead. Bingley and I followed while Jane and Georgiana remained. As we left, I heard Jane ask Lady Kitty a question about her dress, a ruse for keeping the little gossip at bay, I was certain.

"What mean you," Darcy bellowed as he banged into the library, "in keeping the sale of the commission from James's widow?"

Lady Broxbourne gasped while the earl straightened in his chair.

"What mean *you*," Pulham said, rounding on his cousin, "approaching in such a manner at this solemn event and with such slanderous accusations?"

"It is not an accusation," the earl said, rising to his feet. He glanced from me to Darcy. "I would caution you to behave with some decorum, though it is not your way. I would have expected more from you, Fitzwilliam."

Having never heard anyone call Darcy by his Christian name, I was taken aback to remember we shared the family name, his mother—Lady Anne—having been a Fitzwilliam.

The earl nodded at his wife, who rose and departed. I knew I was meant to follow, as a lady alone in such a situation was not proper, yet this conversation was entirely about my future and that of my children. A servant shut the library door behind Lady Broxbourne.

"The commission was purchased to employ James," the earl said, his back stiff. "To provide him with an occupation and a profession."

I stepped forward. "He did his service nobly, suffering wounds and—"

"Yes, yes," the earl said, swatting at the air like I was a gnat interrupting his tea.

"No. Do not dismiss the facts!" My head swam with fury. "Perhaps you do not know the extent of his injur—"

"Elizabeth," Bingley said, his voice hushed, and I checked myself.

The earl narrowed his eyes. "The position is vacant, and now the commission can be sold."

Vacant. The position. Was James no more than the role he played in their theatrics? Or was it their game of chess—all power and advantage?

The earl lowered himself into his chair, the mahogany desk a barrier between us. "The money used to purchase the commission was ours, and the proceeds of the sale shall return to the purchasers."

His dispassionate manner was befuddling. Was this the man who collapsed against his door mere days ago upon seeing me covered in his son's blood? Was the woman who refused to hear this discussion the same one who was so devastated that she—by Jane's account—had to be sedated until this very morning?

Darcy strode to the desk, stabbing at it with his index finger. "Upon his retirement, the money would have gone to James."

"Retirement, yes. He did not retire," the earl said.

"Because he was murdered before he could do so!" All outraged faces turned my way, but I was undeterred. "Was the money to be his merely because you were likely to be dead by then?"

Pulham said to Darcy, "Remove her. She is too overcome with emotion."

"No!" I stepped away from Darcy's reach. "I demand an explanation."

My determination to be proper, to control my temper, was lost in the face of this man who had never been kind to me a day in his life, and was disrespecting the memory of his own son.

"He did not retire," the earl said, pounding a fist on his desk. "You will not profit from your union, brief as it was."

Brief? Was nearly seven years brief? It felt as if my entire life had been entwined with James. Had there been a time before our children and our little house, his service and my work? We had built a life with much sweat and so many tears. They saw none of it and cared not for our toils.

The scene repeated in my mind: Lady Lydia standing with Wickham, both sneering, then her helplessness as the fight began. "His death was the fault of your daughter. Why am I to suffer for that?"

The earl gasped and Pulham pointed to the door. "Leave at once!"

Darcy rounded on his cousin. "She speaks the truth."

"You will leave as well, Cousin!"

"No." Darcy closed the space between them and both men straightened.

Bingley took my elbow and pulled me towards the door. "This is a family matter now." As soon as the door shut, the shouting commenced. Bingley continued dragging me with him, ordering one servant to ready his carriage while demanding that another find his wife. In moments we were in front of the house, I breathless and confounded, he as red-faced as I had seen him in my life.

CHAPTER TWENTY-FOUR

The next afternoon, I brought the children back to our house. All was as it had been the morning of the fair. My shawl was on the floor by the bed, a perpetual source of irritation for James. The water pitcher was mostly full, though it had a few bugs floating on top of the now-dusty water. One of James's stockings poked out from a boot that was in need of a polish. The room felt like an exhibit of thoughtless domesticity long forgotten.

The following days were unbearable. At least one child, usually two or three, needed me at every turn. Though Nora fed and cleaned them, memories of James's final moments, and fears about my children not having enough food or clothing, had me hiding behind closed doors and rushing out of the house to catch my breath or to weep. I covered my mouth so no one would hear my sobs and fought to contain my screams. Nora noticed my red eyes and tear-stained aprons. Occasionally she asked if I was all right, and while she accepted my curt replies and assurances without more enquiries, she did watch me throughout the day as if I might crumble.

Rising in the morning took extraordinary effort, as I knew the moment I opened my eyes that I would not cease working until long after the children were settled into bed for the night. I still slept on my side of the bed, and occasionally punched James's pillow, cursing him for fighting with Mr Wickham, while at other times I held his pillow to me, breathing in his ever-fading scent.

My parenting suffered. I allowed clothes to get dirtier and took longer to soothe the children when they cried. Finding joy in their daily triumphs and silliness eluded me.

We went to Longbourn. Mercifully, Lady Lydia did not come downstairs at all. Margaret and Uncle Gardiner were shocked by the dishevelled state of my children, and Alice's sudden fit at the table over not wanting to eat anything brown. At first I did not react, then I demanded that she leave the table if she had no intention of eating. Thomas put his head on the table and stabbed at his meat with a finger. Margaret attempted to keep up polite conversation, but even she was reduced to silence when no one would answer.

After the dishes had been cleared, I walked outside and found my uncle smoking a pipe. "What is happening at your house, Elizabeth?" he asked with a mix of paternal sternness and utter surprise. I studied my boot, digging a hole in the dirt. "Do you need assistance? The children seem—"

I looked up, imploring. "I need to go away, Uncle."

"What?"

"I need to go. I am asking you to watch over my children."

"For how long?"

"I do not know."

He shook his head in disbelief. "You want to run away. Like always. Like your mother."

"Do not dare to compare us!"

"Then prove yourself otherwise. You are a grown woman, Elizabeth. You cannot run away from challenges like you did when you were a child."

"This is hardly avoiding scraping potatoes."

"No, it is far more serious." He paused, glaring at me. He tapped the tobacco out of his pipe onto the gravel, then swept at it with his foot.

I held myself as still as possible, because if I started to run I did not think I could stop.

THE NEXT DAY, THE CHILDREN AND I CALLED AT Netherfield. I was enjoying tea in the garden with Jane, Bingley, Georgiana, and Darcy until Alice ran to me, screaming, "Thomas hit me!"

"Thomas!"

My son stood with his arms crossed.

"Why did you hit your sister?"

"I tagged her and she was out, but would not accept it."

"But you may not hit her. She is smaller than you, and it is your job to help her, especially now."

He stared at me with wide eyes, bottom lip trembling. "But-but she was out."

"I know, my sweetling, but we cannot hit. Good people use their words; bad people hit."

"Like the man who hit Father?" He wiped his face with his sleeve. "I hate the man. And I hate Alice!"

"No, you do not—"

"Yes! I do!" My young son raged, face crimson. "And I hate games. I hate everything!" He whirled about and ran towards the house. I knew I must follow him, but my legs would not move. What could I say? What could I do? I understood the anger and sorrow within him all too well. There was no fixing this, and all I wanted was to sleep or disappear.

I heard a shuffling behind me. Darcy cleared his throat.

"Pray, might I speak to the boy?"

I nodded, for I knew Darcy would be exactly what Thomas needed and wanted. For a moment I wondered what I would ever do without him.

For the next few days, I attempted to be alert and to focus on the children's needs. Nora cut her hand badly, and I told her to go home to heal, that we would manage without her. I truly believed I could. By mid-week, we had a routine that I thought was working and everyone seemed calmer. Not all of the work needed to be done at once and my primary thought needed to be for my children and our little bereft family. I was determined to survive.

Then one afternoon, I put on my boots to milk the goat before preparing our evening meal, and told Thomas I would return very soon. "Be the man of the house while I am gone, hm?" I smiled at him and he smiled back, his small chest puffing up with pride.

I took a moment to look around the land and consider what could be sold off or traded. The crops and garden would not be enough to feed us, so there was no question of surplus for sale. I would be forced to buy necessities in town. We needed the goat. There was nothing to sell or trade save the furnishings of the house, and they were not worth much.

The truth of my situation—the poverty that my children and I faced—was unavoidable. My mind grew muddled and

I suddenly could not catch my breath. What if the Fitzwilliams did not change their minds about the commission? What would become of us? My breath grew shorter and shorter until I was gasping and my heart throbbed. Was I too young for apoplexy? My vision blurred and I staggered, my mouth dry. I needed water. I knew there was a pump somewhere, but could not remember where it was.

I staggered towards the stream, the same stream where James and I had talked over our problems, the stream where we had brought our babies. I lurched to it and drank, relief flooding through me, making my mind calm for a moment. I strove for serenity, taking in the forest of green. Soon the leaves would change and, as our trees were finally mature, the apples would need picking.

James had been thrilled at the previous year's small crop, and Mr Davis was convinced that this year would be our first true harvest. That orchard had carried our hopes for the future, and my serenity fled with that recollection. I ought to have returned to the house, but could not bring myself to pass the orchard. I scrambled up and ran in the opposite direction.

Breathless, my chest aching, I arrived at a structure—the hunting lodge that Jane and I had stolen into years ago, where James and Darcy came upon us. It seemed even smaller and more rudimentary than my memory, and was all the more welcoming for it. I stumbled inside and fell into the same rocking chair I had awoken from when Darcy burst in—the first time we met—and stared at the fireplace, neatly swept and devoid of a blaze. I willed myself to slow my breath. Slower. Slower. At last, the objects around me stopped shaking. Slower still. I rocked and closed my eyes, pretending I was still a girl of fifteen with Jane at my side, and all my life ahead of me.

An odd thought entered my mind—what if it had been Darcy, and not James, whom I had kissed back then? I would never deny my schoolgirl crush on Darcy. To Jane's confusion, I would blush randomly at the recollection of his lovely eyes and regal demeanour, and at night, I would drift off picturing his face. But James had kissed me at my uncle's wedding, and so much had changed as a result. Darcy was still a great source of comfort, a shelter to me when—

My thoughts broke off as I recognised what I was doing. How could I? How terrible did it make me that, as a new widow, I was thinking of another man? My husband was dead. A man I had married because we were impulsive, and now I was alone because of his anger, too often simmering under the surface. Why did he enter that fight? Why had he not simply let Lady Lydia run off? I was left with nothing. No future. No money. No company. Too many children to manage on my own. I clutched my stomach, fighting the rising sickness and doubled over. Weeping turned to guttural sobs as the bleakness of my circumstances overwhelmed me.

I know not when or how I fell asleep, but I awoke in the dark and immediately felt afraid. I did not know the time and realised that my children were alone and had been for hours. Leaping to my feet, I ran as fast as I could out of the cabin, desperate to reach home. Twigs slashed my face as I raced through the dimly lit woods. I twisted my ankle and continued running. I was overtaken with dread, certain something terrible had happened in my absence.

When I reached the clearing, I saw a lamp burning in the window. None of the children could even reach the matches, so I prayed an adult was inside with them. Was my uncle sitting disapprovingly, awaiting my return? Was a stranger inside doing them harm?

I lifted the latch and threw the door open. My children

were sitting at the table and Darcy was serving them bread. I was so relieved and ashamed of myself, I nearly fell to my knees.

"Mama!" cried Sally.

"My love," I said, going over and kissing her on the cheek. I tickled Henry and he giggled and flapped his arms.

Alice ran and hugged me around the thigh. "We were so worried, Mother. We thought you were never coming back, so we fetched Uncle Darcy."

"Fetched him?"

"Thomas did. He went to Uncle Bingley and Auntie Jane's house."

"Thomas, you went alone?" I asked. He did not answer, but stabbed his knife into the cask of butter. "Thomas, I asked you a question."

"Elizabeth," said Darcy, "I made toast. There is some for you."

He gave me a hard look, so I reached for a slice. I had not eaten in hours. Neither had my children, and guilt twisted my stomach.

"I was just finishing a story when you came in," said Darcy, his voice strained. He let out a long breath and commenced a tale. Milk dribbled out of Henry's mouth as he laughed at something Darcy said. I ate my toast and endeavoured to look as amused as the children without knowing what Darcy was saying.

He went on telling stories until they were finished eating. "It is late," he said to the crowd, though when his eyes flicked to mine, it felt like a castigation. "Time for bed."

"Another story," asked Alice, tugging at his coat sleeve.

"No, you already heard them all," he said.

I noticed once again the warmth and kindness in his brown eyes and the way he soothed the children. Soothed me. It felt wrong, but he was the one I wanted in my home just then. A flash of my earlier despair pricked at me but I fought it back. He was a veritable knight in shining armour to me these days.

Alice rested her head on his arm. "We have not heard them all."

"Perhaps not all, but enough," he said, rising. "Come, help me with your brother and sister."

I rose to assist.

"No, Elizabeth, finish eating. We shall do this." I was not sure if he was punishing me or wanting to give me time alone, but I did need a moment to gather myself. I put water on the stove and located the tea tin. Eventually, Darcy came out and I handed him a steaming mug.

"Let us go outside to talk," he said. I had an overpowering feeling of dread, like when my father summoned me for punishment or a lecture. "Elizabeth, what occurred here?"

How to explain myself? "Well—" My voice broke. Unwilling to let him see me cry again, I only managed to shake my head.

Darcy opened his mouth to speak but checked himself.

I noticed sweat on his brow and upper lip and wondered why I had even bothered to make tea on such a sweltering night. When I was more in control of myself, I asked, "What did Alice mean when she said Thomas fetched you?"

"Around sunset he knocked on the door at Netherfield. Luckily, I was passing through the entry and told the servant not to tell your sister or Bingley. Thomas was frightened, Elizabeth."

My stomach turned.

"He said you told him he was the man of the house, then went out and did not come back."

"Oh God." I moaned. "That was not…I was only going out to look at the fields."

"He thought you found James, or that you died too. Truth be told, I was about to call for help to mount a search."

I blinked rapidly and turned my head away. "He believed I found James?"

"Yes."

"But he knows that James is…perhaps not."

"Not entirely, it seems. He is young, so he might not truly understand the idea of death or perhaps simply wishes —that is hardly the point, is it?"

I sipped my tea, welcoming the burn on my tongue. I deserved pain after what I had done.

"What were you thinking? Where did you go?"

"I…I needed a moment and—" I could not explain what I did not understand. I had lost control of my senses, stumbling about unable to breathe, unable to think. Was I going mad? I feared what he might do if I confessed such a thing. "I-I began to walk and…fell into something of a… well, a panic and then…I guess I must have…must have fallen asleep."

"You left them alone!"

"I know." My hands began to tremble, threatening to spill my tea, and I feared I was having another spell.

He sat on the steps and set his cup down. "At any rate…" He took a deep breath. "Thomas asked if you were at Netherfield and when I said no, he began to cry. He said he was hoping I would be the one to help, and would I come with him? When I arrived, the twins were crying and filthy. Alice was attempting to soothe them. There was no light, no food for them, and no sign of you. And where was Nora?

For all I knew, you were dead, as Thomas said, or you had run off forever."

An image of my mother flashed through my mind, and my legs began to shake so badly that I had to sit.

"I was at a loss, so I cleaned them up as best I could, started a fire, and made toast. It is all I knew how to do. And it was nearly all you had." The judgment in that last statement was thick. "Then you came home all smiles and tickles like nothing was amiss."

"Everything is amiss," I said. "Do not think me insensible to that. I only wished…I wanted to assure them I was well. I was not smiles and tickles on the inside, I assure you."

His clenched jaw only emphasised his elegant, angular face.

"I am so sorry." I worked to keep my voice steady. "I had —I had asked my uncle to help me, to take the children for a while. I feared—" I paused, embarrassed by my need and by the answer. "He said no."

"Why did you not ask me?"

It had not occurred to me and even if it had, I would never have asked such a thing of him.

"Or Jane?"

I shrugged. I could have; I ought to have. Somehow, confessing my need to Jane felt too shameful. It was not rational.

He shook his head, brow furrowed. "You cannot leave them like that."

"I know." Then I whispered the words I had feared so long. "I am just like her."

"Like who?"

"Like my mother." I stared at my laced fingers and the mourning ring, drawn by James's hair entwined within, and tugged until my knuckles ached. "It was grief which drove her away too, you know. I never understood how that could happen until…well, until you begin to see that you are condemned to hurt the ones you love the best in all the world."

"Oh, Elizabeth." His voice was so kind, so understanding that it broke me.

I did not deserve such kindness. I had abandoned my children. Tears spilled down my cheeks and I looked at him helplessly. He reached out and wiped my cheek, a gesture so intimate and tender that I thought I should recoil, but I did not want to. Our eyes met and he blushed. I wondered if his stomach flipped the way mine did. No doubt it was despicable for me to react as I did, but I could not help myself.

He cleared his throat. "You returned. She did not."

"But I…I understand what impulse lay within her and I know now that the impulse lies in me too. What if the next time I—"

He looked at me, eyes beseeching. "Do not. Do not allow it."

I studied him, wishing I did not notice how handsome he was, knowing it was too soon to think of other men but unable to ignore the freckles dotting the bridge of his nose, the fullness of his lips. Truth be told, as much as all of that drew me, it was his goodness that attracted me most of all. Fitzwilliam Darcy had true beauty, both within and without.

He lifted the teacup. "What was it like, if I might ask, living without a mother?"

The question was so personal that I could have been offended, but I wanted to tell him, to have him know about my life. It led to a conversation that began as the moon rose and continued as it travelled across much of the sky. Our eyes grew heavy, and still we talked until he suggested I needed to rest.

"Perhaps…" He paused. "I ought to stay tonight."

I knew why he wished it. He suspected I might run off again, or that my feelings, so near the surface, might again knock me sideways.

He added, "Propriety dictates that I leave, yet I fear it would draw more attention if I was to be seen departing now."

"We are cousins," I said in an attempt to reassure him— or myself. "And we are both widowed. It could not be as scandalous as if we were neither."

"If we were neither, our speaking alone at all would be improper."

I rose, nodding, the heaviness of my lids and limbs overtaking me. "Indeed," I said with a yawn I could not hide. "I know the children would be pleased to have your visit continue. If you desire to remain, I shall move Thomas to my room and you may sleep in his bed."

He agreed to that arrangement and so it was. I wondered, as I lay curled with my son beside me in my bed, how it was that so great a man managed to undress himself without a valet, and lay down in my son's small bed. I wondered even more that he should do these things for me, for my children.

CHAPTER TWENTY-FIVE

T he morning began well. The children were excited
to have Uncle Darcy at the table, and he made
them laugh while I cooked eggs and served the last
of the bread. Shamefully, I could not remember the last
time having James at the table had made everyone so happy.
I was dismayed by the realisation, but could not deny it
nevertheless. Darcy glanced at me every so often, and each
time, it made my heart flutter. Though I knew I should push
the feelings away, it was pleasing to feel something joyous
and I allowed myself the small indulgence.

Suddenly, the back door opened and Nora entered, only
to stop in her tracks as she took in the scene. She curtseyed
to Darcy. "S-sir," she stammered, "what a surprise to see you
here. So early."

His eyes flew wide, and I leapt to my feet. "Yes,
w-well—"

"Uncle Darcy stayed with us because Mother disappeared!" Alice announced.

Nora's gaze flicked from Alice to me to Darcy and back to me, but I had lost my power of words.

Darcy grabbed for the tail-coat he had draped over his chair. "Yes, I did, indeed, stay in the children's room last night." He smoothed his hair, still mussed from a night on a bed far smaller than the one on which I imagined he customarily slept. "Mrs Fitzwilliam was in need of assistance. Have you any sisters or friends looking for employment? With your injury—"

Perhaps fearful that she was losing her position, Nora rushed forward, holding out her bandaged hand. "I am nearly healed, sir."

"That is wonderful news," I said. "Mr Darcy means in addition to you. It seems I am in need of *greater* assistance. There is always so much to be done with so many little ones about."

"Indeed. Indeed," Darcy said, his eyes darting around.

Could he still be flustered by her sudden appearance? I resolved to do what I could to remedy the situation.

"Nora, this requires some discretion. Mr Darcy's being here so early was a favour to me, and as for my struggles...I would not wish for them to be shared."

She shook her head wildly. "No, ma'am. Of course."

I looked at Darcy, hoping he was reassured, but his expression was inscrutable, so I turned back to Nora. "Having employed you for so long," I added as much for his benefit as for hers, "I know I can trust you."

She nodded with equal enthusiasm.

"So," I asked, "have you a sister looking for employment?"

"No, ma'am. I have mostly brothers, and my only unmarried sister is just three, but my cousin is looking for work."

"Bring her tomorrow, if she so desires."

Nora curtseyed again, and scampered off to begin laundry, a task I thought unwise given her still-healing hand, but I knew she wanted to prove her worth. Indeed, it was her silence that would be prized even more than clean linen.

Darcy and I finished eating before we gathered the children for a visit to the stream. Once there he said, "With Nora returned, and since we are, as you mentioned, widowed and related, it seems…it seems I could spend days with you and the children. If you find that agreeable."

The hopeful look in his eyes made warmth spread over me, and I scolded myself for being such a ninny. A great man like Darcy did not harbour secret tendrè for widows prone to neglecting their children and weeping. A man like Darcy would fall in love with a woman dressed in silks with smooth hands and nothing on her mind but what song she might play him after dinner. He was here for my children and the memory of James, and I would do best to remember it.

I agreed to his request and he turned his attention to Henry.

While they played, I mulled over the fact that Thomas had chosen Darcy when he needed help. My middle went soft as I imagined Darcy listening to my son's tale and hurrying to my house, reassuring Thomas all the while, I had no doubt. Nevertheless, I was embarrassed by Darcy's presence, for it exposed my folly, secret though it was beyond the walls of my house. I hated that I had become an object of pity, yet I was in no position to slap away a hand that was willing to help me, much as it shamed me to accept that help.

But would Darcy have hastened to assist anyone? Was it simply that I was his beloved cousin's wife or—dare I hope

—did he come because the person in need was me? *Remember who and what you are. Do not run away with fancies about Darcy that will only leave you bereft.*

DARCY WAS AS GOOD AS HIS WORD AND ARRIVED EACH morning ready to assist in any way required, most enthusiastic if it involved the children. The next fortnight flew by, and I felt lighter than I had in ages. One overcast day, Darcy entered the house without knocking, as had become our custom, and found me with the older children in the kitchen. "Hello, all!"

Alice held out her dough-covered hands. "We are baking!"

Darcy's jaw dropped in mock surprise. "Are you, then? I never would have known." He stepped back out of the kitchen easing off his coat and hanging it on a hook near the door. Not only was he less formally dressed in our home, but he had learned to protect his clothing from my brood.

Alice yelled across the house, "Come help!"

Darcy returned, rolling up his sleeves. "What are we baking?"

Thomas scowled. "Bread. Mother makes us knead."

I fought back a laugh, as did Darcy.

"I shall make you a deal, Thomas," Darcy said. "If we work together on your loaf, we could get it done twice as fast, and then we can study the new book I brought. Is that agreeable?"

Thomas's face lit up, and he kneaded with more vigour. Then he stepped aside to make space for Darcy. "Uncle Darcy, do you know how to knead?" When Darcy shook his head, Thomas instructed him, showing him how to roll from his fingers to the heel of his palms, then how to fold the dough, turn it, and do it all again.

"I think this is rather entertaining," said Darcy.

"Me, too!" Alice threw her hands in the air, flinging dough and flour towards Darcy.

He pulled the bits off his shirt with an indulgent smile.

I asked, "What are you and Thomas reading today?"

"Maps. We were discussing the history of The War of Spanish Succession, so I thought I would show him how the troops moved and the borders changed."

This did not interest me in the least, but Thomas was fascinated by anything Darcy shared. Their work had begun inadvertently with a visit to the library at Netherfield. Upon their return to where Jane, Bingley, and I were having tea, Thomas had excitedly shared what he had seen: globes and maps and tomes containing grand tales, as well as guides to local game, celestial patterns, and myriad natural wonders.

Once Thomas had departed to play, Darcy enquired when I planned on hiring a tutor. I fought my embarrassment, saying I had no means to do so, and no space for a tutor and a child to work. My fear was that Bingley or Darcy would suggest Thomas move to Netherfield, but mercifully Darcy had offered to act as tutor until other arrangements could be made.

I had done my best to teach the older children to read and do basic mathematics, but Thomas's mind was curious beyond my time and limited resources. Though Bingley said Pemberley's library was far superior, Darcy had looked unconcerned, saying Netherfield's was more than sufficient, and so we became its beneficiaries. Thomas thrived under Darcy's care, reminding me of my dear tutor, Miss Taylor, and my happy days at her cottage reading and talking. Thomas's bad dreams and wretched moods faded as his mind was filled with all Darcy could offer.

"Alice," said Darcy, kneading and turning the dough, "I brought you a book about flowers. I know you love to paint them, but no painting in the book." He pointed at her like he was scolding her, then tickled her side.

She threw back her head and giggled, slipping off the stool she was standing on, which only made her giggle harder. When she rose, she had dough all over her apron, arms, and face.

I pursed my lips, caught between a reprimand and a laugh. "Thomas, help her wash up and then you may go with Uncle Darcy." The children ran out the door, and I took hold of Alice's misshapen mound. "I can finish, Darcy."

He lifted his dough towards the bowl I had prepared and dropped it in with a flourish. "No one would believe that I am entertained by such tasks, but I am."

"No one would understand why you do them."

He wiped his hands on a towel. "This was more immediate and satisfying than most of my endeavours." His eyes drifted to the nearly empty bag of flour. "Shall I...have more delivered soon?"

I turned to get fresh towels, swallowing my prideful resistance to the offer. "That would be helpful."

"Anything else?"

Keeping my back to him so he could not see my flush, I said, "Molasses."

"And sugar?"

I nodded and turned back, lifting my eyes with effort.

"No need to hesitate, Elizabeth. Truly. It gives me great pleasure to send whatever you need."

I knew he meant every word, but shame weighed on me

any time money was discussed. Even when he brought the children treats left over from the previous day's tea, I both appreciated and loathed it. When I reacted, he always reassured me, but I struggled not to wince or blush, much as I tried. What never troubled me, however, was his offer to engage my children's minds.

"Thomas must be ready for you," I said. "I shall clean up. And please send Alice back to help."

He bowed and departed, leaving me excited to hear all about their learning as we ate our evening meal.

OVER THE WEEKS FOLLOWING MY DISAPPEARANCE, I attempted to make up for my indiscretion and to prove to my children that I was not going to leave again. I poured great effort into avoiding thoughts of the day I stumbled away, and of James's death. I pushed them aside until everyone was asleep, then I would sit in my bed or at the front of the house looking at the orchard and allow my mind to wander. Some evenings Darcy would remain for a time, sitting next to me deep in his own thoughts or we would talk, depending on our moods.

I often wondered what my sister and Bingley thought of his absence, but when I asked him if we ought to invite them, he made excuses or simply said no. He explained that he preferred the simplicity of our visits, if I did not mind his being my only companion. Naturally, I did not.

Flashes of James's death intruded at the most inopportune times—when I was changing the little ones, getting water, beating eggs, milking the goat—and I felt powerless to stop them. It was a relief to have Darcy to distract and occupy my children when all I could do was look away and choke back tears. Darcy had witnessed the horror of James's last moments, and he confessed that it haunted him as well. We shared this peculiar and unfortunate bond, something no one other than Lady Lydia might understand, and I would not speak to her. She had moved back at long last to the Fitzwilliams' estate, I was told, though under what conditions I knew not.

Autumn was upon us and with it, my sorrow began to lift just a little bit. I forced myself to smile and play, and to notice how soft my children's arms were, how peacefully they slept, how funny they were when they were not behaving dreadfully. We were surviving, albeit barely, and it felt like our lives had begun to heal from our tragedy.

Georgiana had gone to see her beau in Brighton, escorted by an aunt and uncle she deemed dear, but whom Darcy regarded with less pleasure. Still, he felt confident placing her in their care and pleased that his sister would find joy in the reunion. He confided that the young man had written to ask for Georgiana's hand and he had given his permission. It pleased me to imagine sweet Georgiana as a bride and, someday, a mother.

As we sat before the fire one evening, he said, "My anniversary was today."

"It was?" I felt a tingling sadness for him. "I did not know. I am sorry."

He set the book he had been reading in his lap. "My child would have been…" He shook his head as if pushing the memory of it away, and sighed. "That is not important. You once asked me how long it was until I ceased thinking of Anne." He did not lift his eyes from the cover of his book. "This is what I meant. You see me go about my day, but then something reminds me."

I nodded and wished he was a relative like Uncle Gardiner and I could throw an arm around him and we could comfort each other. But I remained as I was.

"Do you miss her?" My cheeks heated with the stupidity of my question. "I mean, of course—"

He looked up at the fire. "I miss having someone."

"Why have you not remarried?"

He shrugged. "I am loath to be in places where I might meet anyone. I despise the Season, balls, dancing, calls with inane chatter, ladies parading and preening to catch my attention." He rolled his eyes and we both laughed. "I daresay I have met all the society women of England and none of them interest me."

I ignored the flare of hope that gave me. "So why do you remain in Meryton?" It took him some time to answer, giving me the opportunity to study him. The crackling fire warmed his skin tone and exaggerated his high cheekbones.

At length he said, "My family."

"But they infuriate you."

He nodded. "That they do, but they are family nevertheless." He opened his book again but did not appear to be reading it. We both knew there was more to say, yet he said nothing.

It was not the first time I imagined how it might be if it was I who kept him here. I reminded myself almost daily of what a foolish notion that was—he could have any lady, beautiful ladies in the latest fashions who did not have more skill with milking than elaborate coiffures, and a past full of tragedy—but it was diverting to think of sometimes.

"And you?"

I had no idea what he meant, and it must have shown in my expression.

"Do you think of marrying again?"

Such a notion! It made me sputter with laughter until I saw it was nothing of humour to him. "It would be quite an endeavour to find any man who wished to shoulder the burden of another man's widow and four children." I raised my eyebrows. "Such a man would have to be quite out of his wits."

His eyes were intent upon me in a way I had not often seen them. "Everyone is out of their wits when they are in love."

Was he speaking of himself or hypothetically? I felt at once hopeful and foolish. To ease my discomfort, I decided to keep my tone light. "I could never love a man who was out of his wits. So you see, it is all quite impossible."

We both chuckled then and I was relieved to have navigated the difficult subject successfully.

"I am glad to see your wit returning," he added.

"My wit? My impudence, rather. It has always been my failing."

"You have never been rude," he said.

"Never been rude?" I laughed. "Sir, I believe you have forgotten most of our early acquaintance."

"You were a child when I met you. A child when you married my cousin, really."

"James and I were both children."

"Children, perhaps, but old enough to fall in love?"

"What an odd question. You of all people know the truth behind our hasty marriage. Not to say I did not have some affection for him when we married, but it was not love that overtook us that day."

He leaned on the arm of his chair, bringing his face— now half in shadow—nearer to mine, which made my heart skip. "You learned to love him then?"

I could not immediately answer, and turned to stare into the fire. "It was never what I thought love was——"

"What is love?"

"Not fear and anger. Forget I said that," I hastened to say. "It is unfair of me to think of the bad when we did have a great deal of good. In any case, it is hardly uncommon."

"Something being common does not mean it is right."

When I turned to look at him, he was still leaning on the arm of the chair, forehead wrinkled with concern. "I only say it to mean that it was between us—both his temper and mine, if I am being fair. And what he saw on the battlefield could only make things that much worse."

Darcy nodded.

"James and I married young, under circumstances neither of us wanted, and we resolved to do our best with it. Both of us were determined to live happily, but love? I have always thought love to be different."

"As have I."

His expression shifted and gave me an odd queasy feeling. Was it longing? No. I could not—would not—imagine what lay behind those eyes. For his sake, as well as my own.

I was growing very attached to Darcy. In many ways, he had become my dearest friend. He was my rescuer, my confidante, my everything, really, though I knew it was foolish—almost mad of me—to think of him in that way. Admitting to the inroads he was making into my heart would only lead to greater despair when he was gone, and I knew that, indeed, one day he would go. He would see that we were safe and he would leave us.

My thoughts caused me to blurt out, "How long do you intend to spend your days here? At my house, that is."

He flushed, and I noticed the trace of a scar on his

cheek left by Wickham's boot. "Have I overstayed my welcome?"

"No! Oh, heavens, no. No." Quite the opposite, in fact, but I could not tell him just how much I enjoyed his company, how quietly reassuring he was, how I felt lost when he departed, empty, alone—no, I certainly could not say any of that. "It is… This situation simply appears, well, odd, I suppose."

"To whom?" He leaned back. "And since when have you cared what other people think?"

"Since always. I never did not care. I simply could not stop myself from doing what I wanted."

We laughed at this truth, and the sparkle in his eyes made my stomach flip, as did the way his hair fell across his brow.

"If you wish for me to depart—"

"It is not that," I said quickly. I had no right to a flipped stomach and a hammering heart. "But…I do not wish for you to visit out of obligation."

"I do not." He gripped his book, his fingertips turning white. "I had not intended to remain this long, and planned to return to Pemberley after the summer's end, but I like it here. I always have. I feel more myself in your home than anywhere else." He cleared his throat and looked away. After a few moments, he said, "I shall leave in a fortnight."

"Oh." The pit in my stomach swelled to a fist. "If you are quite sure."

"Quite."

I wanted to beg him to stay, to argue that we still needed him, to share that I feared being alone again. To express that I relished his company. To say how I felt, that I… But I said nothing, feeling the moment dissipate like steam from a kettle.

In any case, it was likely the right thing to do, to encourage him to be on his way. Keeping him here could only increase these schoolgirl feelings of mine, and that would never do at all.

Darcy rose and leaned on the mantel, staring into the fire while turning the mourning ring he still wore in memory of James. "I have been wanting to tell you something. Something you will not like."

Fear stopped my breath. What more bad news could be endured?

"Wickham is out of jail."

"When?"

"Two days ago."

I sprang to my feet. "But he is a murderer! He murdered the son of a peer and should hang!"

"Not according to the judge."

"There was a trial?" My hands clenched. "Did you testify?"

He pulled at his waistcoat and nodded. "The judge said it appeared to be an accident and ordered Wickham freed."

"An accident?" I cursed softly, and Darcy's eyes flew wide. "Is there anything more we can do? With all of your family's money and influence, surely…"

He shook his head. After a moment, he said, "There is more, if you can manage it."

I slumped with resignation. "Tell me. I wish to know all."

"Lady Lydia left with him. With Wickham."

I gasped. "With Mr Wickham? When?"

"Yesterday. She is gone."

"Heavens to mercy," I whispered. My chest compressed and my breath was stolen from me. Determined not to have a spell like the one that sent me to the hunting lodge, I hurried outside to the pump to splash water on my face. I allowed myself to sink to the soppy ground, knowing I was creating more work for myself when laundry day came, but not caring.

There was no way to change the verdict. Wickham was free. James was dead, and no one would pay for it. Except me. And Darcy. My fatherless children. And yes, the earl and Lady Broxbourne. Was this justice?

CHAPTER TWENTY-SIX

A few days later, there was a knock at the door. Nora was out with Thomas and Alice in the barn, and I was covered in flour, wrist deep in dough. "Darcy, could you answer it?"

"I am dressing Henry!" he called, so I wiped off my hands as best I could, and looked out the window. My heart sank at the sight of Jane, Bingley, Bingley's sister Lady Snowley, and her husband, whose advanced age and lack of dancing ability was forgiven by his sizeable fortune.

I drew in a slow breath and closed my eyes, imagining the laugh James would have had at the situation. He found 'scandalising the small-minded of our class' humorous. I did not quite share the sentiment.

The mourning wreath banged against the door as I opened it, and I noticed Jane's and Bingley's eyes fixed on it. Custom dictated its presence for at least six months. It hurt my heart as I approached my home, but I somehow found myself needing the ritual and the pain it caused. Wiping my hands on my apron, I offered my surprise and welcome.

"Oh! Do you answer the door yourself?" Lady Snowley said, no doubt horrified at my lowness. "How…quaint."

I ignored her, as I had always attempted to do since meeting her at Netherfield many years prior, and instead reached for Jane. She kissed my cheeks warmly.

Once she had released me, I said, "Bingley!" with utter joy, and "Lord Snowley, Lady Snowley," with less. "What brings everyone here?"

I had hoped Jane would speak, but Lady Snowley took it upon herself to explain. "We felt ever so sorry for you after the events that transpired, and your being alone and removed from your acquaintances due to your period of mourning. We are staying with my brother on our way to London and, upon enquiring after you, learned that you continue to live on your own. We decided it would be right to come here and condole with you."

"Quite right," I said dryly, deciding how to match her tone of condescension. "Pray, do come in."

Bingley and Jane were often here, but Lady and Lord Snowley studied the rooms and furnishings, calculating the comments to follow. Memories of this sort of visit were burned into my mind. The cruellest judgments were never shared with the hosts, but whispered and repeated in carriages and parlours. The smallness of my existence would provide a great deal of diversion for the tittering young matrons of Lady Snowley's circle. I suppose she thought it my due, that the brashness of my youth had reduced me to this.

Paining me presently was the fact that there were not enough chairs in our sitting room, as one had been moved to the twins' room for when Darcy and I read them stories, and two others were out front from watching the children play earlier in the day. I was compelled to explain, which sent Bingley scurrying out the door, Lord Snowley being too aged and infirm to assist.

"Elizabeth," said Darcy, entering with Henry, "I cannot quite fasten his— Oh. Greetings."

He halted in the doorway, making an attempt at a well-mannered bow, incongruous and awkward with Henry in his arms and his shirtsleeves on display for all to see. Mercifully, it was cool enough that his stockings and shoes were on.

I walked towards him, wiping my hands again on my encrusted apron, and reached for my son. I felt the eyes of the room boring into my back as I asked, "Would you be so kind as to bring the other chair from the front?" My words were steady, but my eyes were wide, signalling my helpless irritation to him.

His face impassive, he tipped his head to the ladies and, lifting his tail-coat and black mourning cravat from the peg at the door where he had left both upon his arrival as was his custom, he hurried outside. Through the window I saw he and Bingley lean their heads together in animated conference.

I gestured to the available sofa and chairs, and the ladies and Lord Snowley sat while I remained standing. Though I turned to Jane, hoping she might speak, Lady Snowley said, "We were naturally so concerned about Mr Darcy and his family these past four months. And you, too, of course."

"Of course," I said.

She looked with disdain at Henry squirming in my arms. "I am sorry to impose upon you in this manner. I understood you to have help, and therefore hoped a visit would be a welcome distraction from lonely grieving, but it seems I was mistaken on both counts."

"I assure you my grief is quite lonely," I said, each word clipped.

Lady Snowley, chastened, sat back, and Jane took the opportunity to enquire after the children, though Bingley's entrance interrupted my response. He and Darcy set the chairs down, Darcy nodding so I would sit, and Bingley perched at the edge of his. Darcy disappeared into the kitchen, only to emerge with the roughest of my furniture for himself. I wished he had taken the time to get the finer chair from the twins' room but while he recognised his error immediately, it was too late. He stood in front of it stiffly, as if his position could cover it entirely from view.

"Lizzy," Jane said, "Henry has grown so even in a few weeks!"

"Doting on one's children seems to be the fashion these days," Lord Snowley said with a scowl, "something I shall never comprehend."

Lady Snowley reached for her husband's hand and gave it a tepid pat. "On this, we are in agreement."

With perfect timing, Alice and Thomas tore into the room leaping on Darcy and nearly knocking him over. "Play with us, Uncle Darcy!" they shouted. "Yes, play with us!"

Darcy frowned and escorted the children out of the room, whispering reprimands to their great confusion.

"Well, we have some good news for all," Bingley said with a beaming smile towards the direction in which they departed. "We are expecting another." He reached to squeeze Jane's hand.

As I shared my felicitations, Lord Snowley enquired, "Does one share such news in mixed company?"

"My lord," I said, "we are family. I believe any news is welcome among one's relations."

His expression was of a man who was rarely contradicted.

Not inclined to have her husband be the only one present to experience discomfort, Lady Snowley narrowed her eyes. "You seem to be covered in…is it flour? Have you been…baking?"

I looked down, irritated with myself for not having pulled off my apron at some point, the black of my gown only exaggerating the disaster I had made with the flour. "Indeed I have."

"Have you no cook?" Lady Snowley asked, with eyes wide and mouth rounded into a perfect O.

What might she say if I replied that not only was there no cook, there was scarcely money to eat at all? I bit my tongue, knowing no good could come of speaking my mind to her. "I do not," I replied.

"No cook? But how do you manage—"

Jane attempted to change the subject by asking after Lady Snowley's baker, who was by all accounts most accomplished in creating the latest pastries.

"Pardon," said Lady Snowley, "but you must satisfy my curiosity, Mrs Fitzwilliam. I am asking only to understand how you get by." Though her demeanour was the model of concern, her eyes danced with delight in my misfortune.

Darcy, entering again, looked at her with caution.

"I have no cook, no lady's maid, no servant of any kind save our maid-of-all-work." I decided to fully embrace this opportunity to scandalise her and abase myself. "I sew and cook and garden and do some of the washing myself when my children are otherwise safely occupied."

"I wished to hire an additional maid for Mrs Fitzwilliam," said Darcy, "but she dismissed the idea out of hand."

My face burned. I did not want Darcy to make any excuses for me, nor did I want it known how much he was my rescuer. Then I realised he was attempting to excuse himself lest those present thought him less than generous. I was the object of his charity in all ways and there was no use hiding it.

"We had an additional servant, but she married, and the girl recently hired was a fool," I said. Nora's cousin was too slow to learn and often slipped out the door to avoid work. "She created more work than she relieved."

"Then hire another," Lady Snowley said, glancing at a side table, likely inspecting the dust that rested there. "The poor have so many children in need of employment. Surely one of them would do."

I stared at her, again weighing the prudence of speaking my mind.

Bingley asked if he could trouble me for some water and then asked his sister to share the details of a new book she was reading.

Never one to willingly be distracted from her quarry, Lady Snowley said, "I would ask for water, as well, but I would hate for Mrs Fitzwilliam to muddy her shoes pumping more for me."

This slight was too much, and my temper rose though I knew I ought not give way to it. Red tinged the edges of my vision and I choked on the words I wished to say.

"Lady Snowley," Darcy said in deep and grave tones, "you demean the existence that Mrs Fitzwilliam built with my late cousin, a man you once called dear and brave. Surely you do not wish to be cruel to his widow and children now?"

"Cruel?" She tittered, looking around for someone to

share her amusement. "I assure you I meant no such thing. How can it be cruel to merely observe that—"

"Yes, Caroline," I said, using her Christian name for emphasis and insult, "you may take your victory and share the news of my fall to anyone you like, if it pleases you. I answer my own door, I bake my own bread, and I care for my own children. Indeed, it is quite beneath you to even call here, so I release you from that burdensome duty now."

Not even a breath had passed before Lady Snowley was on her feet and ordering the others to follow her. Lord Snowley rose with a groan, one hand supporting his back as he shuffled out, while Jane and Bingley glanced at one other, brows furrowed.

"We ought to remain with Lady Snowley," Bingley said, his usual sparkle dimmed. Jane leaned in and kissed me, promising to return if she could later in the afternoon, though I suspected she would not.

Darcy's face was all solemnity when they had gone. I walked to the dough I had abandoned at the knocking of the door, and rolled it out with more vigour than it warranted. "I could easily forgive her pride, if she had not mortified mine. She is petty and unpleasant."

"And you were graceful in your handling of her, though I was not," he said. He chewed at his bottom lip. "She has become powerful in certain circles."

I continued to hammer at the dough. "How could she possibly hurt me? Such circles as you speak of are as unrelated to me as the populace of the Orient." After a lengthy silence, I added, "You must get tired of coming to my rescue."

"Not at all," he said wryly. "It enlivens my existence. It is why I spend my days here—just hoping for a reason to be the hero."

We both laughed, but I noticed the concern was not quite lifted from his brow. "Thomas and Alice requested a playmate. Entertain them, if you are so inclined, or follow the party and make amends."

He took a few steps towards me, serious now. I lifted the dough into a tart pan while keeping my eyes on him. That I might have involved Darcy in my troubles concerned me, but he had known what he was a part of even while James was still alive, ever since he removed his tail-coat and shoes.

"I ought to follow them." His eyes darted to the door through which the party had departed and back to me, searching my face as if for permission.

"Very well," I said, brushing flour off my apron. "Then I shall bid you farewell."

"I do not wish it. I only feel I should."

"Pray do not let me stop you."

"You do not stop me. I stop myself."

"Darcy," I said. "What do you want to do?"

"What I *want* and what I *must* do not often align." He studied me a moment, then opened his mouth as if he had more to say but clapped it shut. After checking his cravat and smoothing his hair, he turned slowly before walking outside and shutting the door.

I was left unsettled and dismayed by the entire incident. Had Lady Snowley and the rest just encountered Darcy at my house in his shirtsleeves acting the part of a father and husband? No, it was worse. Most men of our station would never be so involved in the care of their children. Likewise, I —born the daughter of a gentleman—was meant to have them ensconced with governesses and tutors so I could spend my days in a drawing room, neither soiled nor troubled.

Yet despite the difficulties of my existence, there was one

thing I loved. I loved these moments that Darcy and I had together and I greatly feared their end, especially now that we had been discovered.

It occurred to me then that, though Lady Snowley and her gossipy circle could not hurt me, they could perhaps hurt him. I resented her more for that possibility than any slight towards me.

CHAPTER TWENTY-SEVEN

D arcy did not return that evening or the next day. I did not want to desire his company, but I could not help myself, and the approaching date of his permanent departure left me feeling adrift. It was best for him, and for that reason I was glad. I would not wish my friendship to injure him.

When he returned at last, he seemed as agitated as I felt, but refused to share the reason for his absence. I suspected it had to do with Lady Snowley and his family, but did not dare ask.

His eyes touched on every furnishing and object in my home, on me, on the children. He kept his tail-coat on and his cravat tight. His brow remained furrowed, even when Thomas asked to go on a walk.

"Indeed," he murmured. "A walk might do us all good. Elizabeth, shall we venture to the shops?" The older children cheered and the younger ones joined because of their siblings' excitement. I had avoided Meryton as best I could since James's death, but I was determined not to show my reluctance or anxiety to Darcy or the children. "People will see us and talk, but damn them all," he said, his voice barely audible as he helped Alice with her shoes.

"Darcy, if you deem it improper, perhaps the woods would be more prudent?"

He shook his head, brow drawn. "No. You are my cousin's widow. There is nothing more to it and nothing to hide."

My heart sank. Nothing more to it. More condemning words had never been spoken. I had thought...perhaps I had allowed myself to hope, stupidly. He was my relation and enjoyed playing the hero, as he said. I would have to be satisfied with that. But could I?

We strolled, and I noticed he chose a path that did not directly pass by Broxbourne. The children stopped to gather and throw leaves, and to chase after chipmunks that scurried out on the lane.

"I spoke with my aunt and uncle," he said at last. "The matter of the commission. They are undeterred."

I had not expected a different outcome, yet still felt a pang of disappointment.

"And..." His voice drifted off, but he stared at me so intently that I stopped walking.

Adjusting Sally in my arms, I asked, "What more?"

His expression softened, his eyes downcast. He let Henry down to toddle after his older siblings and cocked his head. "They accused me of—" He chewed on his lower lip and then whirled around, chasing after Henry and scooping the boy into the air. Henry squealed and giggled, and Darcy jogged to catch up with Thomas, leaving his thought unfinished.

Alice had stopped to trace the tracks of a deer, and I called for her to keep up, needing to know what Darcy had wanted to say or what had been said of him. "Darcy," I called, "what was the accusation?" He glanced over his shoulder and shook his head, leaving me even more desperate to know. How bad could it be? Horrific, if it involved the Fitzwilliams. Darcy had been at my house alone, and they likely knew that. We thought the presence of servants could absolve us of suspicion, but that was foolish.

Or perhaps it was something more. Had they accused him of...caring for me? Could James's family have drawn that conclusion? But how? Could they see it in his eyes? How could they if I could not? Or perhaps I *could* see that he cared for me, but was afraid to admit it. Perhaps Darcy did see me as more than a poor woman in need of assistance, the wife of his deceased cousin; yet if he did, it was wrong. It had only been a few months since James's death.

I walked on, wishing my mind would quiet itself.

On the outskirts of Meryton, we came to Miss Taylor's house. She was in her garden, which was her chosen place any day that it was not raining. "My pupil!" she cried. "I heard of your tragedy, but did not wish to impose with a call. Oh, Lizzy, your very presence here brings me immeasurable happiness." I smiled and went inside the gate to embrace her, trailed by the rest. "You look well, and for that I am relieved. And are these your children, all so grown? And Mr Darcy! You are ageing quite well, young man."

A rare guffaw escaped his lips and he bowed deeply, kissing her hand.

"My word, to be kissed by a man as handsome as yourself is a true gift." She fanned herself like a woman fifty years younger. "Your timing could not be better. I need assistance with this trellis, and I am not too proud to ask you, Mr Darcy, to be the one to do it, if you would be so kind."

He obliged her, leaning the fallen trellis back against the house before pausing to clean dirt from the seam of his boot…and I felt my heart crack open. After all his moments of kindness and goodness, it was almost laughable that watching him brush at his shoe put me over into the realm of love! Yet the act was just like him—careful, thoughtful, and prudent.

Miss Taylor sent him in for her shawl and whispered, "He is a fine man. Is he good to you?"

Dazed as I was by my revelation, I almost missed her question. I snapped back to our conversation and, realising the implication, flushed against my will. "He has been helping so much with the children and—"

"No, I mean good to you." She nudged me with her elbow. "Kind? Generous? Tender?"

I blinked. "Tender? Heavens, Miss Taylor. It is nothing like that, I assure you." I hoped she could not detect the guilt threading my own words.

"Just the ramblings of an old woman, dear," she said, smiling.

"He is James's cousin, and I am a widow with four children."

She shrugged. "You are alone. He is alone."

"He is a gentleman of elevated status with a great estate and large fortune," I replied. "I am his charity, nothing more."

She pressed her lips together, though her eyes danced with delight. Soon we departed, but I was more careful with my gaze as I walked on with him and the children. Even so, I could not help but notice the gentle way he moved through the world and how he made me feel when he was around. I was always calmer, although I did not know if it was just the relief of not being without companionship or if it truly could be attributed to him.

Comparisons to James were inevitable, of course. They had similar builds and heights, and similar looks—so much so that occasionally the flop of Darcy's hair, which had grown far more unruly in recent years—gave me a start. However, James's walk had had a jovial bounce while Darcy's was solid. While James burst into a room and filled it with his emotion, whether joyful or furious, Darcy entered a room with a pensive silence that one might call aloof. I once thought this made Darcy dull, or rude, but I recognised that though his entrance might be quiet, his presence glowed with a warmth which increased if he found the person agreeable. Had he not been known for his exceeding wealth, Darcy was not the kind of man you would notice at a dance or on the street, but he was the kind of man you would cherish as a friend. I did cherish him, and hated when we parted.

My heart fluttered when I considered his fine face and watched him act as a father would with my children. The children who would one day truly be his own, who would rightly call him Father, would be blessed indeed. The thought of him with another woman, having a family of his own someday, made my stomach clench. I distracted myself by fussing over Sally, who had rubbed dirt onto her dress.

On the walk back to my house, as he was sharing a story about Georgiana's music lessons, he took my elbow and guided me around a puddle with such absence of thought that I lost my breath. His caring was inherent to his nature and I was moved. I was in love with him. *I was in love with him!* I had to repeat it to believe it. Darcy. Darcy, whom I had once dreaded and feared; Darcy, whom I had found handsome the moment I set eyes on him; Darcy, who had cared for me and the children, and become the person I most wanted to see and to speak to each day. I loved Darcy. Heavens! What was I to do?

This was dangerous. I was dangerous for him, and my feelings for him were dangerous for me. Besides, it was too soon to have any such feelings for anyone. Disrespectful. In any case, given my situation—quite literally a penniless widow, steps away from relying on the charity of the parish —I was no prize for any man, and certainly not one like Darcy. No, I would bury my thoughts and pretend that all was as it had always been.

THAT EVENING, WHEN HE WAS PUTTING SALLY TO BED, SHE called Darcy 'Dada'. I froze, as did he.

"I am Uncle Darcy, Sally."

"Dad-da-da-da-da."

"Uncle Darcy," I said brightly, Darcy moving aside as I crossed to her. "Your father died and Uncle Darcy is helping at our house for a while." And with that I tucked her in, gave her a kiss, and blew out the candle by her bed.

Once we had left the children and sat by the fire, I could not meet his gaze. "This is confusing for them," I said.

At his silence, I braced myself to say the words I knew would bring pain to us both—necessary pain. "Darcy, you should leave."

"You want me to go?"

I stared at my lap, gathering up what shards of my dignity remained. This was love, it seemed—to do what was best for him, though agony seared every part of me. "You need to depart for good, and not wait another week as planned."

When I had the courage to raise my eyes and meet his intent gaze, he said, "Do not be hasty—"

My stomach churned, for all I wanted was to reach for him, to hold him here, but if I cared for him—and I did—I had to let him go. I had to *force* him to go.

I rose and pulled his coat from its peg. "You said the Snowleys asked you to town. Insisted. You ought to join them and make amends." I thrust the coat at him.

"Elizabeth, I do not care what such persons as the Snowleys think."

"I think you do. I think you should. We are your charity cases, Darcy, and I assure you, we will get by without you."

I threw open the door but he reached around me and slammed it shut. "You cannot think that is all you are—a work of charity."

Our eyes locked. I was not sure what to do or say, or if he was feeling anything between us or merely anxiety at my sudden turn.

"Of course I am. How could I be otherwise? Left penniless by your family, the sons and daughters of your cousin not recognised as the grandchildren of an earl...it is a matter of honour that you have come to my aid, and I thank you for it. But it is no longer needed."

"And this is what you think of me?" Cheeks red, his voice was thick with emotion. "I had not believed myself so easily discarded."

His pain was unbearable, but I had to press on. "I am not discarding you so much as thanking you for all you have done for us and saying it is no longer necessary. Surely you see this is to your benefit?"

"The children need me. If there is some confusion for them, we can continue to correct them. What do you think would be more respectful of James—for me to take care of his family, or leave them alone in penury?"

"James is dead. And it is left to me to decide what his children need and do not need. We do not need you, Darcy. You are free to go. I *insist* you go."

I needed this conversation to end before I changed my mind, yet I was also terrified he would acquiesce and actually depart. I was not quite sure what I feared more—his leaving me alone with the children or the loss of the feelings I had only just allowed myself to name. Nevertheless, he had to go.

Darcy's shoulders slumped. "Thomas needs me. You said he walks around like he has forgotten something except when I am near him."

It was true and it was agonising to acknowledge. "You are not his father." The words prickled my tongue, and I hated them more when Darcy flinched. "He must learn to live as he is, a son without a father."

I laced my fingers together and pulled, needing the pain to focus myself. My husband had not yet been gone a twelve-month. I was still in mourning, and the funeral wreath still hung on my door.

"It is my duty to look after you, for it is my fault James is dead."

I stared at him. "You cannot believe that is true."

"If I had not been so proud, so blinded by fury, I would not have involved myself with Wickham again, and James would not have needed to intervene. He died trying to protect me."

I shook my head. How long had he been carrying the burden of this unspoken guilt? "It was an accident. James's death was not your fault."

He blinked rapidly before averting his gaze. "You will

never convince me of my lack of culpability." After a moment, Darcy glanced towards the children's bedroom. "I need not add to your woes. If my departure is what you wish, I will go."

My heart squeezed, but I resisted the urge to tell him how much I wanted him to stay. How much I wanted *him*.

Darcy tugged at his collar. "For the children's sake, I think it unwise to depart too suddenly. James vanished without explanation and I fear the consequence of my doing so as well."

This was the truth. The sudden disappearance of their father lingered, as Thomas—and occasionally, Alice—panicked when one of us was too long away. His deep brown eyes studied me, and he reached out as if he was going to take hold of me, only to let his hand drop to his side. Then he gave a nearly imperceptible nod and straightened. "I shall return in the morning to bid you all farewell."

And with that, he slipped out into the darkness. I sat down and cried like I had not since James's death. I had lost Darcy—perhaps forever—and the thought was enough to break me.

CHAPTER TWENTY-EIGHT

Darcy, as promised, came to say goodbye the next morning. He would not stay despite the children's pleas, or their hugs and attempts to pull him back towards the house. The little ones were all giggling as they pushed and pulled, but I did not find any of it particularly entertaining, nor did he. I had not seen him look so grim except for the day of James's death. His sunken eyes met mine over and over, yet he said nothing.

"Please write to us!" begged Alice. "I do so love correspondence."

This, said in such an adult manner, broke the tension immeasurably. We both laughed, and Darcy's shoulders relaxed for the first time.

"Her precociousness is outpacing mine," I said.

He smiled. "That might in fact be true, Elizabeth." His smile slipped, though he kept his eyes locked to mine.

"Do not go!" Thomas said, hugging Darcy around the leg.

Darcy stroked the boy's hair. "I must, my boy, forgive

me." His eyes stayed on mine as if begging for me to argue. When I pressed my lips together, he added, "It is best for us all."

IT WAS NOT QUIET AFTER HE LEFT. HOW COULD IT HAVE been? But it was different. Harder. Busier. Fewer laughs for everyone, but we managed fairly well, better than we had just after James passed. Alice and Thomas were able to watch the twins when my attention was on the fire or the boiling laundry or when I had to go to the barn. Sometimes we all went there together, but it was so cold and muddy that I hated to do that. I could never trust that one of them was not going to dance in a puddle or step in dung, creating even more work.

Underlying the work was an air of sadness and longing for what was gone. Each morning the children checked to see if Uncle Darcy had yet arrived, and I reminded them that he had gone to London, which was very far away. One morning I used the words 'went away' which was what I sometimes said about James. A confused Alice asked if he was in heaven like her father. I reassured her that he was merely on an adventure with friends, only to be asked why we could not see him that moment. It was frustrating to them, and—though it had been at my behest—it was devastating to me.

We entertained ourselves by visiting the Gardiners. At dinner the week Darcy left, Alice told my uncle, "Uncle Darcy went away, but not to heaven."

"Oh," he replied, his eyebrows lifted. He looked at me and I shrugged.

"Where did he go?" Margaret asked her.

Alice hopped off her chair and gave a knowing nod. "To

town with Uncle Bingley and Auntie Jane and some horrid snow lady." She curtseyed, then skipped out of the room.

Margaret and Uncle Gardiner looked at me, and I attempted to think of the shortest explanation for the sudden change, and to ignore the nickname they had created for Caroline Snowley. "It was time."

"It was time a while back," said my uncle.

"Edward!" snapped Margaret, and from the quiet slap I could tell she had hit his leg under the table.

His expression remained undeterred. "Why now?"

I did not know how to respond and I did not wish to discuss it with them. It was true Darcy stayed at Netherfield beyond what any of us had expected, but was it too long? I suppose it was. Clearly my uncle thought so, and probably Margaret, though she would never say it. I imagined others believed so as well. But did the fact that others shared the same opinion make his visits, which improved the life of my family, wrong? It did not matter either way. He was no longer in Meryton.

CHRISTMAS WAS COMING. MOST YEARS JAMES HAD BEEN away, but the older children remembered the two occasions when he had been with us. Alice began asking incessantly about Christmas and wanted to plan decorations and foods and make presents for everyone. The adults endeavoured to make December special for the children. Margaret sent to London for paper so Alice could create festive decorations. My uncle took Thomas to cut fir boughs for our mantel. I made new stockings. Lord and Lady Broxbourne even extended an invitation to Christmas dinner at their home. I politely declined, as I am sure they were hoping I would.

Thomas, unlike Alice, began looking more and more

lost. He stopped eating much and did not desire to be a part of Alice's activities. One afternoon a few days before Christmas, Thomas would not get out of bed. I could find nothing wrong with him—no fever, no rash, no cough, no visible animal bite. He simply lay staring at the wall. Alice brought him a gift of holly tied with ribbon. He threw it across the room.

After drying Alice's tears, I asked Thomas what the matter was, as I had done all day, but he refused to answer. I sank onto his bed and asked him what he wanted.

"Father," he whispered. "No one plays the same as he did."

I swallowed the lump in my throat. I thought about them coming back from fishing, covered with mud and grass, Thomas holding his brook trout aloft in victory for me to see. I recalled James teaching him how to groom a horse when Thomas was hardly old enough to stand on his own, and how James nearly fell over laughing when the horse nosed Thomas right off his wobbly feet. I pictured James play-fighting with him, and how often I had wished they would stop for fear that Thomas would get hurt.

"Could I write to Uncle Darcy? I miss him, as well."

"Of course," I said, secretly hoping that a plea from Thomas might bring Darcy back to us.

THE ONLY PLEASING PART OF DECEMBER WAS THE OFFICIAL announcement of Georgiana Darcy's engagement. The wedding would be in August, a date set, I felt confident, so that I could attend. Until the year of mourning was over, it would be unacceptable for me to join a public celebration.

In a letter, Jane described Charles Stanley as an exceptionally kind young man with eight thousand a year, and a keen interest in horses, art, and collecting the beginnings of an enviable library. He also loved to play duets on the pianoforte. It seemed that Georgiana had gained the affection of someone who shared both her interests and her brother's, and one who could keep her in the comforts with which she had been raised. Had the young man's funds been insufficient, I was sure that Darcy would have assisted however he could, yet I was certain he was relieved not to.

My own situation had been eased as well. I came to find that accounts had been set up for me at the dressmaker, the bake shop, the butcher, and the grocer. When I asked, the shopkeepers explained they had been sworn to secrecy by my patron's solicitor, though I believed it was Jane's doing.

I wrote to Jane asking when she would return, telling her I missed her terribly. She assured me they would return after the new year began. She did not say if Darcy would accompany them, and the thought of it consumed many of my waking hours.

CHAPTER TWENTY-NINE

A t the end of January, a knock came at the door. When I opened it, I blinked a few times, unsure of whether to throw my arms about Darcy's neck or send him away. While my deepest desire was to kiss him long and hard (something I had imagined too many times), I knew that was a disastrous idea.

"Darcy." My legs quaked, so I grasped the door frame to steady myself.

I could not discern the expression on his face. Was it agony? Was it hope? But before I could decide, the children attacked him with hugs and stories, hardly allowing him inside.

When at last the hubbub had died down, I invited him inside. "I am pleased to see you, sir. I did not know whether to expect you or not."

"I did not know myself if I should come. It was Thomas's letter which decided the matter for me."

Our conversation proceeded in fits and starts. There was

both too much and too little to be said and any time we began, the children would interrupt us. At length, he said, "I wonder, Elizabeth, if you would consent to me calling on Sundays?"

"But of course."

We were all happy, though I wondered at the change in his habit of a daily visit.

So it began, his weekly visit on Sunday afternoons, conducted in a manner of utmost propriety. He was attired as a gentleman ought to be and he behaved as a gentleman would. The children were attended to by me or by Nora, we served him tea, and we spoke of inconsequential matters. The children begged him not to leave each time, knowing so much of the dreary week was left and they would be stuck inside without their favourite entertainment if he went.

One Sunday, Nora was attempting to train the newly hired servant, Patience, to bake a meat pie. The girl was comically slow to learn, and we endeavoured to ignore Nora's frustration and insults whilst I served tea.

Darcy reached for a spoon and brushed my arm. My breath caught and my stomach tightened. He noticed and asked if I was all right.

"Yes," I said, smoothing my hair. He was used to my shifts in mood, so I hoped he suspected nothing. I attempted to convince myself that I had been alone for many months and that I was reacting to being touched by a man, any man. But I knew that was not true. It was Darcy, for I was in love with him.

Nora sounded as if she was losing her forbearance with Patience, which was difficult to ignore given our close quarters. I suggested we take the children outside given the unseasonably lovely day. After wrestling the little ones into coats and hats and mittens, we walked to the stream. Upon our return to the cottage, he and I stood together in the sunshine, watching the children play.

"I wish James could see them growing and changing," I said. I wondered if I brought him up to put distance between Darcy and myself.

"He did cherish his children," he said, staring at Thomas spinning with Henry.

"Yes. On the days he felt well." I remembered the day Darcy called with my sister and Bingley and spotted my bruises. "I hope his soul is more at peace now than it was on Earth."

Darcy touched my arm, but as I turned to him, Nora came outside. She cleared her throat, making us jump and take a step away from one another, though we had not been standing too close. "Ma'am," she said, her eyes darting between us, "Patience has quit. Shall I look for another girl?"

I nodded and excused myself, explaining to Darcy that Nora would surely need my help now that she was alone again in the kitchen.

MORE AND MORE OFTEN ON THESE LITTLE VISITS, I FOUND myself staring at Darcy, hoping we would have occasion to touch. I felt ridiculous, like I was fifteen again. Each pang of desire was both thrilling, and a betrayal of my husband. I was never able to shake James from the moment, and all attempts to push thoughts of Darcy away by thinking about my life with James only led to feeling lonely again. Worse, comparisons between the men left Darcy appearing far more favourable. I considered asking Darcy to stay away again, yet his visits were something to look forward to for all of us, and in truth I did not want them to end.

When he was gone, I could not stop thinking of his warm eyes topped with those delightfully full brows, or his chin, squared off and dimpled to perfection, best seen up close. Too close. I loved when we had occasion to stand so near that I could smell him, a perfect mix of scented soaps, leather, and manliness. I adored when he absently ran his fingers through the strands of his thick brown hair. My heart raced as I considered these things.

In late February, he departed for Pemberley, prompted by a request from Georgiana that he not leave her alone for her birthday. The house—indeed, Meryton itself—seemed a colder, far lonelier place, the effect heightened by the bleakness of the season. And yet, my passion, my longing for him did not cool.

I had to push him out of my mind, but how?

EACH YEAR, WHEN APRIL ROLLED IN STILL FRIGID, I BECAME impatient. After months of grey and brown, I was ready for verdure and warmth, for long walks among the awakening fields, and for relief from the constant worry for my children's health. This year, I had been uncharacteristically concerned about my own health as well, fearing what would become of the little ones if I took ill or worse. I did consider in that event, their domicile would likely be more beautiful, as I assumed one or more of my relatives would take them in, though I did hope my children would miss me. Or even remember me. They were still so young. Such grim thoughts consumed me, and I endeavoured to stave off such wallowing.

One evening after the children were tucked in bed, I put

on my coat, took hold of a blanket, and sat outside. Had this been November, I might have hurried back inside at the chill, but by April such temperatures seemed a treat. I was delighted to even leave my scarf on its hook.

A horse's nickering and a sudden rustle amongst the shrubs caught my attention. I could see nothing, and a rush of fear crashed over me. "Who is there?" I called out, attempting to sound confident, and possibly armed.

The horse came forward at the click of someone's tongue. Darcy's face glowed in the light thrown from my windows.

"Lord, Darcy, you scared me half to death! What are you doing here?"

After a brief hesitation he dismounted and walked towards me, his horse trailing him. "I am sorry." Then he just stood, shamefaced, his fingers twisting around the reins.

"I had no idea you were at Netherfield."

"Yes, I am." He appeared disinclined to say anything more or offer any explanation.

"Is anything the matter?" I asked. "My sister and Bingley are well?"

"Perfectly so. Nothing is wrong."

My heart still pounded madly—from fear? Excitement? Love? "Then what are you doing here so late?"

"I…" He paused, seeming unsure of whether to go on.

I took a deep breath, still trying to work the fear out of my body.

"I…well, the last I was here, I began to come out here some nights. Just to check on the house. To see that you are safe. It seemed natural to do so now, as well."

"You simply ride here and then just leave?"

He pulled his coat collar closed and nodded.

There was a long pause. I asked, "How often do you do this?"

He dropped his eyes to his boots, so I teased, "That often, is it?" I chuckled, but he did not. He ran his hand down his face and a deep silence lay between us. I waited for him to speak, but when he still offered nothing, I said, "How long have you been in Meryton?"

"I only arrived this afternoon."

"And you intend to remain?"

"My plans are as yet unfixed."

I thrilled at the possibility that he would be near for a time, but wondered why he had not told me of his return. "Would you care to come in?"

"No, I should not."

"You cannot have anywhere to go." I cocked my head. "Unless you are off to the opera? We have so few of those in Meryton. Ah—an assembly, perhaps? But no, those do not begin until May."

"No." He smiled until plaintiveness dimmed his joy. "Yet I ought to leave. It is late."

"Very well, I shall cease to tease you about staying." A sheep bleated in the darkness. "Good night, then," I said, wishing so much he could stay.

"Good night," he said, mounting his horse.

"Darcy, would you like to come to my uncle's for dinner on Saturday?" He hesitated, so I added, "They insisted you join us upon your return."

He held still, then nodded. "I should be delighted." He rode off, disappearing beyond the lantern light.

I went inside, too many emotions battling within me to sleep. I paced to the window and back to the table, sitting, then standing again. I could not catch my breath, wondering if Darcy had returned and was watching from outside. Oddly, I wanted him to be out there, but found it unnerving, as well. It took hours before I slipped off to sleep, and paid for my lack of rest the next day as neither the chores nor the children knew, or cared, how much time I had spent awake in the dark.

CHAPTER THIRTY

After Saturday's meal, Margaret, Jane, and I excused ourselves and went to the drawing room while the men remained at the table. Once alone, I confided in them of my nocturnal visitor, wishing to hear someone say something to encourage my hope. Alas, they both seemed more alarmed than pleased by the intelligence.

"He rides past the house?" Margaret asked incredulously.

"It would seem so," I said. I set aside my teacup, as did she.

"At night?"

"Margaret, you make it seem so…untoward."

"Well, Lizzy, I must admit, it does sound so. Jane, did you know about this?"

Jane stroked her round belly. "Not exactly. We knew he went riding. We could hear the grooms moving about and the departing hoof-beats, but never knew his destination. Charles says he has always been restless. We had no cause to think anything more of it than that."

She and I locked eyes, and I wished we were alone so she could share her thoughts on the matter. Or perhaps I did not, for Jane was always more cautious than I, and I suspected she would advise prudence or perhaps even putting an end to his daylight visits, which I could not tolerate.

My uncle entered, looking for his pouch of tobacco. Margaret stopped him and—to my horror—said, "Edward, Mr Darcy is coming to Lizzy's house."

"And has been for months," he said.

"At night."

"Margaret!" I hissed.

Margaret threw up her hands. "I wish to know if anyone else thinks it odd."

"I wish I had not said anything!"

"What do they do?" he asked. "Lizzy, have you something to hide?"

"Of course not. Nothing. We do nothing," I snapped. "He does not even knock. He simply watches the house, apparently." I reached for my teacup again, desperately wanting to end the conversation.

"That man." Uncle Gardiner shook his head. "Who is going to discuss wasted opportunities with him?"

"Edward!" Margaret gasped.

"It was a joke," he said, his smile fading, but I felt myself blush hot with mortification.

At this most inopportune of moments, Bingley entered, followed by Darcy.

My uncle turned. "Am I to understand, Darcy, that you ride past Lizzy's house under the cover of night?" His voice was full of amusement.

"Uncle!" I gasped, thinking how, in my youth, a man's interest in me had sent this same uncle into such a state that

I was forced to marry before I was ready. Now he was amused?

But that was not my most urgent concern, for Darcy was far from amused. His face reddened and his eyes flew wide, darting about the room as he took in the faces smiling at him. No doubt they all seemed to be mocking him.

"Mr Darcy," I hastened to say, unconsciously reverting to the more formal manner of addressing him. "Forgive me. You were not meant to——"

"Excuse me," he said, his voice clipped. He gave a cursory bow before turning on his heel to leave. I hurried after him, but not before scowling over my shoulder at my indiscreet relations.

I caught up with Darcy in the front hall, where a footman was attempting to help him put on his coat. His arm was caught in the sleeve and he was trying without success to put it on. At the sight of me, he said to the foot-man, tersely, "Leave me."

With a nod, the footman departed. Darcy folded the coat over his arm, and stepped towards me. "It was not easy for me to come here," he said, his voice low, "knowing you had seen me that night outside your house. Honestly, Elizabeth, I thought you would have at least kept that to yourself."

He made for the door but I reached out and grabbed his forearm. My whole body tingled with the contact, and I wondered if he felt the same. "It did not start out as sport," I said, pleading. "Never would I have made it so. But my uncle——"

He flushed again.

I could see he was angry, and did not understand my indiscretion. "I wanted t-to talk about it with someone. I wanted to talk—to talk about you."

Looking at my hand still on his arm, he pulled away slowly. His forlorn eyes met mine, and my stomach twisted. "You need not worry. I shall not come around in that manner in the future."

He walked out the door, and though I wanted to chase after him, I let him go.

MUCH TO MY SURPRISE DARCY RETURNED THE NEXT DAY, AS it was Sunday, although there was an air of solemnity and hauteur about him. "The children expect me," he said as I let him in the door.

He avoided my gaze all day. I stayed away from their play, taking the opportunity to do a great deal of work about the house, yet I did so with an unexpected heaviness of heart. I would glance at him every so often and ache with the desire to talk to him—to apologise, to put things right, to enjoy his company—but he would not allow me that. Even if he had wanted to, the children kept him busy playing 'horse' in a variety of games, their favourite being knights and princesses. Alice was, of course, the damsel in distress.

We ate dinner, keeping our focus on the children, and went through the evening without a private word. After a long time of fussing, and asking for water and more stories, the children finally fell asleep. I invited him out front, for the days were lengthening such that it was still light out and the air seemed mild enough to enjoy for a few minutes at least. All the scents floating on the soft spring breeze were of renewal: grass, primroses, dew. An owl hooted and two doves cooed from across the orchard.

We stood looking out at the trees, which were coming back to life after the winter. "I have always enjoyed the springtime," he said.

"I have as well. The world is coming to life again. It is very…hopeful, is it not?"

He only nodded.

It was not as warm as I had wanted to believe, so I buttoned a few buttons on my coat. Even that was not enough, so I retrieved my scarf. As I wrapped it around my neck, it caught my hair, winding into a loose knot.

Darcy, seeing me struggle, pulled my hair out, and his hand brushed the back of my neck. I wanted nothing more than to take that hand and kiss it. My heart quickened at the thought and I looked away, fearing I would betray myself at any moment. Out of the corner of my eye, I noted him looking at me. He cleared his throat but said nothing, turning his gaze back to the trees.

My head began to throb so I took a few calming breaths, trying to ignore that we were standing so close that the heat of his arm radiated against mine.

I felt Darcy's little finger brush against mine. The touch was soft, tentative; it seemed to be apologetic or perhaps asking for permission. I did not trust myself to look at him still, but neither did I move my hand away.

A few moments later, he wrapped his fingers around mine. The size of his hand made mine feel small and delicate, and I was dizzy with the meaning of it. We stood staring ahead, hands entwined. I finally turned to look at him, taking in his pensive expression, his angular features softened by the fading spring light. His gaze met mine and a shock went through me. I shivered and squeezed his hand tighter, wanting him to know how welcome his touch was.

"Elizabeth." His voice was soft, with eyes that were hopeful and excited and wary. He bent, just slightly, and the scent of his musk teased my senses. I closed my eyes, waiting, waiting for the distance to close between us, for his lips to touch mine as I had dreamed about a thousand times. He caressed my cheek and his breath whispered across my face.

I heard a cry from inside the house.

My eyes flew open and Darcy snatched his hand back. I was still dizzy, imagining his lips on mine, and prayed we might resume our interrupted kiss. Another cry from within produced a low groan from Darcy.

All I wanted was to throw my arms around him and kiss him, ignoring the needs of anyone but ourselves, yet I had a duty. "I ought to…"

He nodded, wincing.

I reached out to touch his arm but pulled back, spinning on my heels and entering the house. Cursing under my breath, I marched to the children's room readying myself to console Henry but discovered that he had rolled over and gone back to sleep, untroubled. I leaned my head against the door-frame and chuckled quietly.

When I walked back to the sitting room, I stopped short, seeing Darcy standing by the fire. I could have easily allowed the broken moment to pass, blaming spring fever for our unconsidered—and likely ill-advised—behaviour. Perhaps that would have been wise.

I chose instead to ignore the voices of doubt that were telling me to be sensible. I joined him, hopeful, sure he would reach out for my hand again or try to kiss me. When he did not, I followed his gaze to the mantelpiece where James's pocket-watch rested.

"James's wife," he said. "You are James's wife."

"Once. Yes, I was his wife, and now I am his widow. For nearly ten months now. Darcy," I said, making him look at me. "He is gone now, never to return. I have made my peace with that and I hope you have too."

"I never should have…" He seemed to deflate as he

pulled away from me, his eyes seemingly drawn back to the watch as if it was James and not a timepiece witnessing our near-indiscretion. He backed away and then turned to pick up the hat he had set on a side table only minutes prior and walked towards the door.

"You are not leaving?" I asked, a hint of desperation in my voice.

"It would be imprudent of me to stay."

"Darcy, should we not discuss—"

"No," he said, his eyes drifting over my shoulder again to the object I now hated most in my house. "We should not."

The next morning, movement outside the sitting room window caught my eye. Darcy was approaching the front door. At his knock, Alice answered, squealed with delight, and leapt on him immediately. I had not slept that night, imagining the passionate kisses I both longed for and feared, and the feelings that filled me with both hope and dismay until I felt almost sick. I did not welcome his appearance just then, but he did not notice—or pretended not to—as he was surrounded by cries of "Uncle Darcy, watch this! Uncle Darcy, pick me up!"

"I know it is not my usual day to visit, but I came to say farewell. Pemberley is in need of my attention, and Georgiana's wedding needs planning."

"By her brother?" I asked, brows raised. He did not hear me over the cries of my children.

"No!" they all shouted, pulling at his coat and trousers. "Do not go, Uncle Darcy!"

"Children, I need to speak to Uncle Darcy outside."

"But—" Thomas frowned.

"Hush now," I said, my tone more harsh than I intended. My disappointment and fatigue were certainly going to make it a difficult day for us all.

With the door closed behind us, I stared at him, arms crossed, awaiting an explanation, something to right the situation. When he did not speak, I asked, "When will you return?"

"I do not know. Perhaps...perhaps never."

Had he struck me, it scarcely could have been more painful. "What?" It was as if all the air had been pushed out of me.

Tugging at the back of his neck, he said, "No. Not never, but...I do not know. It is too difficult to be so close and yet — This is impossible."

I began twisting the mourning ring I still wore on my index finger as I watched Darcy's face flicker with frustration and disappointment. And desire. I hoped I did not fool myself that desire for me still lay within him. "When did this begin for you?" I asked.

"I cannot fix on the hour, or the spot, or the look, or the words, which laid the foundation. It is too long ago. I was in the middle before I knew that I had begun." He drew in a melancholy breath. "I was not looking for love, but there you were. I cannot stop it, I cannot indulge it, so I must put distance between us and hope that time will heal this fever I have."

He turned and walked back into the house to say his goodbyes.

James had always frustrated me with his need to talk over our problems when I wished to sit silently with my thoughts. That would have been preferable just then— Oh, for James's fury and irrationality! I attempted to convince myself that that difference between the cousins, as well as my irritation at the moment, meant Darcy was not the man for me. I thought it might be convenience and loneliness that was pushing me into his arms, but when I walked back in and watched Darcy laughing while trying to break free of the children so he could be on his way, I knew what I wanted and it was him. Stubborn, honourable, kind, gentle, maddeningly rational—I wished for it all.

But I could not speak. I could not admit aloud to the feelings within me, or even feel worthy of them. I had waited too long and the moment was lost. He extricated himself from the children and moved to the door, pausing as if to say something. But I did nothing, and he said nothing. He bowed and strode out, leaving me desolate and filled with regret.

CHAPTER THIRTY-ONE

Preparing for Easter had always been a joyous time, and it came at a perfect moment for the children that year, as they would be with their family more. For me, it was another bittersweet reminder of life without James. And Darcy.

Jane found me standing alone with a cup of tea outside of Netherfield's largest parlour after the children had completed their egg rolls with the eggs they had taken such care to dye that week. The Gardiners' eldest had triumphed, dancing about at the bottom of the hill to the amusement of all, though Thomas insisted they play again.

"Jane, sit," I said. "You ought to rest so close to your confinement. You need your strength."

"I have more energy than I thought possible," she said, holding her protruding stomach. "But I shall heed your advice." She waved, and two servants brought out chairs for us both.

I marvelled at how easily she had adapted to being the mistress of a grand household, and doubted my own ability and interest in such a position. Perhaps I had landed where I was meant to be.

"You seem troubled," she said when we were settled.

I feared she had sensed my gloomy thoughts and shrugged, not desiring to speak of Darcy after the disaster which had ensued the last time I confided in someone.

"Are you thinking of James?"

"Some," I said, guilty that I was not thinking of him in the way she imagined.

"I cannot believe how well you have managed." I could not bring myself to lie, and when I kept my mouth shut, Jane continued. "I know you sought to leave home for a while."

My stomach dropped. "Who told you?"

"Uncle Gardiner. I discussed it with Charles, but we did not act quickly enough. I am terribly sorry."

"No need to apologise. I was grieving and in need of some rest, but I—"

"No, I do owe you an apology. I do not believe we did all we could, and I will never forgive myself for failing you in that regard." She wrung her hands, her cheeks pink.

"Jane, do not blame yourself. You had a new husband and a house to care for, and you have always been the good in my life. You have never ceased to bring me joy. And I have managed."

"What good fortune that Mr Darcy stepped in to help as he did," she said. "Have you heard from him since his return to Pemberley?"

I imagined his lips whispering against mine and my cup fell against the saucer with a clatter. "No. It would not be right for him to write to me, but he did send a note to the children wishing them a happy Easter."

"Lizzy, may I ask you something?"

I nodded.

"You have feelings for him, do you not?"

My eyes flicked to hers before I looked away, for fear that she would see the truth. Children laughed in the distance. "Is it so obvious?"

"Only to me. You are my sister and I know your mind nearly as well as my own. Sometimes better."

We were silent for a moment before she added, in her gently probing way, "He has feelings for you as well, it would seem."

I remembered the sensation of his warm breath on my face the night we nearly kissed. "Is it terrible of me? My husband has not been dead a year, and I am already in love with someone else." My words hung in the air. I pressed my fingertips to my lips as if that might undo my having spoken them. "I am at least ashamed of myself for it."

More joyful sounds from the garden filled the silence. My uncle's laugh. Henry's squeal. Alice's singing. I lingered on the outside of happiness.

Measuring her words, Jane said, "It is complicated, that is a certainty."

I thought again of the implications and possibilities. Darcy and I could decide to be together, constantly haunted by the memory of my dead husband. Or we might sort it out, only to be ostracised by our families or society. The worst possibility was Darcy coming to his senses and realising I was the last woman on earth he should ever be with, leaving me forever.

"Perhaps it is best that you are spending time apart."

Jane's kindly suggestion stung more than any censure could have. I wanted her to tell me that it did not matter, that I should follow my heart and not worry about others or about reason. "It seems Mr Darcy would agree," I said.

I rose and found my way back to the rest of the group, not feeling the least bit festive. Watching the happiness of others filled me with greater loneliness. Would I ever find joy for myself?

THE NEXT MORNING, I WAS BRUSHING CHICKEN COOP FILTH off some eggs when I heard voices in the yard. Lord Broxbourne was walking past the orchard with Mr Richards, a banker I knew from Meryton. I walked out to meet them.

They did not appear to notice my approach, and I heard Mr Richards say, "It will be worth quite a lot in the future, so to sell now would be foolish if the money is not needed right away."

"Good morning," I said, holding my hand over my eyes to block the rising sun.

"Oh, good morning, Elizabeth," said Lord Broxbourne, forcing a smile, the cheer in his voice out of character.

"May I help you?" I asked.

He puffed out his chest. "Not at all. We are managing quite well."

"What, may I ask, are you doing here at my house?" It sounded rude, so I added, "This early, that is. I was not expecting you today." Or ever, I forbore to say, though I could not recall him ever having visited.

"It was the only free time I had this week," said Mr Richards.

I took a few steps closer. "For what?"

"To see the land, of course, and make a recommendation." He was speaking to me like a silly child who did not quite understand the nature of his business.

"Make a recommendation about what?"

"The sale," he said, a bit of a laugh in his voice. When I did not respond, he sobered. "Of this land."

"You want to sell my land?"

"Well, this land here is...part of Broxbourne—" He looked at his lordship. "Is she aware of your plans?"

"My land?" I whispered.

"Well, Mrs Fitzwilliam, I must remind you it is not your land." Lord Broxbourne adjusted his waistcoat. "It is part of the estate and as it is not entailed, I am under no obligation to—"

"It was a wedding gift."

"The house, as you recall, was a gift from Mr Darcy, but the land under it was most certainly not," his lordship replied smoothly.

My breath caught. "How can that be?"

"James signed an agreement before the wedding that said if he vacated the land and we were still alive, the land would return to us."

"He did not vacate the land. He died!"

"Nevertheless," his lordship said, his voice tight, "he is no longer occupying this land, or the house."

I imagined young James, naive and trusting, as he signed the paper. Did he argue? Did he question? Did he think only of his commission and me, of building a family and securing a house for us all to live in? I looked at his father and felt my body burn. "Why would he have agreed to such a thing?"

"We did not offer him an alternative." Lord Broxbourne crossed his arms, his eyes now drifting down the path as if he wished to get on with the unpleasantness and depart. "We had to consider the possibility that he would run off with you to heaven knows where, and the land would end up in the hands of strangers."

"He loved this land," I said, my voice rising. "He never wanted to leave. Did you know him at all?"

"I knew him well enough before you came along," Lord Broxbourne said with a sniff.

"Before I came along? I was always here."

"Yes, you and that ridiculous family of yours."

"My lord," said Mr Richards, whose cheeks and ears were bright red by now, "let us not say things we shall regret." He wiped his neck with his kerchief, his face twitching with discomfort.

Lord Broxbourne kept his withering gaze on me. "I am simply reclaiming what has been in my family for generations, regardless of what this upstart thinks belongs to her. Elizabeth, the two of you were in such a predicament back then that there were no options. Lady Broxbourne and I offered James a piece of our land so he would not be destitute, yet he had the audacity to be offended by our stipulations. He was stubborn as always. Defiant. He said it did not matter what he signed, that the land would be his until the day he di—"

An uneasy silence fell upon us all.

I looked around, taking stock of the place James and I had shared. Quietly I said, "He was a soldier. You knew he could be killed. Surely you did not wish James's children, your grandchildren, to be taken from their home?"

Lord Broxbourne's lips thinned. "Your children are none of my concern. My eldest son has a male heir at last, and Broxbourne shall be his when he is of age."

I am sure I gasped. I had taken so many barbs and so much abuse over the years, but to this disavowal I had no reply. I might have nodded, or perhaps I did not, but I did walk away. Once inside the house, I shut the door and slid to the floor, my eyes drifting around the room: the couch where

James had rocked our children, the spot where Thomas had thrown a toy too hard and dented the wall, the hooks in the kitchen that James had secured so the pots we had scrimped and saved for could be displayed within easy reach. Seven years of memories. Our entire life together. The home we had created was about to be stolen by his own parents! I would have screamed and smashed every object in the place if it would not have terrified the children. Instead, I sat with my fear wondering what was to become of us.

CHAPTER THIRTY-TWO

Two days later, a letter was delivered. Though it would have been improper for him to write me directly, I still hoped it would be from Darcy. I was surprised to see Miss Turner's careful hand requesting I visit her, but to come without the children as she desired my full attention. Nora and Martha were accustomed to the little ones and did not mind, and the journey to the village on my own was delightful. Without constant interruptions, I was able to enjoy the singing of finches and the rustle of wind in the trees, and noted wildflowers on the side of the road I would pick on my way home to decorate our table.

Standing at her gate, all was just as it had been when I was a child. The cottage was made of rough-cut boards that had never been painted, unlike my house, which was yellow with black shutters. Once I asked why she had no shutters; she said she needed no adornments save for her garden—which was currently growing to the point of over-exuberance in every corner of her yard. My garden was modest and tidy, as was the interior of my house, whereas Miss

Taylor's home was cluttered with books, books, and still more books. Her cottage was even smaller than my modest house, with only one bedroom. One charming feature was a loft above the sitting room which, of course, contained more books. The loft was my favourite place when I was young, for large pillows rested on the floor and there was an overstuffed chair perfect for curling up on a rainy day to read.

I recalled the day my father left Jane and me at her house without so much as an explanation. His methods were unforgivable, but I would forever be thankful for their results. The thick scent of roses drew me in, reminding me of days devoted to learning so far in the past. Though I knew she did not care about appearances, I shook the dust off my skirt—still black, for I had no heart to go into half-mourning—and smoothed my hair before knocking on her rough-hewn door.

The expected click of the lock and creak of the hinge preceded her usual embrace. She drew me inside and gestured to my favourite chair—an overstuffed floral print chair that still had an orange stain where I had dropped jam over a decade earlier. Her roomy seat was leather, so worn from use that the arms and headrest had faded from dark brown to a pale sand. Potted plants hung from the ceiling at random intervals throughout the common spaces and sat on windowsills in every room. I reached out to stroke the leaves of a fern sitting atop a stack of books, and I smiled at the familiarity of it all.

After she had fussed about getting me tea and setting out Shrewsbury cake, the butteriness of which I had never been able to replicate, she settled down to talk. She asked after my children, but it was clear that she had brought me there for a particular purpose, and it was not social.

She set aside her teacup with a little clatter and offered a serene smile. "My dear, I am dying."

"What?" My eyes filled with tears. So this was why she had invited me to tea after so long an absence.

"No, no, do not cry," she said, reaching out a hand to pat mine. "I am old and it is my time. Not like your James."

This only made me cry harder. She rubbed my shoulder, cooing that I should not be distressed. When I had collected myself, I was able to say, "But how? Surely not?"

"People grow old and sick. My heart is giving out on me, it seems," she said with a little wheeze. "I shall die. And soon, I hope."

"You hope?"

"Since the end is sure to come, may it be swift and painless."

I could see the toll the conversation was taking on her after a few sentences. I knelt at her feet, grasping her hand. "I cannot bear to lose you."

"Yes, it seems loss is coming to you too often these days." She stroked my hair—she, who ought to have been receiving my comfort and condolences, was instead comforting me. "But, my dear, this is not why I have called you here today. Not exactly."

I pressed my lips to her knuckles. "Please tell me there is no more bad news."

"Bad is such a weak word. Do not I deserve *tragic* or *heart-breaking* at least?"

I sniffed. "Yes, of course. Please, not more star-crossed —no, excoriating—news."

"Excoriating? Not entirely accurate, but I like the sentiment."

I squeezed her hand, too upset to smile as I know she would have wanted.

"I want you to have my house."

"Your house?" Why me? How could it be mine if she lived in it? But she was dying. No, I could not accept a world in which Miss Taylor did not exist, and I could not accept an entire house as a gift!

She lifted my chin with her finger. "You should be beholden to no one. I heard about those miserable, cold-hearted Broxbournes and how they robbed you of your domicile."

"Where did you hear that?" I had told no one—not even Jane or my uncle—as if not speaking of it could make the situation less real. The loss of my house was so profound that I needed to mourn it on my own for a bit more. Eventually I would tell my family. They would express outrage, and they would offer to have us move onto one of their estates or secure us another property. It would all be well intentioned, but I could not face it. Not yet. I still could not believe I was to lose my house—the one made into a home with attention and care and filled with love.

"How did I hear?" Miss Taylor reached for her tea and sipped. "I have my sources." She stopped to catch her breath. "You cannot stay on their land a moment longer—do not wait for them to sell it out from under you. I will not need mine for long, so you must come and live here. Make an old woman happy to know she has righted a wrong even in her last days."

The facts had come so rapidly that it took a moment to think the matter through. "Why me?"

"You were always my bravest pupil and truest of heart. A wasted literary kindred spirit, if you ask me, spending your life buried in drab domesticity. A shame." I opened my mouth to respond, but she held up a hand. "Not to say you did not make the right choice. If I had married and had children, I would not be alone at this time. Being alone in life can be delightful, but facing death alone is a fearful thing, to be certain. So you see, I am alone and in need." She pressed a hand to her chest and, from the rattle, it became clear how difficult breathing was for her. "The property is free and clear. I paid for it years ago. 'Neither a borrower nor a lender be'. Everyone laughs at Polonius, yet there is such wisdom in his dithering. Ah, I digress."

She drew another laboured breath. "In return for this house, land, and, of course, my extraordinary library, I require some caring for in my last days."

She said 'caring for' with her hand set theatrically against her forehead, yet I knew her words to be true. She sobered and took my hands in hers. They were cold despite the mild day, the wrinkled skin soft to the touch.

"I might linger for a while. It will add to your burden, I know, but in the end you will have a home, and I will not have to die alone." Her rapidly blinking eyes betrayed the lightness of tone she had maintained during the conversation.

I rose and threw my arms around her, noting she was more frail than the last time we had embraced. Fighting back more tears, I said into her neck, "I will do it. Even if there were no house, I would help you."

"Good." She patted my back and I released her, returning to my chair. "And since there *is* a house, I shall draw up a new will and be certain all is in order for you to inherit what is mine." She stopped, the wheezing more powerful. "My dear, you will never be beholden to anyone once I am gone."

"Thank you. I will do anything I can for you."

"Just promise me that you shall bury me with Balzac and

Wollstonecraft. I would like something bawdy and something romantic to accompany me to the hereafter."

I nodded and smiled through my tears.

"And one thing more: leave the house to your daughters
so they may never be in need of a place to live or be forced
to marry to keep a roof over their heads."

And so it was that I backed into an answer to my troubles. After leaving, my mind was so occupied that I forgot to
pick any wildflowers, or even notice the birds or the sky. If I
was to care for Miss Taylor starting the next day as we had
agreed, what would become of the children? The cottage
was small—too small for seven of us to move in while Miss
Taylor needed quiet. She claimed to welcome the noise of
children, but I did not believe she realised how loud the four
could get. Additionally, with her books and teacups and
plants everywhere, they were certain to knock things over,
especially the twins. Those two would also be tempted by
the ladder to the loft without the ability to navigate the
rungs safely. No, it would not do. And yet, as I planned to
stay both day and night with Miss Taylor, my children
needed more care than Nora and Martha could offer at my
house.

I changed routes and walked to Longbourn. Margaret
and my uncle received me in the parlour, reacting with
expected fury to the news of the Fitzwilliams selling the
land. Once I explained the situation with Miss Taylor, they
offered any assistance required. If my children stayed at
Longbourn, I could visit with them each day or bring one or
two to the cottage for a short time. The Gardiners had
enough staff that the childrens' presence would not be too
much of a burden. Martha would remain at the estate, and
Nora would stay with me at the cottage, allowing for me to

leave Miss Taylor with a companion when I was required to depart.

I had no answer to how long it would be until the Fitzwilliams cast me out of my house, but I decided to prepare for our departure as soon as possible. On my walk from Longbourn, I made a mental inventory of what could fit into the cottage and what could not, deciding to ask Jane and the Gardiners if they could store most of the furniture.

IT WAS SCARCELY A FORTNIGHT AFTER I MOVED IN THAT MISS Taylor died—in her honour, I shall say instead 'shuffled off this mortal coil'—but it was with joy that her spirit was released. I was reading aloud from Balzac when Miss Taylor held up a hand for me to stop and then pointed to her ear— she had weakened so much that she could not speak. Giggling floated through the cracked window. Thomas and Alice were in the back with Nora chasing the chickens, which they found great fun and Miss Taylor considered charming. Then she squeezed my hand and closed her eyes for the last time.

It was the kind of death that James deserved but did not receive, yet I had been at his side as well. I had held him as he slipped away; he had not been alone on a battlefield or in a rudimentary hospital across the sea. Our final months together were among our most peaceful. I was grateful for that as well.

It was time to let the horror of his last moments go, to let James go, to let everything go. I would remember the past only as it gave me pleasure, and turn my thoughts to raising my children and enjoying the new life that stretched ahead of us. Perhaps, one day, I could find love again. I had found it in Darcy, but it had not found me in return. I could only hope next time I would be more fortunate, but time would tell. Either way, I could be content as Miss Taylor had been content, finding joy in solace, simplicity, and an abundance of good books.

She was gone, but I was not yet ready to alert Dr Thrup or the undertaker, or even Nora and the children, who had grown to love her too. I held her hand, considering the past years. As Miss Taylor's pupil, I had been a wild child—abandoned by my mother, restless, full of anger at the world. Being considerate had once eluded me, whether it was helping with menial kitchen tasks or arriving on time, in favour of losing myself in reading or a walk through the woods. Now I took great pleasure in making the lives of others smoother. Happier. I had more than just Jane to fill my life and, while having the affection of Jane and Miss Taylor had made my youth tolerable, now I had many whom I cared for and who cared for me. She had taught me so many lessons, many of which I was only comprehending now. I owed her a great debt for teaching me the beauty of words, for teaching me patience, love, compassion, and generosity. I would do all I could to honour her legacy.

I do not believe she would have been surprised or cared overmuch that few came to pay their respects. I arranged for her to be buried with her requested books, ignoring the quizzical looks of the vicar. After everyone left, I slipped into the cemetery to strew wildflowers on her grave, and promised her that one day my children would learn to weep over Juliet's funeral bier, whether it was a kitchen table or a riverbank.

CHAPTER THIRTY-THREE

With Miss Taylor gone, I was at liberty to make the house my own. It was bittersweet but necessary work. My uncle had a structure built behind the cottage to store her books. At first I objected to the idea of moving them outside, but he assured me his design would keep them dry, and that his builders were skilled. Before it was finished, the children had attempted to pick their way around the books, but sent them spilling and crashing all too often. I spent hours after the little ones were abed sorting and stacking. I did not have the heart to throw any away, and the shed became a remarkable library in the end—one I would visit every so often just to feel more connected to Miss Taylor.

Most of our belongings would not fit in the house. I brought my own bed, some kitchen tools and pans, mattresses for the children, and our dining table and chairs, but the rest were stored at Netherfield and Longbourn. I retained Miss Taylor's overstuffed chairs, too sentimental to let them go. The children wanted to keep all the plants inside, but just as with the books, I preferred less clutter. I left a few on the windowsills of the sitting room and kitchen, and we moved the rest outside. Sally would go out to visit the plants, talking to them as if they were pets, but eventually gave up the habit.

Clearing out Miss Taylor's clothes gave me pause, as it was the most personal of the tasks. I kept a few shawls and scarves, as well as her spectacles; the rest went to the church for charity. It was less painful and fraught than when James's belongings needed sorting after his death. Thomas had entered my bedroom as I placed his clothing into crates, and asked why I was erasing his father. The question had stopped my breath. It had been a month, which seemed long enough to me, but not to him. I brought Thomas to the bed where I had placed James's uniform, one pair of dress boots, and three waistcoats. "The boots and uniform will be yours someday, if you would like them," I said, running my hand along the red fabric of James's coat. "Uncle Bingley promised to take great care with them until you are old enough. Your brother and sisters will get one waistcoat each. Does that seem satisfactory?"

Little Thomas nodded, brow furrowed, then reached into a crate to pull out a cravat. "May I keep this?"

"Of course." I invited Alice to pick something to save of her father's. She had chosen his hairbrush and used it every day. The twins would not remember James, and I hoped the waistcoats would be enough.

My children had little connexion to Miss Taylor, and none wanted to keep anything of hers except for the books —written for children—we had chosen to keep inside. Those they treasured.

The cottage, bare of the piles of books and plants, felt

naked—but it was far easier to move about and soon became truly ours.

The Gardiners came for tea, and my uncle brought news that my mother was in Meryton. "She would like to come see you."

My stomach seized. "Why?"

He shrugged. "She is ageing. Perhaps feeling guilty? I would never presume to understand my sister."

The next day, I was gripped with apprehension as she approached. She was my mother, such as she was, and I still desired her approval. "Lovely to see you," I said, not sure I believed my own words.

There was warmth in her eyes, with none of the defensive emptiness of our early conversations. "What a magnificent garden!"

I recalled she had a fondness for nature, much as I.

I let her through the gate and gestured to the front door. "Miss Taylor was rather skilled. I hope not to ruin her fine work."

Once inside, she said, "What a stroke of luck to inherit a house." Then she crossed her arms, the cheer fading from her face. "Your father left you nothing and I…well, I have given you nothing but pain."

When I was younger, I would have told her the truth or yelled at her. I would have wanted to add to her agony, to make it clear that her choices had wounded me. I no longer needed such satisfaction.

"At least someone—" Her voice broke and she cleared her throat. "At least someone gave you something real. And love. This woman loved you?" I nodded and she looked out the windows. "Good. Good." She smiled at the riot of flowers and vines which covered the fence and crept around the house. Then she turned and looked at the kitchen.

"It is not large," I said, "but it suits us and no one can take it away from us. The children are satisfied, as am I."

"Children will adapt to anything."

I felt once again like I ought to say something meaningful, or at least reply, but all I could manage was to show her the few rooms in which we lived. I hope I did not fool myself that I had fitted it up prettily.

"It is very sweet," she said, running her hand along a bookshelf. "Perfect for a young woman like you."

"Like me?"

"Independent. Strong."

"Strong-willed?" I asked with a faint smile.

"No. Just strong."

I stood, every muscle tight, waiting to hear more. "I could flatter myself and say that my leaving made you stronger, but that would be a lie. I left. You thrived in spite of me. In spite of your father. As parents, we were lacking."

I rocked back on my heels.

"Nevertheless, you need another husband." She let her eyes drift the length of my black dress. "Not too soon, but do not wait too long, either. You are still young and pretty. Remarkable that you have kept your figure after so many children. There might still be a man willing to have you. Be sure he is wealthy. And that you are given money in a will, not like what happened with Colonel Fitzwilliam, may he rest in peace. That family! Always vindictive. Poor characters all around. And the scandal of the sister. My, my, after the judgment Lady Broxbourne passed on you, well, what a comeuppance!"

I let out a sigh, not wishing to traffic in gossip with a woman whom I had not seen in years.

She pressed her lips together. "You look exhausted. I ought to take my leave." She paused as if waiting for me to disagree. "I know I have no right to ask, but would you—I mean, could you consider—I would like to know my grand-children a little."

I laced my fingers together and pulled, the familiar strain that helped to focus me. "Why now? I asked you before and you re—" I pushed down the anger. "Yes, but truly, Mother, why now?"

She shrugged. "I have had ample time to question myself and admit how horrid I am." She picked up one of Alice's drawings and studied it. "I do not deserve to know you or them, but they deserve a grandparent and have none. Might I be that grandparent to them? And might I get to know you, as well?"

She set down the drawing but I lifted it from the table and handed it back to her. It was true that they had rela-tions, but no true grandparents. I had not known mine and always considered it a loss. "My children do need more people," I said at last. "You may be part of their lives. As for our relationship, well, we shall see."

I was deciding whether to invite her to stay when she declared she would be moving on. "I planned a short visit, not knowing how you might take my request."

I nodded and walked her back outside to the gate. As we neared, she declared, "I will endeavour to spend time with the children. As long as you or a servant is near—I simply cannot imagine caring for all four of them at once!"

I bit my lip to keep from laughing and opened the garden gate. I saw my uncle coming down our little lane with Bingley, and my mother exclaimed her greetings more loudly than was appropriate. I greeted my uncle and Bing-ley. "I was not expecting to see either of you today."

"We have come bearing a letter from Darcy," Bingley

said, his usual cheer dimmed, which gave me pause. What could the letter say? Was he ill? Never to return?

"Mr Darcy?" exclaimed my mother. "A proud, disagreeable man, though he does have ten thousand a year!"

My uncle offered his sister an elbow to escort her away. As they walked, I could still hear my mother prattling. "Of course, Mr Bingley is his dear friend, is he not? How such a gentleman as Mr Bingley could keep company with such a man as that, I cannot comprehend it."

Once they were safely out of view, I asked if all was well with Darcy.

"Yes," Bingley said, his manner somewhat hesitant. "Lizzy, was there some understanding between you before he left?"

I shook my head, recalling the night we nearly kissed.

"Did he express—I thought to send your sister to speak to you, but Jane was with the children and so... No matter. She told me I could enquire, and so here I am. Lizzy, how have you left things with Darcy?"

I sank down on a bench in my garden, unable to explain, for I did not know. So many ups and downs had plagued Darcy and me. Attraction drew us together, even as prudence forced us apart.

Bingley handed me the letter. "I shall leave you to make of this what you will. The pertinent part begins on page two." I ran my fingertip along Darcy's writing, tracing the letters. Bingley added, "I shall go see your children for a moment."

I gave an absent nod, and thought of Darcy's light touch when he had grasped my fingers, tentative at first, then more confident. I thought of the anticipation in his eyes as he leaned in for a kiss that I would have gladly returned. I ached for him, even as I felt a pang of guilt at my desire.

No. I had to cease such foolishness. I would not apologise for finding such a man attractive, for wanting to touch and be touched. It was natural.

I turned to the second page, as instructed.

Plans for Georgiana's wedding are coming along apace, and her joy increases my own. She has endured much loneliness, and I am relieved that her days alone shall soon end.

I am sorry to hear of the passing of Miss Taylor, and sorrier still that my aunt and uncle have treated Elizabeth so abominably. My deepest desire was to negotiate with them on her behalf. However, by the time I had word of her predicament, she had already dispatched her family to Miss Taylor's. I do wish you had informed me of her mistreatment sooner, though I am certain she would not have desired my assistance. It is a quality I admire in her, and yet it leaves me unable to rescue her, which is a great pleasure of mine, it seems. I am relieved to learn from you that Elizabeth finds her current living situa-tion agreeable, but I assure you the matter is not at an end. She is a remarkable woman and I find myself unable to think of anything but working for her peace and for her joy.

Not hearing her voice—I say too much. My hope is to return to Meryton as expeditiously as possible. However long or short, the time shall pass too slowly.

- F. D.

THAT HE CONFESSED SUCH FEELINGS SO FREELY TO BINGLEY surprised me, and I wondered what had been said in other letters or shared confidences.

Not hearing her voice. Heavens! Was it true? Did he miss me? It was clear he had. Did we have an understanding? Not yet, but I felt light-headed, the change from resignation to hope sudden and dizzying. Despite my indiscreet mother and drunken, bankrupt father, despite my lack of refinement and awareness of social graces, despite the misstep that led to my being entangled with James, Darcy loved me. As a mother. As a friend. As myself. I was enough. I never thought I would find someone who did not wish to change me. No, Darcy said that I transformed *him*, that I allowed him to be freer, to be more himself. Together we could thrive and live fully. What I wanted more than anything was him, and somehow he found me worthy of his affection and admiration. I would be forever grateful to him for that.

The thought brought happy tears to my eyes, and I reread his message, exclaiming, "Oh why is he not here even now!"

He would return to Meryton as soon as possible. When he did, I would not let him go again.

Except…except that his family hated me. Not Georgiana, but the Fitzwilliams. Lady Snowley also hated me. They could convince many in society not to accept us. How would he manage? Darcy was so sensitive—the very quality I loved most in him would be our greatest impediment. Could his love for me be greater than all of that?

CHAPTER THIRTY-FOUR

T he fair was upon us once again, but this time its arrival was met with solemnity. The older children were aware of the significance of the day, but asked to attend regardless. Sally and Henry, who knew their father had died that day, had not been told of the details, and so looked forward to the fair with great anticipation. Jane and my uncle thought that going was madness, but I refused to deprive the children of the one entertainment Meryton offered each year.

I sat once again watching our children play in the shade of the willow tree, only this year I did not feel serene. Jane, recovered from the birth of her daughter and recently churched, had been eager to venture away from Netherfield. She put her arm around me and we sat in silence. My thoughts were so chaotic I could not have explained them if she had asked, though Jane rarely intruded on my quiet.

I passed the afternoon listening to music, while others took the children to the booths. I chose not to go with them. My legs trembled on our way in, and I could not manage another pass by the spot where Mr Wickham had killed my husband until it was necessitated by our return home.

Many acknowledged our loss, memorably tied to this day. Some murmured condolences while others merely nodded, their brows knitted. Dr Thrup surveyed the group, bowed to me, and shook my uncle's hand before walking away. I was relieved that he did not tarry.

A shadow fell upon our blanket and I looked up to see the tall, elegant form of Darcy. It took all of my effort not to leap into his arms in front of everyone. I checked my face as best I could, wishing to remain impassive to anyone looking on.

"Mr Darcy!" Jane held out a hand and he helped her to her feet.

He reached for my hand to assist me as well, and when our skin touched, I almost fainted. I breathed deeply to avoid the spectacle, and allowed him to lift me to my feet.

As I remained silent, Jane continued, "We were not expecting to see you before Georgiana's wedding."

"No, but I felt drawn... This being the anniversary—" His fingers drifted to his ribs, and I knew he had to be thinking of a year ago when Mr Wickham stomped on him, desiring to draw blood. "Additionally, it was past time I came to speak to my aunt and uncle about the situation with the house."

Finding my voice, I asked, "You will not do so today, will you?" Much as I hated them, it would be poor form on the anniversary of their son's death.

"I already did. They have offered money to repay the costs I incurred building the house," he said bitterly. "I explained it was not the money, but the principle."

"How did you leave it?" Jane asked.

Jaw clenched, he looked at the crowd around us. "The

conversation, as you can imagine, did not go well. We are at an impasse." Outrage burned from his eyes.

I hugged my arms across my chest as if that gesture might protect me from James's family.

"Will they be at the wedding?"

He nodded. "It would not be right to disinvite them."

I cared not for their feelings, but they were no longer my cross to bear.

We chatted until the sun hovered above the tree-line, at which time Darcy asked if anyone would accompany him to James's grave, and my uncle, Bingley, and I agreed. Jane and Margaret, with the assistance of a few servants, would take the children to their respective homes. Though I wished to be almost anywhere else, it seemed the proper way to mark the occasion. The swish of my skirt and the thud of our feet on dry mid-summer earth filled the silence between us. A frog lurked somewhere in the shadows, announcing itself with an odd, low-pitched croak, like the unoiled hinge of a door swinging slowly in a breeze.

We entered the churchyard and stopped as the family monument came into view. I felt a chill and longed to reach for Darcy, but refrained.

A small bouquet of flowers rested at the foot of the marble door. "Your aunt?" I asked, an image sad enough for me to pity her.

"More likely Lady Mary. She is a thoughtful soul, and one who is comforted by ritual."

"Ought we to say something?" asked Bingley.

We all looked at each other.

My uncle said, "If one of them had to die, it is a relief that it was James rather than Mr Wickham."

That had certainly not been said before. I held my tongue, willing myself to consider his words before reacting.

Taking in our horror, my uncle looked at us with raised eyebrows as if to be sure we understood. "Killing a man changes a person. I believe the guilt would have eaten away at him."

I touched the spot on my wrist where James had bruised me all those years ago. "I believe it did. He was so haunted whenever he returned home from battle."

"Those were soldiers. Killing in combat is—I suspect this might have been worse." Uncle Gardiner rocked on his heels. "We shall never know," he added, and walked away. Bingley followed him to the lane.

I stood amazed at how strange this day had been, and sauntered a few steps after them. Darcy walked up beside me and took my hand, tugging me to a stop. He watched the others disappear around the bend, and whispered, "Elizabeth, may I speak to you a moment?" His gaze drifted towards the grave.

"What are you doing?" I asked, pulling back.

"Elizabeth, you must allow me to tell you how much I ardently admire and love you."

"What? Darcy, not here. Surely not here."

"Yes, here. Can you not feel the power of this place, of this day? It must be here because I want to have James's blessing when I ask for your hand in marriage." I gasped as he took both my hands in his. "There lies James. He cannot be a husband or a father anymore. He cannot be a son or a brother or a cousin. He can no longer give you the love you deserve. But I can. I can and I want to with all my heart, if only you will allow me to do so."

I began to shiver. Of all days, of all places. I could not calm myself enough to remember how Darcy made me feel, could not relish the fact that he was holding my hands, or that he had just asked me to marry him. There was too much within me to form rational thoughts or sensible words. I could not breathe. "Darcy, I—"

"Do you love me, my dearest, loveliest Elizabeth?"

"That is not the question."

"It is."

"No, for it matters not with the impediments before us," I said. "The question is how you will feel when people speak of us, which they will! The gossip will be fierce. Your family will despise us, slight us."

"I do not care about those people."

"You do. I know too well that you do. Your reputation is at risk. You care what others think of you."

"I care only inasmuch as I do not wish to risk Georgiana's happiness. Such impediments are not nearly enough to sacrifice my own happiness. I did that once in marrying Anne. I shall not make that error again." He bent slightly to look into my eyes. "You and James taught me I could be free. I wish to be my truest self. I wish to live out my days loving you no matter the obstacles before us. Together we may conquer them all."

I reached out to caress his handsome, expectant face, unable to believe this moment was real. "Are you certain?"

He nodded. "I love you, Elizabeth. You make me laugh. You make me think. You make me realise that I need not hold myself so tight and follow only what others expect of me. You are so clever and kind. I shall never be lonely or bored with you. What more could a man ask for than to admire the woman with whom he spends his days? And nights." He blushed. "What more could I ask for than to love and to be loved in return?" He paused. "You do love me, do you not?"

I threw myself into his arms. "Yes. Yes! I love you, Darcy. I have loved you for longer than I dared say!"

He held me tighter, and I pressed my lips to his neck, lingering for a moment to take in his scent. He let out a low groan and I stepped back, my eyes flicking to the tomb. I skittered out of his grasp. "Perhaps we could continue this conversation elsewhere."

He gave a perfunctory bow to the tomb, a gesture that made me smile. As we walked away, he asked, "Ought we to tell them about the engagement?"

"Not yet," I murmured, attempting to steady myself.

We joined Bingley and my uncle around the side of the church, and Darcy expressed a desire to look at my new home.

"Bingley, accompany us?" Darcy suggested, for it would be more proper for us to be chaperoned. While laughable, given how often we were alone with only Nora or another servant at my old house, Miss Taylor's—my—cottage was in the village, and I knew we would be more exposed there.

"Jane is expecting my imminent return—" Bingley was as artless as ever, but soon apprehended the meaning of the fierce scowl his friend shot him. "That is, of course I should be glad to accompany you."

Upon our arrival, the children would not unhand Darcy, making it more difficult for him to manoeuvre through the small space, and the scant rooms meant the tour was finished in moments. Even so, he declared it charming.

Almost immediately, Darcy removed his tail-coat and shoes to play bear, the twins' favourite game, for it meant he transformed his fingers into pretend claws and lashed out at their squealing frames until they raced for cover behind me. I prepared cake and tea, and called out warnings when they came too close to the stove.

At length, Bingley insisted he must depart. "Surely with

Nora here, there is no impropriety?" Nora curtseyed to him, and he nodded.

Darcy looked at me, seeking my permission to remain. I suspected it was both to ensure I was comfortable with this arrangement, and to see if I was yet ready to announce our engagement. To answer both, I said, "Bingley, I shall call with the children tomorrow, if you would find that agreeable."

"Visits from you are always agreeable, dear Lizzy." He bowed and kissed my hand, then bade farewell to Darcy and the children.

The sky grew dark, and the children demanded to be tucked in by Uncle Darcy. Alice asked for a story about her father. Thomas punched her when she asked to hear about how he died, and I had to remove him for a scolding and then a consoling. Instead, Darcy shared a story of the wildlife adventures he had shared with James: their hunting journeys, fishing expeditions, and even a tale of a cow that once passed wind right in James's face.

The children shrieked with laughter. That one would be told and retold for months amongst the children.

I suggested it was time for Darcy to depart and blew out their bedside candles before escorting him to the garden gate.

"How was Easter?" I asked, unaccountably overcome by nerves and endeavouring to avoid talk of anything serious.

"Uneventful," he said. "Quiet, really. How was the egg roll? Did Thomas win?"

I shook my head. "Not this time."

"And did they spell out names on their eggs?"

James and Darcy had always used crayons to write letters on eggs and the dye stuck only around the wax, a tradition James brought to our home.

"We did not do it."

"No? That is disappointing," he said. "The children must have missed it."

I sighed. "They missed many things, but they enjoyed themselves."

"I wanted to return," he said, his voice flat, "but you—I did not know what to do about you."

I bit back a laugh. "Do you know now?"

"I thought our discussion in the graveyard answered that." He caressed my cheek, pinning me with his gaze. Those eyes. His eyes pulled me in as always and I wanted to swim in them.

"Good night," I said with a smile, not certain how long I could control myself.

He studied me, amusement—or was it desire?—playing across his face. "Yes. Goodnight." He bowed before unlatching the gate.

I could not let him go. "Darcy!"

He turned back, brows raised. His very look made my heart flutter.

I laughed at myself, and searched for something appropriate to say. "I merely wished to ask if Georgiana had found the right lace to trim her wedding bonnet? She wrote to me in a dither, and I wished to be certain she was satisfied."

"She was, indeed, satisfied." All humour drained away, his face so full of yearning that it frightened me.

"Good. So…goodnight again."

I turned to leave, but Darcy caught my arm, drawing me towards him. My hand brushed against the soft cotton of his shirt, and I stilled. His warmth seeped into my fingers and my gaze drifted from his bright eyes to his mouth, his crooked smile making my stomach quiver. My breath caught.

He bent down and kissed me. It was the gentlest, softest kiss I ever recall receiving. He pulled back slightly, a myriad of emotions flickering across his face. I let my fingers stray until I was holding his back as firmly as he had held mine. He leaned in and kissed me again. I had expected this kiss to be more urgent, but it was as delicate as the first, as if I were a vision he feared would vanish. We moved apart and gazed at one another, both smiling now.

"I have wanted to do that for so long," he said.

This man looked at me with all of the adoration I could ask for, and for a moment it frightened me. Surely I was not worthy of such devotion? But he smiled at me, and tucked my hair behind my ear, and let his fingers trace the loose strands down my shoulders. Perhaps I was not worthy of his adoration, but I would accept it just the same and return it in equal if not greater measure.

I stepped back, choosing prudence over desire. "Darcy, if you spend enough time with me, you might realise that I am trouble."

"I knew you were trouble when you smashed into me at that hunting lodge, and again at the ball."

"Did you admire me for my impertinence?"

"For your daring and the liveliness of your mind, I did. I still do."

"I am in love with you. If you knew when I understood it, you would be ashamed of me."

"I would not"—he smirked—"for well do I know how irresistible I am."

I laughed, glancing down the road to be sure no one was passing and seeing our casual conversation.

He lingered at the gate, waiting, I think, for another kiss, but I bade him goodnight.

"I love you, Fitzwilliam Darcy," I whispered, to which he clutched his heart and beamed before sauntering away.

I hurried into the house. Nora grinned at me from the kitchen, which had a perfect view out the front window. Holding in a laugh, I picked up a doll Alice had left on a side table and tossed it playfully at her. "Not a word," I said, shaking my finger.

"Not even to say he is terribly dashing, and that I wish you two all the happiness in the world?"

"Ah, yes. Those words will do." And with that, I fairly floated down the hall to bed, unable to sleep with thoughts of the day that had brought surprise after surprise, and a proposal from Darcy at last.

CHAPTER THIRTY-FIVE

My children, having never left Hertfordshire, were enchanted by the lengthy journey to Derbyshire for Georgiana's wedding, made bearable only by the luxury of the carriage that Darcy had sent. On the third day, I watched for signs of Darcy's lands with increased anticipation. At last, the coachman announced we had entered Pemberley Woods. We turned at a lodge and ascended nearly half a mile. Where the woods ceased, we saw Pemberley House. Thomas gasped. Alice squealed, "It's a castle!"

And I chuckled. I actually laughed aloud. It was large, and elegant, the most beautiful, stately, perfect house I had ever seen. And it was Darcy's. I knew he had riches, but until this moment, I did not quite realise the extent of it. Here was my family, fresh from a cottage we could hardly move through without bumping into one another, about to enter the grandest place I had ever seen.

"You must behave yourselves when we arrive," I said. "There shall be things of great value and you must—"

"Be quiet and act like little ladies and gentlemen," all four said in unison.

I smiled and touched each of their cheeks before looking back out the window. The handsome stone building stood aside a natural stream, and was backed by wooded hills. I had never seen a place for which nature had done more.

The servants lined up to greet us, and we were each helped down in turn. Alice stood like a perfect lady: head tall, hands at her side, the image of Jane. The little ones reached for my hands, and together we moved forward as Darcy approached with a warm hug for each one of them and a bow to me. I curtseyed, smiling at the formality of it, and wondered if this was for the benefit of his servants or whether the grandeur of the place inspired the change in his behaviour.

"What think you of Pemberley?" he asked. Thomas jumped up and down with glee and Alice, breaking with decorum, placed her hands on her cheeks and twirled. "The children approve. And you, Mrs Fitzwilliam?"

My eyes darted to the perfect line of servants staring straight ahead, their uniforms crisp and immaculate. "Elizabeth," I said, my voice pitched low. "Let us not alter ourselves."

He took my hand, kissing it. "As you wish." Then he clapped. "Come, children! Let me show you my house." He swept Henry into his arms as if the three-year-old had not grown so heavy I could not manage him easily during a tantrum.

Two servants opened the doors and the extent of the grandeur became apparent. We were surrounded by sweeping stairs and painted ceilings, intricately carved rails and a chandelier as large as my kitchen. I battled the urge to laugh again. It was by far the most beautiful place I had been in my life.

"This is the great hall," he said, lowering Henry to the floor, who began racing Thomas almost immediately. I ordered them to stop, but Darcy shrugged, unconcerned that the boys' tumbling could topple one of the many priceless urns along the way. "Pemberley has missed the laughter of children for far too long."

As we walked, I took note of the portraits, wondering which relations were represented. The boys sprinted back at us, barrelling into Darcy, much to his delight.

A respectable looking elderly woman approached, trailed by four young maids. Darcy introduced the oldest as Mrs Reynolds. "My dear and most trusted housekeeper."

She beamed with pleasure at such an introduction." Shall I show your young guests to their rooms?" she asked kindly, but with an urgency I imagined she used to convince not only the staff but also Darcy of pressing matters.

Darcy looked at me and I nodded. "Children, we shall join you later. Follow Mrs Reynolds and the nursemaids to your rooms."

"Nursemaids?" I gasped. "How many did you hire for the week?"

"Seven." He laughed. "You, Jane, and Mrs Gardiner have quite a lot of children, and I desired you all to enjoy the festivities unencumbered."

"Did Jane and Margaret not bring their own nursemaids?"

"One each to assist with routines."

I nodded, marvelling at how strange it all was. I had known him only within my own context and would now need to learn his ways here, in his world.

We walked on a few paces before he turned to me. "Your dress is beautiful, Elizabeth. What a remarkable change it is to see you in colour once again."

I looked down at the cheerful yellow gown, one of five new gowns Jane had insisted on to commemorate the end of my period of mourning. It felt odd to indulge in fashion again, but it reminded me of what I was. I was yet a young woman and it felt good and right to behave as one, walking side by side with my handsome suitor.

We entered the saloon, whose northern aspect rendered it delightful for summer. Its windows opened to the ground, admitting a most refreshing view of the high woody hills behind the house, and of the beautiful oaks and sweet chestnut trees, which were scattered over the intermediate lawn.

"This house is extraordinary," I said at last, and he took my hand in his, relaxed and beaming as we walked on.

He seemed impervious to the witnesses, servants though they were, who stood at each end of the saloon, and I took it as a promising indication that perhaps he was not as rigid a man away from my home as I had feared he might be. "Pemberley was my late mother's passion. She oversaw its design and decoration, highlighting generations of heirlooms and family portraits."

On reaching the spacious lobby above, we entered a pretty sitting room, fitted up with greater elegance and lightness than the apartments below. "This room was just refitted by Georgiana," he said. It was brighter and devoid of the grave painted faces of Darcys and de Bourghs, for which I was grateful.

We walked on and, at his nod, a servant threw open the doors to a final room on the hall. Books of various sizes, inscribed with gold lettering and bound in every imaginable jewel tone, lined the shelves, which reached as high as the thirty-foot ceiling. There were rolling ladders and fixed ladders, globes and maps, stuffed birds and stuffed chairs.

"What a delightful library you have!" I exclaimed, thinking of how Miss Taylor's collection, small in comparison, had recently overwhelmed me.

"It ought to be good," he said, turning in a circle. "It has been the work of many generations."

"And then you have added so much to it yourself. You are always acquiring books."

"I cannot comprehend the neglect of a family library in such days as these."

I wondered if he was referring to me—for I had had no time for books while I was married to James, or even now—or if he meant my father, who had a library, though nothing as astonishing as this. Yet Darcy's face was devoid of prejudice. He seemed to delight in my amazement and gripped my hand even tighter.

I walked in, trailing my fingers over the spines, reading a few of them and imagining myself with time to read again. Oh to imagine such luxury!

Darcy, it seemed, had other ideas besides reading. He tugged me between two larger shelves and said, "Elizabeth, how I have longed to be alone with you."

I closed my eyes as he pressed his lips to mine.

A gentle but firm rapping noise interrupted us. Darcy looked heavenward before composing himself. "Come in."

Mrs Reynolds entered. "Mrs Fitzwilliam's family and Miss Darcy all await you in the parlour."

He adjusted his waistcoat and drew himself up to full height before extending an elbow to me, a much more acceptable way for us to walk together. "I apologise for not sharing that they had arrived earlier in the day. I wished for a few moments alone with you." As we left the library, he snuck a kiss onto my cheek, and I giggled. He was so cheerful and affectionate, I felt like I was floating through the elaborate passageways to the parlour, confident that nothing could go awry.

"There is more to see, including the nursery, which is well appointed. There are still the gardens to explore, and the gallery, in which my collection of art is displayed. My mother collected statues, but my contribution to Pemberley has been the addition of sculptures that match my taste. Acquiring them has brought me great pleasure."

"I look forward to seeing it. A man's taste in art is quite telling."

"And when I chose bedrooms," he said, his tone arch, "I admit I resisted the urge to place you in one with a secret adjoining corridor to mine."

Laughter floated to us from the drawing room, but before we entered, he took my hand once again and kissed it, his eyes lingering on my face. "My joy at being reunited with you is limitless," he said, and swept us into the parlour to join his guests.

THE NEXT WEEK WAS A WHIRLWIND OF LAVISH MEALS, WALKS in the gardens and the surrounding lands (though we never saw all, as we learned it was ten miles around), and sports. The men hunted and fished, while we ladies were left to play croquet and shuttlecock. I had not the appropriate outfit for each activity, but none present seemed to mind. Against fashion, I visited with my children for hours early in the day while the other ladies rose at their leisure and dressed and breakfasted in their rooms. I actually looked forward to lengthy dinners and visits in the drawing room, though I enjoyed sneaking off to the gallery to appreciate the sculptures, occasionally with Darcy. No one seemed to notice or, if they did, they were kind enough not to remark upon it.

Accompanied by his family (including two younger sisters, both charming and sweet), Georgiana's intended arrived four days before the wedding. In the evenings, Georgiana showed off her skill at the pianoforte, and her future husband, Charles, delighted us by singing along with a voice both pure and strong. Standing in the candlelight, engrossed in their song, they regarded one other with a gentle affection I never had with James, but hoped for with Darcy. These last evenings were filled with music and lively conversation, and I could not remember a time I felt so full of joy and free.

The most thrilling moment was when Bingley proposed dancing, and Darcy declared he would sit out. When I enquired why, he tilted his head. "Because you do not know the dances, my dear."

"But I certainly do!" I replied. "Darcy, you wound me."

He knew I was only teasing him but narrowed his eyes. "You do? How?"

"Jane brought her dance master from London, and he spent the past weeks teaching me." Jane's exultation at the news of my engagement had been followed by a flurry of good-natured demands that I learn to be a proper lady, and promises that she would help me in any way she could. "I am sure to falter occasionally, especially with the most complex patterns, but I know a great many dances now."

Darcy turned to Jane and Bingley, who confirmed this with delighted nods.

"Then we shall dance indeed!" Darcy's smile was brighter than I had ever seen it.

Though I did step the wrong way every now and again,

no one seemed to mind, and we all laughed and clapped, and twirled the night away. It was the happiest I remember being.

Everything changed with the arrival of more guests, the Fitzwilliams and Snowleys among them.

CHAPTER THIRTY-SIX

T ension was palpable the moment the dining room
table was extended and set for the large party.
Darcy reverted to his stiff posture and formal
manners, rarely speaking. I was seated quite far from him,
but still we managed to exchange a glance or two. More
unsettling was his refusal to return even the smallest of
smiles.

After dinner, I was relegated to the ladies' parlour where
the conversation was dreadfully dull when it was not
outright cruel. Matters improved when a card game was
proposed and most joined. Between my limited means and
lack of knowledge of the rules, I was only too happy to
decline a seat at a table and began to read. In the week we
had been at Pemberley, I had read a book a day, an
extraordinary indulgence.

Darcy sat out the game as well, but every time he moved
in my direction, Lady Broxbourne or Lady Snowley would
ask him a question or insist he advise them on the hand they
ought to play. Tiring of their game, I excused myself to

stroll in the hall, marvelling again at the portraits of Darcy's relations.

Upon my return, I passed one of the small sitting rooms and heard familiar voices. I froze and then stepped closer to the door, leaning my ear ever closer.

"She has no spell on me. And I have little wish to speak to you on the matter."

"Your wishes are not of my concern, and I shall have my say." It was Lady Broxbourne. "Tell me at once, are you engaged to her? Tell me the rumours are untrue, for I could not bear it."

How could she insert herself into my romantic life after having stolen my home and my land? When would this woman cease trying to take from me all that I loved?

"I am engaged to her. I asked and she accepted, thereby making me the happiest of men."

"Fitzwilliam, I am shocked and astonished. She trapped my son into marriage, ruined his life—"

Anger licked up my neck, yet I remained rooted beside the slightly ajar door.

"I do not see it so," he replied tersely. "James knew what he was about and she was merely a child. It is she who has borne the brunt of the matter, living in penury, raising your grandchildren to be delightful young creatures—and all while being cast aside by you who ought to have done better by your son."

"I will not sit here and listen to you defend her."

"Then let us agree to importune one another no further on this subject. She will be my wife, and if you choose not to accept that, then you will need to absent yourself from Pemberley."

I heard his footsteps approach and pressed my back against the wall.

"Not so hasty, if you please. I have by no means done."

I fought the urge to ask her to leave myself.

"I am no stranger to the particulars of your sleeping under the same roof whilst she was playing the grieving widow."

How could she know about the one occasion nearly a year earlier? I winced, imagining what Darcy's reaction might be.

"Is such a girl to be married to my nephew? Heaven and earth!—of what are you thinking? Is the name Darcy to be thus polluted?"

What he said I knew not, but Lady Broxbourne gasped and accused him of insolence.

"Once Lady Snowley and I publicise that you nearly lived at her house soon after her husband's death, no one will ever visit with you, call on you, speak to you. You will be utterly alone, an outcast. Acquaintances far lower than you will not deign to speak to you at gatherings. Should you throw a ball, no one shall attend. Should you write a letter, no one shall answer it. Such snubs have happened. The humiliation would be so complete you would wish yourself dead."

My mind raced. Caroline Snowley and Lady Broxbourne would vex me to the end of my days.

"I shall dare you to try," he said calmly. He exited the room, stopping short at the sight of me. I reached out to him, wanting to smooth the creases in his forehead, to mop his sweating brow, to whisper to him until his wild eyes returned to their natural beauty, but he uttered a few inaudible words to me and hurried down the hall.

THE MORNING OF THE WEDDING WAS CLEAR AND NOT TOO warm, a perfect day for sweet Georgiana, but as I donned my pale green gown trimmed with fine lace, I felt ill. I had hoped to speak to Darcy but he had been occupied the whole of the evening, with what I knew not.

After the church service, the breakfast was as elegant as would be expected in such a place as Pemberley. As I still had not had any opportunity to speak to Darcy in private, old fears began to intrude. Had he decided his aunt was right about me?

It was in the midst of such unhappy thoughts that Lady Snowley stepped into my path as I left the drawing room. My every muscle tensed. "Caroline, I have no stomach for you right now."

She lifted her pointy chin. "Eliza," she said. "Really. You must think of Darcy. Think of the ruination you will bring upon him, and the shame to his family name."

She looked over my gown with such a sour expression that I doubted its loveliness. True, it was less uselessly fine than her own costume, but excess would never be my fashion, no matter how rich I might be.

"Why must you always seek to make me unhappy? What is it about me that you hate so much?"

She smirked and leaned in. "I will destroy you both if you will not give him up."

"I do not fear you, Caroline," I said. "I have not forgotten where you came from, though it seems you have."

I turned on my heel, determined to find Darcy. I peered into the billiard room where I heard the voices of men in full enjoyment of liquor and games. At last I found him exiting the library with Lord Broxbourne and Bingley, his face grave, his back ramrod straight. "Elizabeth!"

Lord Broxbourne excused himself, unable to look at me as he passed.

My heart lurched, wondering what new threats he had made against us. "I must speak to you." To my great relief, he smiled, and reached for my hand.

"Darcy," Bingley asked, "shall I join Jane?"

"No, good news ought to be shared in a crowd."

"Good news?" I asked, too overjoyed by the feel of his hand holding mine to understand immediately. "But Lord Broxbourne looked miserable."

"And indeed he is," Darcy said with a grin. "For he has lost the war. Elizabeth, James did, indeed, make provisions for you. My solicitor has spent the past months battling with the Fitzwilliams for information. Investigations were made and threats issued, but to no avail. Last night, however, Lord Broxbourne apparently enjoyed one port too many and confessed to Lord Stanford that James had indeed drawn up a will. There was an agreement about a legacy—money which undeniably belonged to James—that you, as his widow, are entitled to. What Lord Broxbourne did not consider fully was Lord Stanford's loyalties to me, his dear friend from university days—"

"*Our* dear friend from Cambridge," Bingley said with a meaningful look.

"Yes, yes," he said, squeezing Bingley's shoulder with the hand that did not hold mine. "He did not consider that Lord Stanford would share the information with me. Stanford did so just after the ceremony, and Bingley and I confronted Lord Broxbourne. Lord Broxbourne confessed it was true. The money shall be yours! It is not a fortune—and I will, of course, provide for all of the children's needs, so the amount is inconsequential—but it is the principle of it. We have prevailed."

He paused, giving me time to take in the news. "Is this not wonderful?"

"Y-yes," I said, still working it through my mind. "But, Darcy, what about…"

My eyes flicked towards Bingley, unsure whether he knew about the conversation Darcy had had with Lady Broxbourne and Caroline. "After the threats against you last night, I was…well, I was fearful that you had decided to break our engagement."

His jaw dropped slightly. "Lizzy, good heavens, no. I simply dared not say a word until the confrontation was at an end and the agreement was finalised."

I felt faint. "Dearest, do not keep things from me, whether out of fear or a desire to protect me. I am strong and would rather know than be left guessing."

He took my hands and pressed his perfect lips to my knuckles. "And I swear to you: no more secrets."

"But Darcy," I said, still shaken, "you heard Lady Broxbourne and Lady Snowley. I know not why they hate me so much, but I am sure they will never give up. They are set on destroying me, and you by association. Their message is clear: to be with me could mean no more parties, no more Seasons in town, no callers. They are powerful and could likely sway society."

He shook his head. "I shared with Lord Broxbourne what my aunt had threatened, and assured him that I could destroy the Fitzwilliam reputation by sharing widely how they turned their backs on their son and grandchildren, how they did all they could to see those grandchildren destitute without even bread to eat. Your children are the grandchildren of an earl! And yet they were not being given their due because of his wife's vindictiveness. It is not the behaviour of a gentleman, much less one of noble birth, and society would have much to say about that were it known. He has agreed that, no matter their feelings, there will be nary another word against you in public. We are free of them, my dearest."

"My goodness," I said, unable to believe the turn of events. Stepping closer to him, I took his face in my hands. "Never has anyone cared for me and the children the way you do. I am so very fortunate."

Bingley cleared his throat and excused himself, claiming he heard Jane calling for him.

"I love you so, Darcy, that I cannot understand what I have done to deserve you. It frightens me, how much my happiness, and that of my children, depends upon you."

"My dear Elizabeth, you deserve all the love and care I can give. I am delighted to have the honour of caring for you and loving you for the rest of our days." He stroked his finger along my cheek, then kissed my left eyebrow and my right, before brushing his lips across mine.

I shivered slightly, sure that he could see the force of my adoration for him blazing in my eyes. I kissed him behind his ear. Upon his cheek. Lingered on his lips. I breathed in his scent and sighed.

EPILOGUE

One Year Later

Crying woke me, as it did too often, but I did not mind. Baby Grace had a kindly disposition and delicate blonde curls, reminding me more of Georgiana than myself or Darcy. All she wanted was to be held close and soothed, which Darcy and I were all too willing to do. Grace had been easy and welcome from the beginning.

It was drizzling the afternoon I told Darcy I was expecting, so we had taken our tea in the brightest of the sitting rooms. I ought to have waited until his mouth was not full, for he nearly choked on a biscuit.

Once he had recovered, his eyes welled up and he reached for my hand. "Dearest Elizabeth, you have no idea — After all these years, to be father to a child of my own I…I am overwhelmed." His gaze drifted to my stomach, a dreamy grin on his face. Almost immediately, however, the grin slipped away and he dropped to his knees, clutching at my hands. "I fear—I cannot lose you, Elizabeth. I cannot!

We ought to have been more careful. I need not have any children of my blood. Yours are enough. I cannot bear to lose you!" He let go of me to cover his face so I would not see him cry.

I kissed his head and ran my fingers through his hair. He had been grieving his lost child all along, something I had not appreciated enough, and so assured him in that moment and every day until Grace's healthy delivery that all would be well. I was never sick or exhausted, perhaps owing to the fact that I was not bent over boiling laundry or kneading dough while heavy with child, nor worried about how I could afford a bit of meat or new shoes for the other babes underfoot.

The night Grace was born, she lay swaddled on the mattress between Darcy and me, and the other children clambered onto the bed to admire our latest addition. We would gather in such a fashion every so often—beginning with the six of us, then seven, and eventually nine of us in total—birthdays and Christmas mornings, and occasionally during thunderstorms or on a snowy day. Our practice continued until Alice married twelve years later. That night, as they always did, the children asked for stories of their births and early lives, and we obliged. In this way, we kept James's memory alive.

A favourite story to tell and retell was of my wedding to Darcy. Thomas and Alice remembered the details vividly, and Henry and Sally claimed to recall, though I suspect much was from the recounting of the day over the years.

After Georgiana's wedding, Darcy had asked us to stay on (along with the Bingleys and the Gardiners), and set the wedding date for a month off, giving Georgiana and Charles the chance to return from their honeymoon.

Whether or not to invite my mother had been a source

of some tension, but Darcy's sense of propriety had prevailed. To my relief, she wrote that a summer cold would keep her away. I did not know whether to believe her, though Darcy said my marrying a man with ten thousand a year would have thrilled her endlessly, and missing it must have pained her. The Fitzwilliams and the Snowleys were not invited. Even if they had been, they would not have come. Unfortunately, Lord Snowley's gambling had rendered them penniless at the same time that Caroline was scandalised by rumours of a 'criminal affection for a menial servant'. I dared not ask the meaning of such an accusation, but privately laughed with my husband over the implications. It was somewhat gratifying to know that thanks to her own foolishness, the very threats she had made against us came true for her.

I had worn a gown of grey picked out with silver thread for my wedding. It was so perfect I was reluctant to wear it again lest it be ruined, but Darcy said it brought him such happy memories that he wanted to see it as often as possible. We compromised; I wore it to the occasional assembly and, when we were in London, to the opera.

I carried a bouquet of flowers from Pemberley's gardens, a mix of ferns, roses, peonies, and delphinium, along with sage and ivy. The same ribbon used to tie it was woven through Alice's and Sally's hair, which delighted them. The boys only cared that there would be sipping chocolate after, a delicacy they had come to associate with celebrations. It remains a favourite treat.

Jane and I climbed into a carriage with the girls, and I assumed we would travel straight to the church. To my surprise, the driver turned onto a different path and into a clearing I had not known existed, since Darcy always claimed there was a swamp in the area that needed draining. Given Pemberley's size, there was always new ground to explore, and new sights to see, so I thought nothing of that.

A sun-dappled structure awaited us at the east side of the pasture, and as we approached, my breath caught. It was Miss Taylor's cottage. My cottage! Darcy had had it dismantled, transported, and reassembled, knowing how dear it was to me.

It was beyond belief. Miss Taylor's plantings, of course, were missing, but seeds and cuttings had been taken and Pemberley's land would soon boast a small slice of Meryton in its midst.

In what had been the garden of the original structure, an arch had been erected—and under it stood the vicar and Darcy, flanked by Bingley.

"Our house!" Sally cried out with delight.

Alice clapped. "Did it arrive by magic?"

Darcy stood, beaming, and I knew it had been his sort of magic. Happy tears slid down my cheeks and I told my girls it was indeed magic.

My uncle Gardiner waited at the gate with Thomas and Henry, and after the girls and Jane went through, the men of my life walked me down the makeshift aisle towards the man I loved. I wept so much during the few steps I needed to take that I feared tripping.

A look of alarm crossed the vicar's face and he asked if I had come of my own free will.

"Yes," I exclaimed, and Bingley handed me a kerchief. "Darcy, you did this for me?"

"I would do anything for you," he said, reaching for my hand. I squeezed it, then turned to kiss each of my children before joining him under the arch. I was in a daze, but knew how different this wedding felt than my first. There were no doubts and no fears. I had chosen this man and this life, and he had chosen me.

We said our vows, and when the vicar pronounced us man and wife, Sally rushed forward and hugged Darcy around the knees, prompting all of the children to join in as we kissed each other above their heads and laughed.

Laughter filled our days, along with reading and art and walks and appreciating nature. All the things I dreamed of when I had hidden in the woods to escape from my drunken father and to mourn the absence of my mother had come to fruition. No, my life exceeded even those wild hopes. My beloved Jane remained dear, and I made friends, true friends, as I met more of Darcy's circle. When people stared at me now, it was out of admiration and envy rather than scorn.

Another wail from baby Grace brought me back to the present.

"Shall I take her?" Darcy asked, attempting to sit up in his midnight stupor.

"No," I said, kissing his shoulder. "Go back to sleep."

He closed his eyes, shifting so he could rest a hand on my hip. Even after all of these months, he still sought my touch, and I relished it. "Do you still love me as much as I love you?" he asked, a dreamy half-smile on his face.

"Always and forever, Darcy," I whispered, more content than I had ever been.

The favour of your review would be greatly appreciated.

Subscribers to the Quills & Quartos mailing list receive advance notice of new releases and sales, and exclusive bonus content and short stories. To join, visit us at www.QuillsandQuartos.com

ACKNOWLEDGMENTS

Thanks to Amy D'Orazio and Jan Ashton for believing my tale was worth their time, for answering questions about history, and for instructing me on what can and cannot be changed from the original. Marcelle Wong, you are a patient and instructive editor with great gifts and even better advice. Thanks to Jennifer Altman for introducing me to this genre and to Quills & Quartos. To my friends who have read drafts and supported this story in its many incarnations. Sage and Joanna, this book is clean, so you don't have to be embarrassed while reading your mom's writing! Jonathan, you are the best cheerleader a girl could ask for.

ABOUT THE AUTHOR

Michelle Ray is a middle school literature teacher who also directs plays, writes stories, and sees as many Broadway shows as she can. She grew up in Los Angeles and went to the awesome Westlake School for Girls where theater had the cachet of football and the girls were in charge of everything. She lives with her husband and daughters near Washington DC, and dreams of traveling anywhere and everywhere.

ALSO BY MICHELLE RAY

Falling for Hamlet

Passion, romance, drama, humor, and tragedy intertwine in this compulsively readable Hamlet *retelling, from the perspective of a strong-willed, modern-day Ophelia.*

Meet Ophelia, high school senior, daughter of the Danish king's most trusted adviser, and longtime girlfriend of Prince Hamlet of Denmark. She lives a glamorous life and has a royal social circle, and her beautiful face is splashed across magazines and television screens. But it comes with a price-her life is ruled not only by Hamlet's fame and his overbearing royal family but also by the paparazzi who hound them wherever they go.

After the sudden and suspicious death of his father, the king, the devastatingly handsome Hamlet spirals dangerously toward madness, and Ophelia finds herself torn, with no one to turn to. All Ophelia wants is to live a normal life. But when you date a prince, you have to play your part. Ophelia rides out this crazy roller coaster life, and lives to tell her story in live television interviews.

A World on Fire

Six lands, three religions, one true love. (Based on real events.)

1497. The Mediterranean is in upheaval, and Beatríz finds herself in the midst of the turmoil. Expelled from Spain not five years earlier along with the rest of the country's Jews, she is terrified to learn of Portugal's decree that all Jews must convert to Christianity. Beatríz has promised her fiancé, Yusef, a merchant at sea, that she will wait for him in Lisbon, but when events spiral out of control, Beatríz must choose conversion, death, or separation. If she stays, what of her identity? If she goes, how will she find Yusef again? Leaving offers dangers: land wars, civil wars, religious wars, not to mention plagues, pirates, starvation, and others who would desire her conversion to Christianity or Islam. The world is on fire. Which way to turn?

Outlaw

Outlaw is based on the true story of Rose Dunn. Raised in a family of minor outlaws who taught her to shoot, rope, ride, and steal, everything changes for Rose when she meets Bittercreek Newcomb, a member of the Dolan Gang. If she chooses him, the robberies, deaths, and risk of arrest will intensify. If she chooses to leave him or her family, she will be completely alone in 1890s Oklahoma, an inhospitable place for a young woman. She must decide if she can continue the life of crime she has begun to doubt, and what the consequences will be if she turns her back on everyone she loves.

Much Ado About Something

Beatriz and Ben don't see eye to eye on much, but they do agree on one thing: they can't stand each other. No way are they going to date again. Ever. But when Beatriz's cousin Hope starts at Messina Prep, everything changes. Not only does she want to fix Beatriz's love life, but she also attracts the attention of Ben's best friend Clay…and the two cruelest guys at school.

Mac/Beth: The Price of Fame Shouldn't Be Murder

Duncan King's death was an accident. It was. I know everyone wants to blame me for it. Make me out to be some evil schemer, but that's not how it was. I'm just like any other teenage girl. Except that I'm on TV. And my boyfriend is a movie star. Sure, we're ambitious. Sure, we like to get our way. But that doesn't mean we're murderers. Well, not me anyway. I never meant for all those people to die. Especially not Duncan.